Breaking the Surface

Matt Hebert

ISBN: 1530568498
ISBN 13: 9781530568499
Library of Congress Control Number: 2016909267
LCCN Imprint Name: Omaha, Nebraska

To my dear and loving wife, Gabriella: Thank you for your patience, support, and all the hours you allowed me to seclude myself in the loft to finish this. You are the spark that lights my fire.

And in loving memory of Victor Beatty: Your enthusiasm and anticipation of this sequel will live in my heart forever. You will always be a shining light to others.

Part One
High and Low

Chapter One
Spearhead

Tears filled Mahana's dark, weathered eyes as the submarine carrying his niece disappeared into the ocean's broken twilight. He had just finished a silent prayer when his ship, *The Beluga,* was rocked by a deep explosion. The fading light of the sun was suddenly replaced by a cloud of fire and debris. Mahana hurried along, a line of his bravest warriors following in his wake. One of the warriors forced a radio into Mahana's great, brown hand. Most of the others began to pour into the attack subs that waited around them.

"Status, please." He said quickly into the radio. His tone was hurried, but it did not falter under such pressure. It would take more than one torpedo to take out *The Beluga.*

"*Recon sub. Gov'ment. Set the deck guns to 'em and drove right into us.*" Said a voice on the other end of the transmission.

Mahana chuckled, noting, "Must have da mano's worried. Dey're sendin' out da suicide crew." He turned to the warrior on his right, saying, "Get da hole patched, and get da patrol ring out to tree-hundred meters." The young man ran off to a staircase ahead.

Mahana continued quickly behind him. After three flights, two of his newest allies ran in from the adjoining deck. Jonah Feldman spoke first; his reluctant partner Linx was at his side.

"Sembado? Kaluna? Are they alright?" Jonah asked. His tone was panicked and anxious.

"I only just saw dem dip below da waves before de attack. I tink dey made der escape," Mahana replied, slowing his pace so that he would not lose his breath. "We got to keep da distraction alive. Linx, I want you down in one of dose subs. I need half my boys to stick wit da security perimeter, the rest I want forming a spear head down below wit you."

"On it." Linx replied, all too ready to get into the action. He immediately reversed course, and was a whole flight down before Jonah could protest.

"Wait!" Jonah shouted. He was a half flight between the other two men. Mahana and Linx both stopped, looking harried and impatient. Jonah took his chance to speak, saying, "I'm not going to wait around here and let one more young man die by my inaction! I'm going with Linx."

Mahana chuckled loudly as he continued up the stairs. "Suit yaself!" he shouted back down.

Linx looked exasperated, but said nothing. He turned and continued running down the stairs as fast as he could, a flustered Jonah right behind him.

Jonah followed Linx down to the submarine dock level. Mahana and his men had outfitted a portion of *The Beluga's* hull so that small submarines could be dispatched from within. The two men quickly made their way down the dock as Linx carefully picked over his choices of available craft.

"Perfect," he said, making his way to the last submarine. It was a normal-sized two-seater, but its engines were wildly disproportionate to the rest of the body.

"Perfect," Jonah echoed, eyeing the massive engines suspiciously as he climbed in the cockpit.

Linx finally acknowledged Jonah with a quick list of commands as they prepared the submarine for departure. Jonah obliged, squeezing into the second control seat next to Linx. Mahana's surrounding crew signaled them out to the exit port, and the two unlikely allies bobbed out of *The Beluga's* belly and immediately dove below the waves. Linx flipped another switch and the massive engines rumbled into their second stage. The submarine shuddered under the surface, shedding thousands of tiny bubbles as it did. They continued down below *The Beluga's* keel before leveling out. The two men sat in total silence as Linx finished preparing the engines for full use, but he finally dropped his stony front, asking, "You ready, man?" In that moment, Jonah knew that Linx's question held more reconciliation than he could have otherwise mustered.

"Ready to go." Jonah responded.

"Good. I'll need you to call out Mahana's orders, and get at least twelve of his boys with us in formation. Did you hear everything he said?"

"Yes. Let's get out ahead of *The Beluga* first."

Linx showed agreement by throttling up the engines and rocketing them forward.

Up above, Mahana was being greeted into the bridge. He listened to the radio orders given by Jonah, and watched a dozen of the patrol subs that had been circling his ship break off and race after Linx and Jonah's submerged vessel. He got on the ships intercom, readying the crew for the next maneuver.

"Dis is Mahana. We're patchin' da side and headed straight for the tankers. Prepare to attack, my friends." A battle cry could be heard rolling across the ship. Mahana closed his eyes and prayed.

Chapter Two
The Scenic Route

Sembado opened his eyes, his hand still clung to the key around his neck. His thoughts quickly passed from *The Beluga* to his family to his grandfather's lock box waiting deep in the bowels of the complex, and then back to his family. It had been months since he had seen them, and last he knew the complex's security czar, Fabian, had posted his best henchmen right at Sembado's family's front door. He hoped – prayed – dearly that they were okay. Being alive would be a good first step.

"Sembado!" Kaluna said with exasperation.

"Deeks. What?"

"I said I have to go to the bathroom. Take the controls."

"Sorry. Go ahead."

She smacked him on the back of the head as she went. The small second cabin in the back of the sub was not designed as a bathroom, but Kaluna's people had outfitted it with a double evacuation chamber. A door was opened on the inside, the small chamber was filled, and then closed again. After that, the secondary, exterior hatch was opened with a lever so that the contents could be evacuated into the open ocean water. It was a crude system, but did allow for prolonged trips. Kaluna confined herself in the closet-like space. As Sembado took control, he checked the radar for activity. *The Beluga* was nearly off their screen, and a smaller group of blips could be seen ahead of it. They were just starting to create a v-shaped formation ahead of the ship. The depth gauge dropped past one hundred feet as Sembado continued to take the submarine down to cruising depth. They were headed due south at fifty-seven knots. Their goal was to circle around and approach the complex from the southwest. To his surprise, a scan of the oxygen and power levels showed that both were approaching fifty percent. He assumed that Mahana had put them in a fully commissioned vessel. He was just comparing their remaining resources to their current navigational plan when Kaluna returned from the back. Sembado shared his concerns with her.

"I didn't realize the sub wasn't completely topped off with O2 and power. I'm not sure we will have enough of either to complete our route as planned."

Kaluna furrowed her brow and began clicking through the navigation system to make the proper calculations. She pursed her lips and breathed quietly for a few moments before responding to Sembado.

"It is possible to pull the route in closer to the complex, but I don't think we should go as close as the nav is telling us to. If we continue making our circle around south and watch the oxygen level, we should be able to adjust towards the end of the trip."

"But don't you think the computer is going to calculate closer than we can?" Sembado replied. His tone was not sarcastic, but a genuine question. He had been raised in a culture that valued the advice of machines much more than Kaluna's people did.

"No I don't." she replied flatly. The two friends sat quietly. Kaluna's silence was one of measured resolve; Sembado was simply trying to hold back further objections. Kaluna seemed well aware of this as she quickly elaborated on her original answer.

"Those calculations are based on assumptions that are programmed into the computer. The rate of oxygen consumption per person and breaths per minute are nearly twice what I myself actually use. It's not taking into account the fact that I am using the current to our advantage, and on top of that—it is programmed with a safety factor of almost one point five. I'm sorry, but if you are concerned about O2 levels then we should probably keep the talking to a minimum." When she was finished, Kaluna sat with a sour look on her mouth as if she had just eaten an under ripe banana. Sembado knew that her knowledge of modern electronics far outweighed her interest in discussing their finer points. He continued to sit quietly as they went, fighting to keep a smirk off of his face all the while.

Chapter Three
The Whites of Their Eyes

"I think he might have blown an engine," Jonah said, pointing to the submarine on the radar screen in between him and Linx. "The others have left him behind." The two had been leading the spearhead attack for nearly half an hour with *The Beluga* fighting to keep pace. The submarine that Jonah pointed to was one of a small pod that they had been driving back to the complex. Its companions had set to overdrive, and had been cleared off the radar since the pursuit began.

As they continued to close the gap on their prey, the submarine started to fade into their sightline out of the front viewing shield.

"Look, there he is!" Jonah shouted.

Linx pressed the accelerator paddle all the way down and set two small torpedoes right at the submarine before Jonah had time to protest. Jonah turned with disbelief from the torpedoes, to Linx, and then back. The two finned rods hit the submarine dead center, exploding in a large bubble of fiery turmoil. Jonah and Linx's submarine shuddered from the blast, and they were on their way before the bubbles from the attack could even reach the surface.

Jonah continued to stutter in disapproval as their accompanying submarines radioed in compliments to Linx's accuracy.

"Uh-uh-unacceptable!" Jonah finally shouted.

Linx rolled his eyes. He provided one simple response before Jonah could protest further, "Just think of Meligose."

Jonah shot him a piercing glare, and then closed his eyes and curled his lip as the thought started to settle in. He gritted his teeth and opened his eyes.

"Nice shot," he growled.

"That's it." Linx responded, "Put that anger to some use. You have to focus it or you won't know who to be angry at, will you?"

"Fabian." Jonah said. It was almost a whisper.

"That's right, man. Every one of these goons we kill is one less finger on that eel's crooked fist." He held up the back of his hand to Jonah with his ring finger curled in. Jonah studied it with a smile, nodding with grim approval. The smugness quickly faded from his face as he pointed to the radar again. A mass of blips had appeared on the radar and grew by the second. Linx continued his sinister smile as he addressed Mahana over the radio.

"Beluga, this is Spearhead. We've reached the complex. Prepare the volley, and launch on my mark."

"Roga' dat, Spearhead." Mahana said back over the radio. "Da volley is ready and waitin'."

Jonah continued to watch the radar as Linx looked out ahead through the Pacific murk.

"They've turned around! Here they come!" Jonah shouted. "Here they come…"

"Fire volley!" Linx shouted into the radio.

Mahana watched from the bridge as the deck of *The Beluga* erupted in fire. Thirty rocket launchers fired simultaneously, releasing the volley of torpedoes high into the air. They splashed down a thousand meters ahead. Two more rounds of rockets followed, one after the other.

Linx brought the submarine to a near stop as ninety torpedoes found their targets ahead. Faint outlines of submarines were suddenly highlighted by clusters of explosions. The line of explosions reached out to the left and right as each torpedo found a unique target amongst the large group of government submarines. A handful of the rockets continued downward, exploding just in time to rend gaping holes in the complex's containment net. Jonah and Linx's submarine rocked terribly as the explosions continued. They braced themselves against the console and each other.

Linx throttled the engine back up as the explosions subsided. They could see a number of escaping submarines through the mangled debris ahead. Many of the government submarines were using the recently created holes in the containment net to escape down to a safer depth.

Linx called orders out through the radio, and soon he and the other attack submarines had formed circles around the openings in the net. As they settled into their defensive formations, *The Beluga* slowed to a stop directly above, casting a massive shadow over everything.

Chapter Four
Short of Breath

It had been nearly four hours since Sembado and Kaluna had left *The Beluga*, and the oxygen and power levels were now very low. Sembado grew increasingly nervous. He had only experienced a loss of power once in a submarine, and it was terribly unpleasant. A large fish had become wedged in the intake of his father's submarine, and the subsequent mechanical failure had rendered the backup power useless. Without power for the radio, he and his father had to sit for several hours before a passing submarine took notice.

Kaluna was still very quiet as her technique for conserving oxygen was reaching its limit. They still had over ten miles to go on their current route, and even after disabling the lights and extraneous accessories, their power consumption was tracking to strand them a challenging distance from the complex.

"Keep at it. I'll be right back." Sembado said, giving her a reassuring pat on the shoulder. She reached up and placed her hand on his for a short moment. Sembado moved to the back of the sub, checking every side compartment, drawer, and stowing hatch he could. To his surprise, he found exactly what he was looking for: oxygen tanks. They were both very small. One was only a twenty minute supply, and that was if it was full.   The other had a half hour max. Digging through the shelves further produced some hand fins and a pressure gauge.

Sembado plopped back down in his seat with his arms full of gear. He set the hand fins between him and Kaluna, and started fumbling with the pressure gauge and tanks. The twenty minute tank was full up, but the thirty minute tank was only half full. The good news was that air times were typically calibrated for a full body, fast-paced swim. The bad news was that Sembado and Kaluna might have to employ the tanks before they even got into the water to swim.

"Maybe we should go ahead and get these masks fitted while we can." Sembado said.

"At this rate we are going to run out of fuel before we do oxygen," Kaluna responded. "Let's save those for when we have to swim the rest."

Sembado's stomach turned. It was the first time in the discussion of their contingency plan that Kaluna had not said "if". It seemed that they had both come to the same inevitable conclusion.

"Well, at least you can take the bigger air tank." Sembado said, passing the twenty minute canister to Kaluna.

"What sense does that make?" She responded. "I'm smaller than you, and will use much less O2."

"Yea, but you aren't accounting for my leg," Sembado said back. "It doesn't use oxygen like the other one, and its battery is full of juice." Kaluna accepted the fuller tank begrudgingly.

"Twenty minutes of air means we need to get well within a mile if we are going to stand a chance." said Kaluna. Sembado nodded in agreement adding, "It should be doable if the current continues to help."

"It's been backing off since we changed direction. I don't think we're gaining much more than a mile per hour now." said Kaluna. Sembado said nothing, but gripped her hand tightly.

They continued on in silence, each very aware of their own heart rate, breathing rate, and oxygen consumption. Sembado was afraid that holding Kaluna's hand was going to be the death of him.

Even at their slow speed, the final stretch was quickly reduced, but with just over a mile to go, the submarine started to activate its automatic shutdown procedures. Sembado and Kaluna exchanged nervous looks as the already dark submarine shuddered for the last time and died. They drifted quietly while situating their finned gloves, oxygen masks, and backpacks. Then they waited.

Several minutes of Sembado studying the wrinkles on his knuckles had passed, and finally Kaluna reached out and touched his shoulder. The submarine had stopped. With a nod, she motioned for him to follow her to the back and they began to turn valves and levers to get the submarine to fill as slowly as possible. They struggled through the dark, but Kaluna's prowess won out, and water started gushing in from the back of the vessel. As it did, the back end fell first and Sembado and Kaluna soon found themselves standing close together on the rear wall. The water rose quickly past their legs. Suddenly, residual pressure in the submarine's piping was released and a loud bang echoed throughout the cabin. Sembado cringed at the sound, and opened his eyes to find Kaluna hugging him tightly around the middle. She opened her eyes to look around, but even after she realized they were okay she did not let go. Sembado returned the embrace and they remained close while the cold salt water climbed her chest and then his. With their air tanks activated, they fumbled through the dark water to find the hatch. Kaluna took the lead, groping in the dark with one hand, and holding on to Sembado with the other as the submarine continued to fall. They torqued on the handle together, and it gave way with a muffled creak and a hiss. They pushed out together, and climbed out of the sinking submarine as calmly as possible. There was more light available outside, and Sembado swam in a small circle as he gained his bearings. He finished his turn to find a familiar sight: the giant, shadowy complex, stretching its metallic tendrils organically across his vision. The sheer size of it overwhelmed him, as he had not had this encompassing of a view for quite a while. Kaluna tugged at his arm and they began swimming.

They began with a measured pace, but they both struggled to not check their O2 meters every ten seconds.

Their attempted distance was the longest swim they had done in months, and the lack of preparation was no help. While Sembado's lungs did burn, his real source of discomfort was the amount of heat coming off of his prosthetic. It seemed to be compensating more and more for his other leg, but as it did, its power source began to heat up. Sembado tried regulating his power back to his real leg, but the further they went, the more his bionic limb took over. He had eight minutes of air left. They slowed just long enough for Kaluna to indicate that she was already down to five.

Despite her attempts at remaining calm, it was clear that Kaluna was incredibly uncomfortable with their situation. Sembado was finally able to convince her to switch tanks after explaining that his new leg's battery was doing most of the work.

The further they went, the more they had to stop, and soon they were making very poor progress. Sembado found himself experiencing more frustration than fear. They had reached the first few chambers of the complex, but were unfamiliar with the location, and could not find a depressurizing pod right away. They started moving along the outside of the structure, desperate for anything like a utility hatch or access port, but they found nothing. Sembado angrily propelled himself along with his leg; he struggled to slow his pace for Kaluna.

We wouldn't be in this situation if the islanders had prepared a sub for us. Mahana knew we would be leaving.

16

Sembado had one minute of air left. Kaluna had stopped. Her breaths were becoming more labored and then slow. Just as they made eye contact, her eyes began to roll, and Sembado's heart began to race. He grabbed her small frame as it started to drift and held her tight. He looked around frantically, and suddenly caught a glimpse of light shining out through a porthole. He kicked desperately with his bionic leg, and it shot him forward like never before. His biggest challenge was steering with Kaluna in his arms. He swam furiously toward the light, and within moments had reached it. His leg was in excruciating pain where the power source from his prosthetic met the skin. He peered inside the hole, and looking back was a confused face. A boy looked out in disbelief and Sembado desperately motioned to Kaluna. The boy disappeared from the window, and just as anger and despair began to consume Sembado, a hatchway next to him blew open with an explosion of bubbles. He quickly moved Kaluna inside the small chamber, barely squeezing in himself. The chamber closed with both of them inside, but nothing happened. Sembado's oxygen meter read zero.

Chapter Five
Disappearing Act

Mahana looked out the windows of *The Beluga*'s bridge. His fleet of surface vessels circled the ship in strategic patterns. Luxury yachts sat with their deck guns trained on the water. A few larger fishing boats sat poised with torpedoes hanging vertically over their sides. Shadows of submarines weaved back and forth under the surface crafts. Tears welled in Mahana's big brown eyes. He was preparing to send more of his men, his people, into battle than ever before. Many of them were going to die. And somewhere down below the surface, below his attack subs, and below the containment net, his beloved niece was preparing for the most difficult challenge of her life.

***

Jonah and Linx sat poised with their submarine's weapons aimed at the hole in the containment net.

"But there has to be a way to disarm those orbs," Jonah said, renewing an earlier argument.

"Yes, Jonah, there is." said Linx. He smacked the back of his head against his seat in frustration. "And that's why

Sembado and Kaluna are going back for Hyron's notebook. And that's why we are here."

"Well, yea, I know, but couldn't we try one of those electro...mag..." Jonah argued.

"No," Linx interrupted. "EMP would disable our submarine as well. Don't you think we thought of that?! Just sit tight, and be ready to pull back. I'll keep on the guns so that you don't have to hurt anyone."

Jonah did not respond. They sat in silence until Linx looked over to see Jonah sitting with his head down, tears dripping from his eyes. Linx sighed and put his hand on Jonah's shoulder.

"Hey, I'm sorry. You didn't ask for this any more than I did. I know. You're just trying to help, but you have got to trust this plan. You have to trust Sembado."

Jonah sighed as he brought his head up, and pushed it back against the seat. He focused his intense, watery gaze on the ceiling of the submarine as he spoke.

"I do trust Sembado. And Kaluna. That doesn't mean I have to be happy about what they're doing or where they are. I don't mean to beat a dead dolphin, but I lost my son. I don't intend on losing anyone else's."

"Yea, I get it. I just don't think..." Linx was interrupted by the collision warning system. He scrambled to respond, but Jonah had already started pulling back on the steering yolk. As he did, a slender torpedo shot right past the nose of their submarine and continued straight up. Just after it left their field of vision, they heard a dull bang. They waited for an explosion, but none came. Linx started flipping switches, arming a handful of small torpedoes under each wing. As Jonah pulled back, he dropped the back end of the submarine so that they could move up and away from the containment net. As they accelerated upward, the next submarine above them came into view. It drifted listlessly while shadows of other crafts swirled in the surrounding water. The drifting submarine had been pierced just under the cockpit by the torpedo that missed Jonah and Linx, but the hull was still intact. They steered close enough to the adjacent sub to get a view inside, but it was empty. They exchanged an ominous glance, and Linx grabbed the radio. Just as he did the radio exploded with chatter, cutting into on an ongoing exchange.

"…distance, and back to the surface!"

"Has Linx called in yet?"

"This is Linx! Jonah and I are okay. Repeat maneuver."

"We are heading back to the surface for a regroup."

"No we are not!" said Linx. There was radio silence, so he continued his orders. "Swing around your tail ends and keep the enemy in your sights. You will have a better chance to deflect and counter. We will back away from the net for now, but if we have to go under it, we will."

Linx and Jonah took the lead and were soon flanked on every side by a mix of pilots from Mahana's islander group and Linx's rebellious Elephants' guild.

"Light up your weapons, everything you've got," Linx commanded.

For the second time, they sat poised and waiting, but from this distance the hole in the net was barely visible. Linx snapped his head to the right as the vacant submarine drifted into his peripheral vision. His eyes darted back to the hole in the net, but he continued to consider the empty sub. It was a small, single person vessel; the cockpit was only big enough for the pilot to sit. There was no extra cabin like the submarine he and Jonah were piloting. He grimaced at the thought of the embedded torpedo being orb-tipped, but it would have been slower and the pilot would have had time to radio for help.

"Head's up!" Jonah said, echoing through Linx's headset. There was some kind of movement and activity beyond the net, but it was too far away to see. The radar only showed a couple of very small vessels on the other side; too few for an attack.

Suddenly an orange beam shot through the murk and started piercing the net. The laser danced around the net in a large circle, burning through each cable it passed. Linx gave the order for the pod of submarines to back away and spread out as the circle being cut in the net grew to one hundred feet in diameter. As the edge of the severed piece became separated from the rest of the net, it drifted in the ambient flow of the ocean. Within minutes the entire circumference had been cut. For more than a minute there was only a deafening calm. Then the pause was broken by a series of clawed cables shooting out from behind the net. The claws grasped the separated piece of net, paused momentarily, and then retracted quickly, yanking the net

21

back beyond the briny gloom. Jonah fidgeted with the yolk. Linx flipped the trigger guard off of his most powerful torpedoes.

Dull circles of light bobbed in the distance. They were pale and faint. As the lights came closer, they multiplied. Soon dozens of submarine navigation lights were shining out from beyond the freshly cut circle, and moving steadily toward the attackers. Linx directed his group to each lock onto a primary target, and to have a second identified. He gave Jonah the signal to pull forward toward their enemies, and gave the order to take the first shot. As the group of rebels released their first volley of torpedoes, the government submarines accelerated rapidly. Some preformed evasive maneuvers, others were hit directly. Linx's group scattered in defensive patterns, engaging each of their targets and avoiding stray torpedoes as they were shot off in all directions. Jonah navigated alongside a friendly submarine as part of a duel attack maneuver, but before they could execute, the other submarine was hit in its far side by a torpedo. It stuck in the hull without exploding and the pilot, an Elephant escapee from the complex, looked over and radioed in the good news.

"Superficial damage, but I'm..." Before he could continue the tip of the embedded torpedo exploded with a blue flash. An electric blue orb, about eight feet in diameter, appeared and then vanished. The pilot was nowhere to be seen, and his submarine drifted to a stop as Jonah and Linx exchanged looks of horror. Linx immediately sent out a distress and retreat message to his brigade.

"I want full retreat to *The Beluga* now! They've upgraded their dissolving orbs to be instantaneous!" As soon as Linx's transmission went out, an enemy submarine appeared from above and made a course straight for his submarine. Linx fired a quick burst of small, explosive rockets, but the other submarine had already released its own attack. Before the enemy torpedo could strike, Jonah grabbed Linx by the shirt and jerked him out of his seat. He threw Linx to the back of the submarine cabin with all his strength. Linx landed hard on his back and his head bounced off the floor just as the torpedo struck the front of the submarine. He looked up just in time to see Jonah stand up straight and proud. His sun-burned face was highlighted by his wispy blond hair which was all outlined by the sparkling blue water above. His face wore a stoic grimace. It was honor. And in a flash, the orb consumed him.

Chapter Six
Would You Like Some Tuna Meatballs?

Sembado hit the floor in a heap, gasping desperately as he ripped off his restrictive swimming gear. His head pounded painfully and he struggled to take in his surroundings; his eyes were clenched in burning pain. As he fumbled around for support, his hands found Kaluna's small, limp frame. His eyes shot open and he spun around on one knee. He frantically searched for a pulse, but could not find one. She was not breathing either. He looked around for something, anything to use to revive her. It was only then that he noticed the boy standing next to him. He stood hunched with his hands on his knees, excitedly observing Sembado's struggles. The boy, about twelve years old, asked Sembado for instruction.

"We need to resuscitate her. Do you have a revival capacitor?" said Sembado.

"Yea, but it's kinda old," The boy replied.

"Doesn't matter. Go get it! Now!"

The boy retreated from Sembado's sharp tone, and ran away down the corridor. Sembado realized he was in a housing chamber. The boy had let them in the garbage expelling gate. He looked back to Kaluna to see that her golden brown skin was taking on a terrifying ashy hue. He was just starting to panic when the boy returned with a large case and a towel. Sembado yanked the case from the boy's hands and dropped it on the floor. The case popped open, revealing a small, sealed bag and a small battery with tangled electrodes. As Sembado fumbled with the bag, the boy used the towel to sop up the excess water on and around Kaluna. Sembado grabbed the towel from the boy and quickly dried his arms and hands. He rolled Kaluna on her back and unzipped her wet suit from her neck to her navel. He pulled it open to reveal her chest and stomach, taking care to maintain her modesty. He turned to the case and grabbed the sealed bag, ripping it open over Kaluna's chest. The contents of the bag, a pale yellow powder, were sprinkled all over her skin. The powder quickly absorbed any remaining moisture, leaving her skin dry and chalky. Sembado brushed away the sticky residue and turned back to the case. He separated the ends of the electrodes and pulled on the tangled mess. It was a sufficient enough snag to pull one of the electrodes out of its socket. Sembado swore, pulling at the wires and fitting the plug back into its port. He flipped on the main switch. The backlight on the power meter came on, but revealed a less than desired charge. Sembado sighed and swore under his breath. The boy fidgeted nervously, backing away a little. Sembado placed one probe at the base of Kaluna's left breast, and flipped a secondary switch on the box. The action light was lit a yellow orange. It was not ready. He tried anyway, placing the secondary probe against her chest quickly. He grimaced as he did, waiting for the jolt to hit her. Nothing happened. He shouted again, throwing the probes apart and turning over the machine. There was a cavity on the back where the power plug connected. Sembado yanked it out. He fumbled through the accessory pouches that lay across his chest, finally producing a small utility knife. He used the knife to cut the head off of the power cord, and he quickly separated and stripped the two wires. He extended his prosthetic leg and used the knife to pry open the battery compartment in the calf. When he had the battery terminals exposed, he wrapped one wire around each probe, being careful to not move his leg. Once the wires were connected, he laid on his back next to Kaluna, carefully yet quickly cycling his leg in the air. The limb quickly came up to temperature again. Small amounts of smoke and water vapor emanated from the connection. He sat up to see that the resuscitation pack was responding. It was not quite charged for use so Sembado laid back down and continued his hurried bicycle kicks. In less than a minute he was up and had his leg disconnected. The machine was back on and ready for use. He sat, poised at the last step, and took a deep breath, pleading for success. As soon as the second probe touched Kaluna's skin, her body gave one large jerk, and recoiled, curling up in the fetal position. Her tired eyes opened and Sembado met them with a smile. She looked around wearily, and reached out to him. He moved over to her, and cradled her small frame, helping her zip up her wetsuit. She pushed her face against his chest, her arms curled up in front of her, and Sembado squeezed her tightly.

The boy stood at a distance, looking concerned. Sembado gave him a reassuring nod, and the boy smiled a timid smirk.

"Who are you?" the boy asked.

Sembado paused. He leaned his cheek against Kaluna's head and closed his eyes. He opened them to address the boy and answered, "Friends."

The boy smiled again.

"My name is Tae."

"Thank you for saving us, Tae. We are grateful."

"Do you want something to eat? My mom made tuna meatballs last night. They're my favorite."

"Bathroom," Sembado responded. His adrenaline was starting to overwhelm his stomach. Kaluna struggled to sit upright by herself, but allowed Tae to show Sembado to the bathroom. This housing chamber was the same layout as Sembado's family's. Sembado shut the bathroom door and turned to the toilet just in time for the vomit to come. He dropped his pants and turned to sit on the toilet. His limbs shook uncontrollably. When he was finished relieving himself, he washed his hands and went back out to the main chamber. He found that Tae had moved Kaluna to a sofa and had given her a large blanket. She sat quietly, wrapped tightly, and stared at the floor. Her bloodshot eyes did not blink.

Tae stepped out of the room as Sembado came in. Sembado went to Kaluna's side and sat beside her. Only when his arm was around her did she break her trance-like stare. She let out a sigh and leaned against him.

"We have to get out of here," she said.

Sembado let out a single chuckle. Kaluna was always focused on her objective.

"We will," Sembado replied. "As soon you're feeling better."

"One hour," Kaluna responded. "And we need to figure out where we are."

"Well, I'm pretty sure we're on the other side of the complex from my sector," Sembado said. "But that doesn't help too much."

Just then, Tae walked back in carrying a tray.

"I brought the tuna balls," he said happily. "We can eat them while we wait for our district's penalty officer to arrive."

Sembado and Kaluna both dropped the little meat balls they each held.

"I'm sorry!" said Tae. "Are they too hot?"

Kaluna stood up, whipping off the blanket and frantically collecting her equipment.

"I said I'm sorry!" Tae said, picking the meat balls up off the floor. "I can get something else."

"Tae, it's not the meat balls. We just...we need to go," said Sembado. He was quickly helping Kaluna collect their wet belongings.

"But you need to be here when the penalty officers arrive so they can file a report! How are they supposed to file their report?" Tae pleaded.

Sembado looked at Tae, into his eyes. They were filled with genuine concern. He had no idea. There were so many things he wanted to share with the young boy, but there was no time. Kaluna was just starting to tug on his sleeve.

"*Sembado.*" It was just a whisper.

Sembado placed a hand on either of Tae's shoulders and knelt down so they could see eye to eye. Tae's eyes, welling with tears, searched longingly for answers to the questions he didn't even know he should be asking. Sembado smiled a warm, calming smile.

"Tae." He paused as a single tear rolled down the boy's flawless skin. "It's going to be okay. Just tell them we left, and that we are heading to the Civillion if they need to find us. Can you do that?"

"I...I think so," Tae said, wiping his nose with his sleeve. Sembado pulled Tae towards him for a hug, but was not prepared for how tightly the boy hugged him back.

"Alright..." Sembado coughed with short breath. "We'd better get going." Tae responded by squeezing harder, but he eventually let go.

When Sembado stood up, he found that Kaluna was attempting to collect their small, sopping backpacks, but was already looking fatigued. She did not resist Sembado's offer to take the waterlogged bags. The two friends were ready to go and about to leave when Tae ran back in with a small bag of tuna balls.

"The Civillion is a long walk," he said. Sembado laughed and gave the boy one more quick hug before he and Kaluna slipped out the front door.

They quickly made their way to the closest stairwell and wayfinding station. Kaluna teetered against Sembado as they found their bearings.

"Are you going to be up to this?" Sembado asked. It was not a critical comment, but genuine concern for her wellbeing. She pressed her forehead against his shoulder, and was silent for a moment.

"I think a short break somewhere is going to be worth not limping along the whole time." said Kaluna. While Sembado completely agreed, he was a little surprised at the answer. Being honest about her limitations was not normally Kaluna's strong suit. Sembado waited to respond as a stranger walked by.

"Well, I don't think we could be any further away from the grow houses. We might as well take that break as soon as possible, but let's get out of here first," Sembado said. Just then, a pair of penalty officers came around the corner at the other end of the hall.

Chapter Seven
A Rolling Boil

Linx cried out in agony as nothing but a foul stench filled the space where Jonah had just been standing. He clung to himself and fought to crawl forward as his grief enveloped him. There was no time to react. He wailed unintelligibly. How could he have done anything? He began to weep. There was no body to cling to. There was no body.

Linx had personally witnessed countless losses in his service to the Elephant's guild. The very first one was Jean M'Gereg's son. His name was Andrel and he had exposed Linx to the Elephant's agenda and trained him through his first several assignments. Andrel, Linx, and Linx's brother Reece were on a mission to steal an advanced penalty officer access card. The pick-up had gone bad and the young men had to fight off two penalty officers by hand. Linx had sprayed one of the Pens in the face with assault foam, and Andrel was locked in hand-to-hand combat with the other. With three quick blows to the face Andrel had nearly subdued the officer, but then the desperate adversary lashed out with a knife, slicing a deep gash across Andrel's neck. Linx sprayed this penalty officer's face with the foam as well, and kicked him in the throat. He turned to see Reece running far away down the corridor. Linx screamed after his brother, but Andrel needed his help. The strong young man had his hand clasped firmly on his wound, but blood was running freely between his fingers. They moved as quickly as they could to get away from the two incapacitated officers, but they did not get far. Linx was able to make it over two corridors and down three flights of stairs before collapsing under the weight of Andrel's solid frame. Andrel did not cry out or grimace once. He merely looked angry. Linx laid against the steel stairs with Andrel between his legs, helping put pressure on the giant gash. He nearly had his mentor in a head lock to maintain the force as he had no idea what he was doing, and soon the life had drained from Andrel's eyes. Linx was overcome by loss, failure, anger at his brother's betrayal, but at least he had a body to cling to.

Those old feelings boiled to the surface as the focused rage and seething vengeance of every death that Linx had ever seen washed over his spirit. Jonah had died with purpose. That purpose was to allow Linx to succeed. He would not fail.

Linx clinched his fists as he wrestled back into the control chair.

"Abort last command! I repeat. Do not retreat! We will focus a dive through the hole in the containment net. Your priority is defense as we move forward. At any sign of a torpedo, blast it with explosive rockets. We aren't losing one more man to those goddeeked flash-spheres! Acknowledge order!"

A report of emboldened confirmations came rolling through the headset as Linx assumed the tip of a new attack maneuver.

He ignored the pod of enemy subs to his left and right as he accelerated forward. He had the throttle pushed to its maximum and smiled a dark grin as he thought about how uncomfortable his recently departed battle-mate would have been with his current speed. His submarine's massive engines rumbled to life as they kicked into overdrive. The attack squad struggled to keep pace as Linx shot through the hole in the net and barreled toward the complex.

The confusion of the government submarine pilots could not have been more obvious. A number of them merely circled overhead while only a handful made an attempt at pursuit. Linx put his finger on his call button, ordering *The Beluga* to release another volley of rockets. As Linx and his gang continued down, they encountered pairs of government subs which they dispatched handily. Their discretion was tested to its limit as they repeatedly held their fire for random escaping submarines that appeared laden with civilians. Several could be spotted heading for the net breach. As Linx skimmed down over the upper levels of the complex, he pulled back up to re-challenge his pursuers. His formation followed suit and soon they were in a steep climb back up. As soon as they were turned around, the government subs that had avoided Mahana's most recent volley were headed straight at them.

The lead sub had released a torpedo directly at Linx who was able to veer away at the last second. As he did, the torpedo detonated, sending a large flash-orb through the hull of Linx's submarine. Linx grimaced and leaned to the far side, but the orb had only just encompassed the empty copilot seat.

Renewed with rage over his fresh loss, Linx screamed out loud as he released every last rocket and torpedo he had left. His immediate wingmen followed suit and suddenly Linx and his companions were chasing their wave of missiles as they collided with their targets. Linx maintained full pressure on the accelerator as he steered directly through the damage and debris he had just caused. Errant submarine pieces bounced off his viewing shield, but soon he had a clear view of *The Beluga*, and he radioed to Mahana to prepare to receive his battle-worn brigade.

***

"Welcome back, bruddas," Mahana said as he hoisted Linx out of his submarine. He was difficult to hear over the loud victory song being sung around him. He then poked his head in the submarine, immediately pulling it back out in dismay. "Where's Jonah?" As the celebration continued around them, Linx fought to describe what had happened to Jonah and the others. As he did, Mahana leaned against Linx with his heavy frame and wept. The celebration was cut short when a body that had been partially dissolved was hauled out of a nearby submarine.

A number of escaped submarines had returned with the battle brigade and were making their way into *The Beluga*'s underbelly port. Several of the submarines were captained by Elephant guild members. The escapees shuffled out of the submarines and while the civilians were escorted away to be processed, the Elephant members joined the surging crowd of warriors that was now following Mahana and Linx to the upper battle deck. Their victory song had given way to angry battle chant that echoed in the cavernous docking chamber.

Mahana and Linx walked with their heads close together as they continued to share information.

"Dis flow of new tanka's ain't gonna stop." said Mahana. Linx nodded in agreement as Mahana continued, "We're gonna have to move on to da main land soona than expected, but not if da government can still track us down. And dees new flash-spheres got me feelin' real uneasy."

"We have to have a more secure situation in the complex." said Linx. "Sembado and Kaluna need us to maintain the distraction. That is still key."

Mahana's face flushed at the mention of his beloved niece, but he motioned for Linx to continue.

"I volunteer to head a strike team to actually invade the complex. Everything we've heard points to Fabian steadily losing control. All we need is one good push to knock him off balance. Let me get down there and see what kind of trouble I can stir up for him. Once we can get a resistance to overwhelm him, we will be free to lead the escapees to the mainland."

Mahana clinched his jaw the way that he did when he was thinking. He took a long time to respond.

"I agree to da strike team, but you gotta be wary. Da closer Fabian gets to defeat, da more desperate and dangerous he'll be. As far as da escapees go, I tink dey're fate should be in der own hands. We should only bring dem to da mainland if dat's der wish. Some might just wanna stay tankers in da tank," he said, finishing with a chuckle. The two leaders and their procession continued to the control deck, recruiting warriors for Linx's strike team along the way.

Chapter Eight
Shoulder Pad

Sembado and Kaluna wasted no time turning away from the approaching penalty officers, but did so as casually as possible. Kaluna leaned into Sembado as they went; their current situation had only exacerbated her anxiety. With his arm around her torso, Sembado lifted her as much as he could without making her uncomfortable. Their awkward shuffle must have seemed too suspicious because one of the two penalty officers called for them to stop. Sembado nearly found himself adhering to his lifetime of fear. Less than a year ago he would have complied immediately as he knew nothing of the Elephants, their cause, or their present struggle against the tyrannical government. Staying out of trouble with authority had been his greatest achievement. But now he quickened his pace. Kaluna squeezed him tight as he bounced them along between his real leg and the more powerful prosthetic. The penalty officers called out a second warning which was followed by a steady banging. They were starting to trot down the corridor in their heavy boots.

Sembado rushed Kaluna to the next stairwell.

"Start moving down," he said. He pulled the door shut, listening for her muffled steps as she made slow progress downward. The sound was lost in the noise behind him. The two penalty officers had slowed to a stop, but were now taking turns barking orders at him.

Sembado clenched his jaw and closed his eyes tightly as he thought of Kaluna struggling on the other side of the door. She had always tried so hard for him, for herself, for her people.

"You will put your hands above your head or you *will* face penalties," said one of the officers. His voice was gravelly and dark. This was not one of the young, bewildered officers that Sembado had encountered in the past.

Sembado opened his eyes. Before he could do anything else, one of the officers stepped forward and pinned him against the stairwell door. Sembado thought of Mahana leading his people on the surface with Linx and Jonah Feldman at his side as they fought to give him and Kaluna the opportunity they needed. The officer had one hand on the back of Sembado's neck and the other on his wrist. Sembado fought against the restraint, but the other officer joined the struggle and soon the two men had Sembado's arms crossed behind his back and were applying a restraint to his wrists.

"Stop squirmin' or I'll shock ya," said the penalty officer with the gravelly voice. He produced an electric baton and activated it next to Sembado's ear so that he could hear the hum. Sembado thought of his deceased friend Meligose.

"Deron, I don't think we're supposed to use the shock stick unless..." said the other officer in a light, boyish voice.

"Shut the hell up, Banes, or I'll put it to you too."

Sembado thought of the murderous coward, Gerard Hutch. He jerked one hand free, catching the lead officer in the chin with his elbow.

The officer wasted no time in applying the shock stick to the back of Sembado's neck. The electrode met the skin right next to the receiving sensor for Sembado's prosthetic. His entire body stiffened with excruciating pain, but the powered leg collapsed from the impulse and Sembado fell hard on his left side. The convulsions continued for a moment while he lay on the floor. His leg twitched back and forth in a steady rhythm.

"Deeks, Deron! He's got a fake leg. The last thing the boss is gonna want is excessive force on a damn handicap." The younger officer said.

"I said shut up, Banes! Hutch don't give a damn about some crippled kid."

Sembado opened his eyes.

Are these guys really answering to Gerard Hutch?!

He used his leg to spring up while rotating in midair. He landed in front of the older officer and immediately backhanded the shock stick out of his hand. The officer responded with a right hook across Sembado's mouth, sending him back against the stairwell door. The room spun. Through his blurred vision, Sembado could just barely see the younger officer trying to hold the older one back.

"Get your damn hands off me you little eel!"

"Seriously, Deron! Just stop!"

Deron shoved Banes to the floor, bringing his momentum back again to strike another staggering blow. This one landed in Sembado's stomach and he doubled over, his lungs devoid of air. The officer grabbed him by the hair and stood him up.

"Still think he's just some handicap, Banes? Look at this." Deron said. He held Sembado's arm out so that his young counterpart could see the Elephant symbol. Once again Sembado was forced against the door. Banes had returned and was appeasing Deron by helping secure the restraints.

"I bet Gerard'll be surprised that we found one in this sector!" Banes squeaked.

Sembado snapped out of his haze. His blood ran hot and then cold. The officers had just pulled the restraint snug, pinching both his wrists painfully.

Suddenly Sembado jumped up, planting his bionic foot on the steel door in front of him for just a second before kicking off with all his might. The force of the robotic limb shot Sembado and the two ill-prepared penalty officers backwards over ten feet. The three bodies landed in a heap. Sembado was the first to stir, rolling off the other two men as his hands were still tied. The younger officer lay motionless and unconscious. His skin was tight and flushed. His brown hair was tossed across his ears. He looked very young. Sembado began to stumble down the hall. His mechanical leg did most of the work, but it seared his flesh with the heat of its performance. His chest burned with anger.

"Don't go any further you little cuss," the older guard said. His gruff voice was even hoarser than before.

Sembado stopped. He pivoted on his real leg to face his opponent. He turned to find the guard had his pistol sited halfway up his torso. The young guard remained motionless on the floor. Just as Sembado's panic and fear and rage started to boil over and turn into one, his bionic leg responded. It recoiled quickly, bringing him into a crouched position; the leg was nearly doubled in half. The officer dropped his weapons to maintain his aim on Sembado, but before he could follow through, Sembado sprung forward with all of the power his leg could offer. He shot toward the penalty officer at breakneck speed while a new pulse of heat rippled through his body. He was barely in control, having to drop his head to maintain his trajectory as he was completely airborne. He closed the twenty-foot gap to the officer in an instant. The officer was able to squeeze off one round before Sembado's shoulder struck him square in the chest; a sickening crunch emanated from the impact. Sembado continued flying further, hit the floor, and rolled to a stop. The restraint on his wrists was broken and hung from one arm.

Sembado's head swam as he stood up and squared his shoulders to the officer. He began making steady, deliberate steps as he gained his bearings.

The officer was just getting to his feet. His chest plate was shattered and blood trickled down one corner of his mouth. He looked angry, but fearful.

Sembado quickened his trot as the officer fumbled on the ground for his sidearm. Just as the officer grabbed his pistol and stood up, Sembado planted his normal foot on the ground and brought his powerful leg up to kick the man in the chest. The powerful blast sent Sembado back on his rear, but he was able to watch the officer fly backwards several yards and collapse to the floor, his arms wrapped around his fractured sternum. Sembado collected himself once more, and marched past the officers, stepping over their broken bodies. He grabbed their handguns as he went, and hurried to the stairwell.

Sembado found Kaluna three and half flights down; she was fighting to go further. He brought her to the next landing where they embraced. He winced and recoiled when she hung around his severely bruised shoulder. The impact to the officer's armor had not been easy on him. Kaluna fought against her fatigue as she searched one of their bags for a couple frayed garments. Her movements were clumsy. She wrapped the articles of clothing around Sembado's right shoulder as he explained the incredible abilities his leg had provided.

"My cousins must have made a few tweaks," she said weakly. Before Sembado could respond, Kaluna's eyes drifted behind her eyelids and she teetered into him, unconscious. Sembado did his best to support Kaluna while he slung the bags over his unbruised shoulder, and collecting her in his arms to continue down the stairs. He gritted through the heat of his powerful appendage as he used its strength to make faster progress despite the extra load.

Sembado knew that Kaluna's condition was beyond a quick recovery, but fast and friendly medical treatment was going to be a rare commodity on this mission, let alone a place to bed down for a while. Sembado carried Kaluna to the next wayfinding station, pausing just long enough to locate her people's district on the map.

If the government is having trouble just keeping regular citizens under control, perhaps the islanders have put up a strong fight too.

The fate of the islanders' quarter had not been discussed since Sembado first fled the complex. Once he and his friends had arrived on the Hawaiian Islands, the fate of the remaining refugees had been forgotten; at least by Sembado. At this point, he was not even sure if there was an islanders' quarter to return to, but that was the only place to which he could confidently carry Kaluna. They would provide the protection and care she needed. Sembado quickened his pace even more. He had discovered an ideal gait at which he could make six foot strides without jostling Kaluna too much. In addition to strength and power, his bionic limb offered a great deal of finesse if he concentrated hard enough on his landings.

Sembado slowed his speed to a slow strut as he surveyed his surroundings. He had come a long way, and recognized this area as that which surrounded the 4D virtual reality arena that he used to frequent with his friends. He continued to glance around corners as he went. This area was always busy with pedestrian traffic, and the sight of him carrying Kaluna was suspicious enough by itself, but Sembado was becoming more surprised by the minute. He had traveled over a mile without sight of a single person.

He continued to creep along, Kaluna's limp frame huddled against his chest. Suddenly to his right, he heard a noise; it was a low, muffled banging. He moved through the intersection he was passing and carefully set Kaluna in a nearby communication alcove. He returned to the intersection, and peeked his head around the corner. The banging noise was louder; it was getting closer. Two intersections down, a handful of people appeared. They backed into the intersection; each held a handgun. They fired another barrage of shots. This time the noise was loud enough to be uncomfortable. Sembado put his hands over his ears, and watched the group carefully. He heard orders and directions being shouted as the group turned away from the fight and headed his way. He quickly ducked around the corner and picked up Kaluna. He stood back into the communication booth as much as possible. Soon the group of people ran by, firing more shots behind them as they went. In addition to the terrible noise, Sembado was surprised to see that all five people running by were armor-clad young women. They ran past Sembado and Kaluna without notice. Sembado was in no mood to meet the female warriors or their pursuers and he quickly headed away from the main corridor.

Upon further examination of the corridors he passed, Sembado had come to the conclusion that this part of the complex had become a regular warzone. Every residential chamber he passed had its front door blown in. Looting and burning had occurred in many of them. He paused at an elevator tube; the doors had been removed. He squeezed Kaluna tight as he chanced a peak in the empty elevator shaft. A glance up and down revealed countless levels, with no elevator car to be seen. All of the adjacent floors had also had their doors removed.

Suddenly Sembado heard a crunch behind him. He froze. Someone had stepped on the debris strewn all about the floor of the elevator lobby behind him.

"Don't move." said a husky voice. There was something strange about the tone. "Now, turn slowly," the voice commanded, and Sembado complied. He turned to see a diminutive figure in black combat gear. The size of the person's frame continued to baffle him as he took in the helmet, the combat rifle, and the bright blue symbol painted across the figure's ample chest.

That's a young woman, maybe just a girl.

The figure seemed just as perplexed by the appearance of Sembado, his leg, and the petite brown woman that lay in his arms. Before the stranger could say anything else, an explosion rocked the corridor behind her. She turned quickly, falling to one knee and siting her rifle in one fluid movement.

Sembado held Kaluna tighter than ever, and backed away from the noise. His foot kicked some rubble over the edge of the elevator shaft. He turned to face the opening. As gunfire erupted behind him, he took aim at an open door across the shaft and one floor up. With one powerful leap, Sembado's bionic limb sprung him and Kaluna across the twenty-foot distance in a moment. The landing was painful, but mostly because of the overheated power supply.

Once he landed, Sembado took a moment to glance back down the elevator tube. The young woman had backed her way up to the edge of the shaft. She returned one final spray of gunfire before jumping backwards down the opening. It was only then that Sembado realized she had a rope attached to a body harness, and he watched as she repelled down the dimly lit shaft, disappearing into the darkness. Sembado resituated Kaluna as he turned to continue cautiously down the next corridor.

This portion of the complex was still unfamiliar to Sembado, but it was much quieter, and while Sembado was able to maintain a very good pace, he was not sure of his direction. A brief pause at a wayfinding station showed that they were actually headed straight for the island refugees' district.

Sembado checked Kaluna's vitals. Her pulse and breathing were both steady, but weak. He hoisted her higher into his arms as he made his way quietly down the next corridor. Sembado started to feel on edge from the silence and lack of activity. The last few months had provided an endless stream of chaos, pain, and struggle. The unexpected calm allowed his thoughts to wander.

Sembado had never been alone against his will, and even with Kaluna in his arms, the lack of company made him feel isolated. He longed to be talking to his friends, to be scolded by his parents. He missed his grandfather very much. As he walked along, he situated Kaluna's hand so that it fell into his. Even when he held it with a light squeeze, it did not feel like the warm grip to which he had grown accustom. Kaluna was here in his arms and he could not hold her hand, embrace her body, or gaze into her incredibly green eyes.

"Who's that!" said a voice from just ahead. It sounded less than official, and Sembado tightened his hold on Kaluna's light frame. He prepared to get Kaluna to the floor as quickly as possible, in order to make a preemptive strike. He started to roll his padded shoulder, but the voice cried out again, "Kaluna!"

Chapter Nine
The Descent

"The plan was to keep them distracted so Sembado and Kaluna could find the journal!" Linx said to Mahana. His tone had become elevated. He paced in front of the panoramic windows of *The Beluga's* bridge.

"I know what da plan was, Linx, but tings have changed." Mahana responded. His voice was growing exasperated also. "We haven't heard from da Elephants in da complex in days, almost weeks. We have dis new group down dere, and we don't know who dey are or what dey want. Da government has dese new flash weapons. And now we have dese penalty officers turnin' demselves in. Dis new guy is da tird defector to come forward. Dese guys want to take out Fabian jus' as much as you and me."

Linx said nothing, but let out a deep sigh as he gazed out on to the ever expanding network of vessels that surrounded *The Beluga*. They rippled with the ocean swells like one giant patchwork fabric.

"What was da plan to turn into?" Mahana continued. "You wanted me to send you down dere to jus' stir stuff up? Try and rally support? According to dese defectors, da entire complex is a war zone."

"We don't even know these guys!" Linx snapped back. "And I don't think our plans should be based on hearsay from some so-called defectors. We know nothing about this Markus guy."

"Ya, we do. He's one of Fabian's higha'-ups, and word is dis guy has been workin' his way up trew Fabian's ranks for years."

"Oh, great! Yea, that's not suspicious at all. Why didn't we just send Sembado and Kaluna straight to him!?"

"Linx, calm down, man. One o' da d'fected penalty offica's is Markus's nephew. His younga brudda snuck out wit him. We'll hold the olda brudda here while you take da young man wit ya. He knows where to find da next contact who will put ya in touch wit Markus. I have a couple of my boys ready to go wit ya, but keep the team small, huh?"

"You don't think the younger nephew would just sell us out?" Linx asked.

"I've talked to dese guys myself," said Mahana. "Dey have it in der eyes. Fabian's taken family from dem too. Please. You want to take a team down der? Fine. But at least go with a solid head on yer shoulda's and a solid plan."

Linx straightened up and squared his shoulders. He looked Mahana in the eye, saying "Where's this younger brother?"

"He's wit Jellene down in da dockin' bay. He really loves those subs," he said with a chuckle.

"I'll go check him out." Linx said. He left Mahana alone. The islander let out a long sigh as he peered out from his great vantage. He closed his eyes.

"God help us."

***

Mahana and Linx renewed their discussion quietly while the crowd of young men and women congregated on the platform around them. The cavernous surface dock in the underbelly of *The Beluga* echoed with excited chatter. The infiltration was upon them.

First, Linx and his team would make contact with the defectors. The coup would be as swift and clean as possible, but they would need help. After Linx made the initial contact, additional support would arrive from the surface and provide the necessary guns to help keep peace during the transition. Finally, they would locate Sembado and Kaluna to see if they had discovered any answers to the anti-weapon in order to eliminate their use in the future. The last step in the plan was still being kept between Mahana and Linx. Sembado and Kaluna's objective was too important to make public knowledge yet. They had agreed that even Sembado's name being used around the defected agents would be too risky.

Mahana and Linx briefed the group on the details of the mission as mechanical crews serviced the surrounding fleet of submarines to full repair. The crowd fell silent as

Linx energized a microphone that was broadcasted to all of their headsets.

"We will not be forcing our way into the complex." The silent response to his statement was deafening, even over the roar of the sea outside. He continued, "There is enough chaos for our friends down there as it is. With all the people coming to the surface, we think our team should be able to get in unnoticed. We will approach and enter the three identified access points at random intervals. Once we access the complex, we will rendezvous at Mahana's district. You *will* minimize weapons fire. Our goal here is to use as passive techniques as possible. We will be subversive, but only with as peaceful means as possible."

Mahana expressed his continued approval by nodding at every statement Linx made. He listened on as Linx continued his speech.

"We have received word that there may be several penalty officers who are willing to defect, but we may encounter normal citizens who wish to remain in the complex, and may still support the government..." Linx trailed off as the murmuring in the crowd approached an unruly tone. Mahana took the microphone and continued for him.

"Hey!" Mahana said firmly. The crowd fell silent again; first Mahana's people, and then the rest. "We ain't playin' judge an' jury here. If dese people we meet, your brudda's and sista's, want to stay, let 'em. Each an' every one o' you is here because you're sick of bein' told what to do, right? So I'm sure not gonna be tellin' anyone else der bidniss."

Even with Mahana's commanding voice, objections could be heard throughout the crowd. Mahana silenced them quickly.

"Ya tink it's gonna be hard?"

There were a few obstinate replies, and Mahana wasted no time in addressing the doubters directly. He stepped down into the parting mass of people, and walked directly to the loudest, boldest objector. Linx followed in his wake.

"You tink it'd be easier to show strength?" Mahana asked the man. The man surveyed those around him. He was not nervous, but calculating.

"Yes," the man replied.

"Into da mic, friend," Mahana said, staring straight into the man's eyes. The man paused, staring back, and then responded directly into the microphone.

"Yes, I think it would easier if we weren't worried about everyone's feelings," said the man. His comment was followed by a few shouted approvals.

"So did ya gov'ment," Mahana said flatly. Even more approvals echoed throughout the dock. The mechanics had stopped working, and sat with their headsets tuned into the showdown. The man tried to offer a valiant retort.

"Yea, but they abused it. There's nothing wrong with government control if it's done correctly," the man said. He could barely finish before he was showered in boos.

The mechanics were especially dissatisfied, and soon they returned to their work.

Mahana put his hands on the man's shoulders.

"Brudda, ya don't sound too different from da people whose freedom ya's arguin' 'gainst. Now, ya deserve ya say, but so does eryone else, even if it means having to wait an' listen a while. Ya gonna have to be watchin' ya brudda's backs more den eva'." As the words soaked in, the man broke eye contact with Mahana for the first time, and looked down at his shoes instead. Mahana reaffirmed his grip on the man's shoulders.

"Hey, look at me." said Mahana. The man lifted tear-filled eyes to meet Mahana's as the islander continued, "Fabian's days are numbered."

One unified cheer erupted from the crowd.

"And his crooked crowd of friends betta' watch *deir* backs!" Mahana added. The man's face broke into a smile as he choked back more tears. Mahana hugged him in a tight squeeze. He turned to hold the man in a one-armed embrace, and grabbed an unsuspecting Linx with the other. With his two companions held tightly at his sides, Mahana roared one last slogan, "Now let's go lib'rate some tankas!"

The crowd began moving as one, each person rallied to their team leader, and the group was quickly divided into submarine-sized squads. Linx took his team to their craft as the mechanic on top came down to meet him. The mechanic was a middle-aged woman named Jellene. She was an escapee from the complex who used to repair submarines for the penalty officers. She and Linx had quickly bonded over their shared hatred of Gerard Hutch.

"Wish I could take you with me, Jell," said Linx, as his team clambered into the vehicle. They exchanged a long, sincere hug.

"You and me both, Lefty," she replied, wiping her hands on her tool smock. "But I need to help get this thing sea worthy or she ain't never gonna make it to the mainland," she said, pointing to the rest of the ship with her thumb. Linx smiled and nodded, but did not know how to end the exchange.

"Get the hell out of here," she said, punching him in the shoulder. Linx climbed into the submarine door, and turned to pull it shut.

"Hey, Lefty." Jellene shouted. Linx paused to prop the door back open. He looked at her expectantly.

"If you find Hutch, kick his ass for me," she said with a smirk.

"For you and the whole world," Linx said smugly. He closed and sealed the hatch for good, and his crew began their shove-off procedures.

Mahana and Jellene watched as Linx's submarine led the procession out of *The Beluga*'s belly. While Linx and the others were down below, Mahana and Jellene had plenty to do in order to prepare for the influx of boarders, and the long journey ahead.

Inside their submarine, Linx and his crew were acclimating to their surroundings. It had been a day and a half since Linx was last underwater; a day and a half since he had seen Jonah.

Linx's team consisted of Mahana's two islanders, the defector's younger brother, and one more escapee. The team was diverse, but some of the most skilled Linx had ever met. His pilot was a talented one; one of Mahana's best. His name was Puolo. He and the other islander, Kala, had been the first to welcome Linx into Mahana's ranks. Linx sat at the copilot's position as Puolo flipped switches and called out operational orders. Although Linx took comfort in the competence of his crew as they worked seamlessly around him, he found himself clenching his teeth as the submarine made its initial plunge. While the twilight fire of the setting sun had submitted to the evening's murk, the bright track lights on the submarine's exterior cut through the salty deep with ease. Linx could see a dozen shadows ahead; additional submarines awaiting his lead in the descent.

Puolo brought the nose of the submarine down masterfully: quickly but without turbulence. Linx's tensions faded as his crew adjusted to a steady dive. The task ahead was not the chaotic violence that he was used to, but going unnoticed would be a pleasant change of pace. The descent was quiet and uneventful, save for the few instances where the radar technician, Rita, had called out random escape submarines as they safely passed without incident. The most recent passing submarine had apparently come too close, as Rita had exclaimed loud enough to draw laughter from the rest of the crew. Linx turned and consoled her. She was a good solider, but he also knew her to be high-strung. For the past three weeks, Linx had watched the blonde vixen consistently call-out every one of her male counterparts that had disrespected her. In the dozen cases that Linx had observed, five of them ended in a fist fight with Rita winning each and every one. When her pride was not being challenged, she was one of the most focused warriors Linx had ever seen. He only hoped that she would be as much of an asset given the clandestine nature of their current mission. She sat and fidgeted with her radar controls; her hands were used to being occupied by a weapon.

Linx turned back to his front. He smiled at the memory of Rita's last fight. The young man she had bested in fisticuffs was well-deserving of his beating. Linx smiled even more at the thought of Rita getting her calloused hands on Gerard Hutch. That would be more than adequate for Jellene.

Just ahead at the viewing shield, the lighted sea water passed by calmly. Flotsam and jetsam rushed past the glass as they slowed their approach to the containment net. On Linx's signal, Puolo executed a vertical dive through the tattered opening that Linx had passed through just over a day before, right after losing Jonah. Linx felt his heart become hard, the weight of Jonah's loss seemed to physically affect his chest. It was only then that he realized Puolo had accelerated the dive toward the complex. The other islander, Kala, radioed back to the trailing submarines. His order was for them to hold back while the leading team advanced to the first depressurized landing pod. Even as they were making their final approach, two different submarines were making a frantic escape.

As the water in the landing pod was evacuating, Linx set his eyes on the last member of the team, the brother of the defected informant – Markus's nephew. Linx was still unsure of the young man's trust, but he had been adamant to join the mission and serve his purpose. While his combat opportunities were few, he had assured Linx that he had several hundred hours logged in his local 4D arena. For their trip back into the complex he had foregone his typical large afro for tight, orderly corn-rows. From what Linx could gather, the young man was usually light-spirited, but the loss of his family and escaping with his brother had made his life grimmer than he could have ever imagined. Linx also got the distinct feeling that his young comrade longed to return to the complex; he frequently lurked in the submarine bay whenever possible. His name was Kreymond.

Chapter Ten
Lahalo

Sembado heard motion around him before he opened his eyes. He had fallen asleep sometime in the night. He recoiled slightly as bright light glared through his eyelids. He cracked them open, first one and then the other. A crowd of old women stood and cooed around Kaluna's rest bed. Kaluna had finally come to and was trying to respectfully dismiss the women's concern. Sembado's heart jumped as he saw her conscious eyes blinking away the same bright light that bothered his. One of the old ladies took notice, and soon the lights in the room were dimmed slightly. The women took turns making their last appeals for Kaluna to eat this or rest that on her forehead before they filed out of the room. When the last woman walked out, Kaluna closed her eyes and pushed her head back against her pillow. Sembado let out a chuckle. She turned her head and opened her eyes.

"What are you laughing at?" she asked.

"Nothing. It's just funny to see people fawn over you for a change. You're normally better at avoiding attention," Sembado said smugly.

"Well, when you bring me here unconscious and let them put me up in one of their damn sick beds, it's kind of hard for me to resist," she responded sourly. "How long have I been out?"

"Just a day. You were in pretty bad shape when I caught up with you." Sembado said.

"I remember...you were very angry," said Kaluna.

Sembado shook his head and then dropped it, saying, "Yea. I don't know what that was. Even though I defeated those Pens, I almost felt...powerless over it." He rubbed his fake leg. "I don't know if it's the heat or what, but this thing has me feeling kind of uneasy."

Kaluna twisted her mouth as she pondered the prosthetic.

"I could ask one of my cousins to look at it," she said.

"Yea. Maybe," said Sembado. "I almost feel like I'm getting feedback in this thing," he added. He moved over to the bed so that he could show her the receiver at the base of his head. Kaluna tried touching it, but it was too hot.

"Ow! Doesn't that hurt?" she asked, pulling her hand away.

"It's not hot on the skin side, but the leg is. Maybe there's a wire crossed?"

"I don't know," said Kaluna, shaking her head. "Let my cousins look at it."

"Yea. Okay," he said.

Then Kaluna wrinkled her nose.

"Hey, I appreciate you waiting here while I recovered, but you need to shower. You smell awful," she said, pulling her head away from him.

"What?" he said incredulously. He smelled under the armpit of his shirt. "I do not. Wait. What is that?" He sniffed all around his clothes before finding and revealing a bag full of smashed tuna meat balls. "Hungry?" he asked with a smile.

Kaluna feigned vomiting.

"No. I'm all set. Poor Tae," she said.

"Yea. He was clueless," Sembado added, shaking his head. "I think I'll take a shower anyways."

***

After he had bathed, Sembado returned with a tray full of food, and he and Kaluna spent the remainder of the morning snacking while talking about his prosthetic's feats of strength, the state of the complex, the band of female warriors Sembado had seen, and their strange symbol.

"Do you think they're pro-government?" Kaluna asked.

"I'm almost positive they're not," Sembado said, "but I haven't talked to anyone about how Elephant-friendly they are either."

"So let's go find out," she said, setting the tray aside and pushing off her blankets.

"Are you sure?" he said, preparing to brace her as she stood.

"I passed out. I didn't get hit by a submarine. You're starting to act like my old tutu," she said with a furrowed brow.

As they walked out into the islanders' common space, Sembado was careful to use his prosthetic as little as possible. His real leg was already sore after its lack of use over the past few days. Luckily they were taking ample breaks as almost every islander they passed wanted to take a moment to greet Kaluna and say a prayer for her speedy recovery. Most of the well-wishers also offered him and Kaluna yet another secret recipe for recuperation. Kaluna would thank them gracefully and pass the food off to Sembado. Soon both of his arms were cradling a small feast worth of morsels, snacks, and salves to apply. At the next encounter, Kaluna simply stuffed the sweet bread she was given right into Sembado's mouth. This elicited enough laughter from the crowd that the two were able to move along without having to stop again.

Kaluna led Sembado into a quarter of the islanders' domain to which he had never been. The sight of one heavily armed soldier after another told him that this was their military sector.

"I have never seen the warriors with this many weapons." Kaluna whispered. "This must be from the unrest out in the complex." They continued turning this way and that, each guard acknowledged Kaluna respectfully and helped ease Sembado's load with a grin. By the time they had reached their destination, Sembado was left with a single coconut-dusted rice cake. They stopped at a beaded entrance that was flanked by two men holding assault rifles. A voice from behind the beads beckoned them inside.

"E komo mai!" said the voice.

The dim light inside was made worse by the cloud of electronic cigar smoke that hung in the air like thick whale's milk. Beyond the smoke was a face; a large face that let out a familiar chuckle.

The man greeted Kaluna in their native language. Kaluna introduced Sembado to Lahalo. He was Mahana's one and only son. He offered them e-cigars and rum, both of which they declined.

"We got lots to talk about, cuz. How's papa doin' up there on da surface?"

"We have not seen him in two days." Kaluna said solemnly. "He was under attack when we left him."

"Yea, I know. I already got word from him," Lahalo said, letting out another signature laugh. "I was just seein' what you knew."

Sembado was entertained by this more sarcastic spitting image of Mahana. Kaluna was less than amused.

"Well how is he? What's going on up there?" Kaluna said scornfully.

"Not up there, cuz. Down here. He's sendin' down a strike team to try and turn da tide on da masta' tanka'. They should be arrivin' soon. Pops is still up in *da Beluga* though. Dis ol' fish tank is leakin' like a fish *net*," Lahalo said as he released another cloud of smoke. Kaluna glared at Lahalo while Sembado wafted the smoke away. "Don't worry 'bout Mahana," Lahalo said, putting down the cigar, and straightening up in his seat. "He might be old an' crusty, but he's still got his wits," he finished with a chuckle.

Kaluna maintained her icy stare. Lahalo stiffened, quietly returning the glare. Sembado decided to break the silence.

"So what's the situation with access in and out of the complex?" Sembado asked.

The awkward silence persisted, but Lahalo finally broke the stare-off with a sigh, focusing his attention on Sembado for the first time. He let out another deep sigh and dropped his eyes.

"I was really sad to hear about ol' Hyron," Lahalo said as he raised his eyes to Sembado's. "He was a good man. One of da best. Used to help sneak me batteries for deez," he said, indicating the e-cigar that sat on its glass stand. A small ring of smoke still hung above it. Sembado watched the thick smoke dance around. The smell was sweet and heavy.

"So does Fabian have this place on lockdown or what?" Sembado asked. He used a flat tone to indicate that he, like Kaluna, was only there for vital business. Lahalo pursed his lips, and looked back and forth from Sembado to Kaluna. He shook his head.

"The masta' tanka' gave up on containment right away. Mahana's been takin' on hundreds a day. Maybe thousands already. They're havin' to stay on their own crafts. *Da Beluga*'s already run outta space." Lahalo said.

"Then why hasn't Fabian been brought down yet?" Sembado asked suspiciously.

"Those tanka's makin' it up to the surface are nothing. There's still millions of people down here, and da pens have been focusing all their energies on controllin' the inside. Mahana could have da world's biggest fleet. Doesn't mean he can break down da door. He'd kill everyone. Tried tellin' him that," said Lahalo smugly.

"But you said that Mahana had people coming down. How are they gonna get in?" Sembado asked.

"Mahana's tryin' some *covert* approach. Thinks gettin' four or five of his folks in at a time is gonna make a difference," Lahalo said with a chuckle.

"Well he's counting on just the two of us to turn this whole thing around. Maybe four or five at a time will do," Sembado said defiantly.

"Yea. I know all about ya little scavanga' hunt. Sounds like ya gramps was keepin' some mighty fine secrets. I'd like to send some of my guys to help." Lahalo said. For the first time in their exchange he spoke with true gravity.

Sembado and Kaluna exchanged a look, and Sembado cleared his throat to speak. Before he could, Kaluna answered.

"No. This is supposed to be *quiet*. If we have a team with us then it will look like we are looking for something." She spoke with clear resolve.

"Then why da hell'd ya come? You don't want my help, and ya actin' like I whizzed in ya breakfast," Lahalo snapped. His tone was not playful.

"We wanted to see if *your* father was okay," Kaluna shot back.

"Well now ya know. He's doin' what he loves. The ol' sap is takin' on more tanka's than he knows what to do with," Lahalo said picking up the cigar from the stand and taking a long drag.

Kaluna continued to sit, arms crossed, and stare at Lahalo quietly. Lahalo stared at the wall above Kaluna's head as he puffed the cigar and played with the smoke in his mouth. Sembado sat quietly, not knowing what to do with his hands. Lahalo started letting out a long intricate smoke ring, but finished by quickly blowing out the rest.

"Seriously, Luna, if ya just gonna sit here and bus' my coconuts, why don't ya just take ya boyfriend and go." Lahalo said. He was not being mean this time. Sembado almost detected defeat in his voice. Sembado also detected heat in his own stomach at the sound of the word *boyfriend*.

Kaluna took little notice, and answered Lahalo without missing a beat, saying, "We aren't going anywhere until you fix his leg. I don't know what you guys did to it, but it's overheating and giving him feedback."

Lahalo perked up, setting the cigar down once again so that he could move around the table to look at Sembado's prosthetic.

"Damn, I almost forgot about dat thing." Lahalo said. "How's she treatin' ya?"

"Well, like Luna said, it's been overheating. At my knee and the head unit," Sembado said, indicating the sensor on his neck. Lahalo moved around behind Sembado, poking and prodding unabashedly. He ran his fingers across the sensor at the base of Sembado's skull.

"Damn, that thing *is* hot!" Lahalo said as he called in one of his cohorts. They were able to pry the sensor open, making small adjustments and asking Sembado questions as they went.

"What kind of feedback ya gettin'?"

"Does it burn all the time or just when you been usin' it?"

"How many times have you had to recharge it?"

Sembado sat and described each episode of prolonged use: swimming to the complex, defeating the penalty officers, escaping up the elevator shaft. Lahalo and his crony sat and listened tentatively like children. Sembado went on to describe the associated heat and burning that came with each exertion, and also the overwhelming anger that he struggled to control. Lahalo and his mate exchanged sheepish and worried looks.

"What?" Sembado asked pointedly. "What did you do?"

"Ah, calm down, we can fix it," Lahalo said.

"What did you do?" Kaluna demanded.

"We added a couple extra battery cells... and the overheating mighta reversed da signal to his brain... but he should be fine." Lahalo said quickly.

Sembado immediately hated the feeling of the prosthetic and the sensor around his neck. Kaluna calmly helped him detach both as his hands were starting to shake uncontrollably. Anger and anxiety began welling up inside, and his leg was just starting to kick and flex by itself when Kaluna disconnected the brain sensor.

"Seriously man, we can fix it. Betta' than eva'." Lahalo said timidly.

"Just get him a crutch or somethin'." Kaluna said.

Sembado sat staring at the cigar, clenching his fists painfully.

Lahalo's assistant disappeared while Lahalo fidgeted with the prosthetic quietly, avoiding eye contact with Sembado who still had his steely stare fixed on the glass cigar stand. Sembado's entire body felt restless and numb all at once. He focused so hard on the glass stand that all feeling seemed to leave him. The only sensation he was aware of was a distant softness; a cool touch somewhere on his back. He turned his head slowly to see that Kaluna was making small circles on his back with her hand. She continued to glare at Lahalo.

Within moments, Lahalo's assistant had returned, his arms encumbered with bulky objects. He let the items spill out on the table.

The first item was another prosthetic. This one was completely manual, and featured leather and wood components. There was also an old aluminum crutch, its foam padding was stained black and yellow. Something at the bottom of the pile caught Sembado's eye. As Kaluna picked up the old wooden prosthetic the item below was revealed. It was a cane, a beautifully intricate cane with an ornate wooden handle and a stainless steel body that showed fine etchings even in the murky light of the room.

Sembado took the cane in his hand, and moved it this way and that to expose all of the fine details. As he turned it to one side, the handle began to move. It slid out of the body, and Sembado caught it and pulled it out completely, revealing a finely sharpened blade.

Sembado grinned as he looked it over, showing it to Kaluna. She did not look amused.

"Ha! I haven't seen that in ages," Lahalo chuckled, adding, "that used to be old Kalu's!"

"Who?" Sembado asked.

"My dad," said Kaluna. It was barely a whisper.

Sembado immediately sheathed the cane, and set it on the floor, away from Kaluna. Lahalo took the opportunity to change the subject.

"So ya'll should be settin' out pretty quick then. I've seen those lil' spheres in action and we gotta put an end to it," he said in his most business-worthy tone yet. "Go ahead and use these relics for now," he said as he indicated the cane and wooden leg. "I'll get this robo-kicker fixed right away. I don't think you should be goin' on ya lil' scavenger hunt without it."

"I think that's up to him." Kaluna said forcefully.

Sembado wanted to speak for himself, but he was still processing the drawbacks to the power that the leg provided.

Even in the covert scenario that lay ahead, it would be useful in covering more ground in less time. But then Kaluna wouldn't be able to keep up. Unless I carried her. No--that would look too suspicious.

"I could take the powered leg and just go by myself," he said. Lahalo nodded approvingly. Kaluna glared at Sembado.

"I'm not letting you go alone." she said.

"Luna, he's got a good point," offered Lahalo quietly. He seemed to finally understand the seriousness of the mission, and of Sembado and Kaluna's bond. "You said yourself that a team would be suspicious. Well, one is less suspicious than two. Especially if they see ginger here walking around with you. I'm sorry to say it, cuz, but even with his red hair, you stick out more than he does."

Kaluna tightened her mouth and looked reproachfully at Lahalo. Sembado took advantage of the silence.

"I know exactly where I'm going, and I will be back before you know it. I'm much more familiar with that part of the complex than you anyway, and if all else fails, I'll be able to find somewhere near the Civillion to hide," Sembado said as reasonably as he could.

"Whoa, I hate to stop ya there, but da Civillion's a bad choice. Da pens have fortified her pretty good, and have control o'er that whole hub," Lahalo said. "Let me show you a better route. Maybe that'd give Kaluna some peace o' mind," he said as he moved the prosthetics and cigar stand off the table. He reached under the edge of the table and flipped a couple switches. Suddenly the table came to life, a bright blue screen gave way to black and then white. The room was brightly illuminated and the smoke that still hung in the air was highlighted like wispy ghosts. Lahalo maneuvered deftly through the navigation program and soon a familiar map of the complex, of Sembado's district, was stretched to the extents of the table. As Lahalo continued to refine the resolution, Sembado caught sight of Kaluna. She sat with her arms crossed, staring straight at him. Tears welled in her eyes.

"This wasn't the plan," she hissed.

"Neither was you almost dying," Sembado snapped back. "It'll be okay, but I'm not going to continue to put you at risk when I don't have to."

"That's not your call. I'm not yours to take care of," she said.

Lahalo struggled to mind his own business as he clicked and refined the screen with less purpose.

"And I didn't take care of you in the water? Bringing you back? Carrying you here!?" Sembado felt the indignant rage growing inside him again.

What is she talking about? This isn't about me or her. It's about us. We're supposed to take care of each other.

Lahalo ignored them, and started pointing out suggested areas to avoid and others that were safe.

"Da areas you see here in red are under da control of my people and ya Elephants. Now, without Mahana and Hyron, around ain't been so easy to gather them together, but we been pretty good at stayin' out each other's way."

Sembado abandoned his argument with Kaluna to focus on the map, something he had control over. Lahalo panned the screen over to the Civillion.

"Everythin' you see in green is under da masta' tanka's power. They were losin' some ground last couple weeks, but since they moved inside, they done a good job of slowin' our progress and shorin' up their lines."

Sembado's eyes poured over the map as he tried to memorize which corridors were safe and which were contested. He panned and zoomed the screen as he needed, and soon found himself directing the map to his old home. He moved down the layers of the map. As he approached the level his family lived on, he was relieved to see that his allies had control of that part of the district. He was confused, however, to find the levels near and including his family's corridor were highlighted not red or green, but blue. He looked up at Lahalo with concerned eyes.

"What is blue? Does that mean the territory is disputed?" he asked.

Lahalo sat back in his seat, crossed his arms, and let out a sigh.

"No." He said. "Blue is... somethin' else. Someone else really."

"Who?" Sembado implored. "Are they friendly or what?"

"They call themselves *the Spring*," Lahalo said dramatically. He carefully moved through the map, making quick selections from a group of time-coded archives. "Here," he said. "Watch the progress of da colors."

He began clicking through the series of snap shots. The first was dated several months back, just after Sembado had left for the surface. It showed the majority of the complex highlighted green with the islanders' village representing most of the red territory. As he clicked through the weeks, little red areas began to appear all over the map. Some were eliminated over time, while others grew and formed together. The red and green territories ebbed and flowed over time, with the Elephant and islander progress slowing more recently. In the current screen shot shown on the display, little blue dots had appeared throughout both the government and rebel zones.

"This is from two months ago. This is when we first started trackin' da Spring. They aren't really with us, but they ain't with Fabian either," Lahalo said, scratching his chin. "They shoot at us *and* pens, but they never shoot first. Just seem keen on endin' whatever fight they find."

"Do they have a symbol of some kind?" Sembado asked.

"Uh. Yea, actually. They do," Lahalo said curiously. "How'd you know?"

"I saw one of them," Sembado said, redirecting his statement at Kaluna. "When we were on our way here. She had the chance to shoot, but didn't."

"Probably because you were carrying me," Kaluna said dejectedly.

"She has a point," Lahalo said. "Those girls never fire on da unarmed."

"Girls?" Sembado said

"Yep. Best we can figure – every last one of them is female. Ain't no one ever seen a man runnin' with da Spring."

"Sounds like a good idea to me," Kaluna said.

Lahalo let out a chuckle.

"They've actually made better progress against da pens than we have lately." Lahalo admitted.

Sembado had moved the time sequence back to the present where his family's home was well within the Spring's influence. He continued to move around the map idly, finding places he was familiar with in order to identify who controlled those areas. He was slightly amused to see the 4D arena was under control of the resistance. He thought about Zetvez, and wondered if he was okay – or even alive.

"You study up there, friend," Lahalo said, gathering the powered prosthetic and leaving the room.

"It's Sembado!" Sembado yelled after him.

"Whatever ya say, ginger!" was the response that came back.

Chapter Eleven
In Through the Out Door

Linx and his crew were poised at the submarine door while the chamber outside still contained a foot of water. Kala held the door while Rita stood by his side with a handgun held at arm's length. They were barely able to crack the door before it was pulled from their hands. Outside was a man with a child in one arm. A crowd of twenty stood behind him. They were ankle deep in water, and appeared tired and desperate. The two groups stared in befuddlement.

Shouting could be heard from beyond the chamber. Both Linx's crew and the group of escapees froze. The commotion grew until one muffled voice could be heard pleading. The voice was interrupted by a repeated command. The voices were barely audible over the sound of the remaining water gurgling into the floor drains. When the water had finished draining, the voices could no longer be heard. The silence in the chamber pressed on their ears. Suddenly, one final plea was cut short by a single gunshot. Even as the piercing crack rang out, it was replaced by a stomach-turning scream.

"Get in," whispered Linx. Everyone looked around at him. "Get in. Get to the surface. Tell the people on the ship that Linx sent you." The man carrying the child continued to gawk. "Well, you wanted the damn submarine didn't you? Take it! Now!" Linx said, directing his people off the sub and out of the way. The group of haggard escapees piled into the submarine. The last few passengers were afforded nothing but standing room. Linx helped close the hatch while his team quickly finished loading and securing their weapons.

The team moved to the exit door. It was kicked open as they approached it. Rita was at the head of the line and wasted no time laying down heavy fire. One penalty officer collapsed through the door. The body was kicked and prodded into the chamber, and the door was closed behind it. Linx and his team kept their weapons trained on the door, but suddenly their attention was on the floor as cool sea water began to percolate out of the vents through which it had just drained.

"So much for sneakin' in," Rita hissed.

The escapees peered out the windows of the submarine with concern as the chamber quickly filled with water.

"They're gonna try and drown us!" Linx shouted to the passengers as he worked his way back to the submarine. "Give us the spare air tanks! Hurry!"

By the time he reached the submarine, the water was waist deep and was approaching the bottom of the submarine's main hatch. The passengers cracked the door and feebly tossed out two air tanks and masks. They splashed into the water in front of Linx. Water was just beginning to pour inside the submarine when they shut and sealed the hatch quickly. Linx banged on the hatch with his fist.

"This isn't enough! We need five!" He screamed as the water climbed his chest. His team had gathered behind him. They stood quietly as the water approached some of their chins.

"What are we gonna do?" Kreymond nervously cried out.

"We will have to pass and share until the depressurizing pod cycles back to dry lock," said Linx, and he handed the air tanks out. One to Rita. One to Kreymond.

"But they could hold it open forever from inside!" Kreymond shot back. He had moved up next to Linx and was starting to claw and beat on the hatch.

"Then we'll have to swim out and find another way in." Linx said firmly.

"We would never..." Kreymond started to say before the top hatch of the submarine opened and three air tanks flew out, one after the other, and splashed down behind the team.

"Thank you!" Linx yelled, but the hatch was already pulled closed shut. "See?" he said to Kreymond, water lapping at his mouth. "Calm down." Linx quickly addressed the entire group, "Let's ride the water to the top of the chamber before wasting any O2." The team, including Kreymond, concurred, and they were soon bobbing off the floor. The submarine was floating too, and the passengers had turned on the lights. Linx and his team tried to maintain composure as they treaded water to the top of the room. The light from the submarine cast their shadows on the remaining wall surface. The multi-layered shades danced in and out of focus as the water splashed and climbed to the ceiling.

There was only a foot of space left to the ceiling when Linx called out his order.

"Alright – masks on!"

The team quickly and efficiently fit the breathing masks to their faces. They followed Linx as he used the pipes on the ceiling to move away from the large breaching door out of which the submarine would soon exit.

The vibrations through the water indicated that the submarines main engine had been engaged. The team found a space between some mechanical equipment to shelter. They held on and watched as the submarine pilot gained his control. The chamber filled, and the equalizing process was over. Linx and his crew focused as their chests were introduced to the full weight of their current ocean depth. This was the first time Linx had felt the crush in months. He nearly passed out.

The large, exterior chamber door split into pieces as it retracted back into the walls around it. The submarine wasted no time in departing, and Linx's team watched as it zipped out of sight. To Linx's surprise, the door began to close almost immediately. He and his team worked their way out of the confines of the ceiling equipment and swam down to the door from which the Pens had attacked. A resounding thud indicated that the large exit door was closed, and they all turned to confirm it. They waited for the bubbles to blow out of the floor vents, but the chamber water did not evacuate. Linx began to share some of Kreymond's panic as he realized the penalty officers had trapped them in the depressurizing pod and were going to wait for their air to run out. The thought seemed to spread throughout the group as each member did what they could to express their growing anxiety. Hand gestures and wild eyes were tossed from person to person. No one could find a comforting response. Linx attempted to calm the team, and indicated for them to move back to the pipes so that they did not waste energy kicking their legs. Rita had to nearly drag Kreymond by the arm. As they swam back up to the mechanical units, a series of tinny, sharp cracks echoed through the water. The noise multiplied and grew, becoming nearly uncomfortable. They had just reached the piping and were making efforts to plug their ears from the loud knocking noise. Kreymond expressed concern and curiosity, but Linx could only shrug and communicate his guess with a pointed hand-gesture: *gun fire.*

Without warning, an explosion rocked the chamber. A large orange flash blew the small, interior door in before the water pressure pushed the mangled door into the corridor. Linx held tight to the closest pipe as all the water in the chamber blew through the door and into the complex beyond. The suction, pressure change, and noise were excruciatingly painful on their ears. Linx was able to steal a glance at Rita fighting to keep Kreymond in place. She had just gotten him to lock his fingers around a pipe when the pull of the water sucked her away. Her screams were muted over the rush of water as she was carried out of the doorway with the rushing current. The chamber was half empty by the time the complex's safety measures had responded. A series of doorways beyond the corridor had been sealed and the rush of water was slowing to a stop. Water continued to move out of the chamber as it equalized with the surrounding corridors. Linx fought through his hazy confusion to release his grip on the pipe he held. He fell to the water below, splashing through five feet before he hit the floor. He stood up in the neck-deep water and fought with the pain in his ears. His team followed his lead, each landing gracelessly in a splash.

"What happened?" shouted Puolo as he helped Kala to his feet.

"An explosion," said Kala loudly. He fought to unclog his ears. "Someone blew the door off."

"Rita – is she okay?" Kreymond asked.

"The current sucked her out the door," Linx responded. "We have to go find her. Let's move."

The four young men made cumbersome progress through the deep water. They approached the damaged doorway to the corridor. The complex's emergency system was beginning to bilge the excess water; the industrial pumps were removed a foot of water per minute. Linx had the team pause at the doorway until the pumps stopped. There were signs of the recent chaos in the corridor beyond. The remnants of the exploded door were embedded in the adjacent wall. Several bodies lay piled against a door to another corridor. Linx ordered the team to the pile and they removed one dead penalty officer after another, nine in all. Each one was riddled with gunshot wounds.

"No Rita," said Linx. "Let's move down to the other blocked corridors and see if we can unlock any of these emergency hatches. More pens could be coming so keep your guns up."

They moved back past the depressurizing chamber to the other end of the corridor. The console outside the door was flashing warning signs about the pressure regulator inside the chamber. At the other end of the corridor, they found a similar pile of penalty officers. They moved the top body out of the way to reveal a female form, but it was not Rita. It was a young woman in heavy armor with a large blue swirl painted across her chest. She too had suffered several bullet wounds, and a large spherical wound on her abdomen indicated an orb attack.

"Who the hell is she?" Linx said as he crouched near the pile of corpses.

A sound came from the other end of the corridor. The door was opening and someone was pushing the bodies out of the way. Linx stood and readied his weapon; his team mimicked him. Suddenly the door behind them opened too. A squad of women stood with rifles pointed at them. The blue symbol was painted haphazardly across each of their chest plates. Two women in the back supported Rita under each arm. Linx and the women's leader locked eyes; hers were a piercing blue.

"You better come with us," she said.

Chapter Twelve
The Secret is Out

Sembado walked to the next corridor and paused. He had moved beyond Lahalo's territory and into contested space. According to the islanders, the entire sector that surrounded the grow houses had been under constant attack ever since the government started rationing food.

"There's no shortage," Lahalo had said. *"They're makin' just as much food as ever and with less mouths to feed now that so many have left. They're just tryin' to scare the tanka's that are still here. Lotta use that does. They just have people starvin' and panickin' now."*

Sembado watched two figures run across an intersection a quarter mile away. When they had disappeared, he continued on. He was careful to use his powered prosthetic as little as possible. Lahalo's helpers had made some adjustments, but Sembado could still sense an unnecessary strength hiding inside. It took more focus than he thought to maintain a balanced use between his two legs. His leading shoulder was padded just in case.

The islanders had fabricated a much more practical garment.

He checked the navigator Lahalo had given him at Kaluna's behest. It had calculated a direct route to the grow houses, but Sembado was using his discretion to avoid trouble areas. Lahalo had overlaid the latest territories map on the navigator, but had admitted that they were out of date. According to the device, Sembado was running on the edge between a contested region and Spring territory. Beyond that were the grow houses which were, according to the data, under government control. He thought of Kaluna and the heated words they had exchanged before he left.

"And if you get even a sense of trouble?" Kaluna had asked.

"I know. I'll come right back," Sembado had said. *"I'll be fine."*

"Don't get fed up with me," Kaluna snapped. *"You know I wouldn't be doing this if you'd just let me go with you."*

"Yea, well, it's not happening," Sembado shot back. *"I'll be back in a couple hours, we'll go through the journal, and get the info back to Mahana and the Elephants."*

Sembado meant to keep his time commitment, but he had already been gone an hour because of his insistence to not engage his bionic limb more than necessary. He heard gun shots down a corridor to his right, and checked the navigator before turning away from the disturbance. He was just rounding the corner when he collided with someone who was running the other way. Sembado bounced off of the heavily armored figure and spun into the wall. He was able to brace himself against the wall before falling, but he dropped the navigator in the process.

The other person had landed against the opposite wall and was now pointing their rifle at Sembado's chest. The navigator was at their feet. The figure, a woman, wore the same blue symbol on her chest that Sembado had seen days before. The two stood, awkwardly braced against opposite walls for several tense moments. More gun shots could be heard; they were closer than before. Sembado looked away to the source of the noise. The woman did not flinch. She just kept her rifle trained on Sembado's chest. He looked back at her and swallowed hard.

"You're with the Spring?" he asked as timidly as possible. She did not move. "I'm just trying to find some food for my family," Sembado said meekly. The woman jerked away from the wall, squared her weight over her feet, and threw up her tinted visor. She narrowed her eyes at Sembado as if trying to read his thoughts. He carefully pointed to her feet where the navigator had landed. "S-see," he stuttered. She reached down, and grabbed it. She maintained eye contact the entire time. She moved the navigator up to her eyes so that she could see Sembado while she studied it. One glance at it made her shoot her stare back at Sembado.

"Plenty of info here," she said. "Too bad it's so out of date. We've taken grow levels A through G from the government. They're fighting with the Elephants for the lower levels." She tossed the navigator back to Sembado who nearly bumbled it as he caught it.

"What about J?" he asked.

"What about J?" she replied.

"Do you know who controls that level?" he asked.

"I just said it's contested," she said.

"Oh, right. Sorry," Sembado said, pretending to push buttons on the navigator. When he sneaked a glance at her face, she was looking away to where the gun fire had been. Sembado made an awkward motion for a good-bye before turning in an attempt to slip away.

"Hey!" she said, and he turned back around, pretending to nearly drop the navigator. He stood still and erect. She still had the gun pointed at him, but quickly dropped the muzzle. She extended her left hand to him, and he took it carefully before shaking it. "Good luck finding something to eat," she said, but before he could respond, she twisted his left forearm upward, exposing his Elephant's mark. "Just finding food for your family, huh?" she said, squeezing his hand firmly. The armor on her glove slid and popped in a way that pinched and contorted his hand painfully. Before he could think, his prosthetic leg propelled him up and away from her. The powerful thrust and her firm grip coupled to pull her arm from its socket. She cried out as Sembado ricocheted off the wall; the padded shoulder took most of the impact. He landed, tumbled forward, and took off in a sprint, tucking his key-adorned necklace back under his shirt.

Sembado abandoned his attempts to suppress his bionic leg as he fled. The adjustments Lahalo's people had made were more apparent at full speed. While Sembado was running faster than he could ever manage naturally, his strides were much shorter than when he had carried Kaluna at this pace. Despite the governed speed, he quickly put several twists and turns through corridors between himself and the Spring solider. As the heat began to build on his severed knee, he slowed to a trot, and then to a hurried gait.

Sembado passed through the gateway to the grow chamber sector. He was on level F which, according to his unfortunate acquaintance, meant that he was still in Spring territory. He saw two people ahead and ducked into a stairwell. He used his powered leg to jump down a half-flight at a time. Each landing, with much focus, was nearly silent. He increased his speed when he heard a door open a few flights above him. Within moments he landed at J, and carefully cracked the door open. It was silent outside, but the smell of smoke hung in the air. He moved out into the corridor and began moving his way toward the actual grow chambers. He passed another stairwell and realized that he was running down the same stretch of corridor through which he was unwittingly chased by the Elephants nearly a year ago. He followed the curved hallway to the door marked:

GROW CHAMBERS—KEEP DOOR CLOSED.

He pulled the door open, and darted inside. What was a field of seven foot corn stalks the year before had been replaced by waist deep, golden-yellow wheat. Sembado was overwhelmed by the sweet, pungent aroma. The muffled clatter of gunfire encouraged him to move more quickly towards the far end of the room. The bright grow lights that hung over the crops flickered. Sembado hurried to a hatch in the floor. He paused for a moment as he remembered following his grandfather down this very hole. The lights flickered again, and the sound of heavier gun fire reverberated through the chamber. Sembado lifted the vent, climbed halfway down the access ladder, and pulled the lid over himself.

Once he had both feet firmly on the floor, Sembado held the navigator high over his head to project the light from the screen as far as possible. He fumbled blindly along the wall to find a switch that he was sure he remembered existing. He kicked something solid and loose by mistake. He reached down to find it was a flashlight. He clicked it on and quickly surveyed the space. Not much had changed since he had last been in the J-vent. The steady hiss of the equipment around him did little to mask the muffled knocking of battle above and beyond. He quickly worked his way deeper into the room and found the projector assembly his grandfather and old Jean M'Gereg had used to educate him. There were some loose boxes full of recovered documents. He moved the beam of the flashlight up and down as he scanned the racks of mechanical equipment that housed random piles of his grandfather's memorabilia.

Then he saw it, stashed between some fertilizer pumps and a water line: his grandfather's lockbox. Sembado moved to it as chills ran up his arms and across his chest. His face contorted involuntarily as his emotions welled up unexpectedly. He pulled the key and chain from around his neck. His hands were shaking uncontrollably. He held the box firmly under one arm while inserting the key with the other hand. With a little coercion, it fed into the lock smoothly. He closed his eyes and used minimal force to turn the key. He felt each mechanical piece work into its designed position, and then he heard a click. He opened the box and set it on a nearby shelf so that he could examine the contents.

On top of the pile of items was the small tool that Grandfather had used to administer Sembado's Elephant tattoo. Tears welled in his eyes as he picked it up and set it aside. The next few articles were photographs. They were printed on old digital media film, but were very well cared for. Sembado was able to recognize a very young version of his grandfather, his grandmother, and a little girl that he could only assume was his mother. He had never seen a picture of her when she was young. He tucked the handful of photos away and moved on to the most-prized treasure: his grandfather's tattered old journal. He carefully picked it up as if it might shatter. It was reddish brown and the cheap pleather cover had split and curled, but Sembado did not care. His tears broke away, rolled down his face, and dripped onto the musty book. Sembado froze. He could hear voices from up above. He cautiously extinguished his flash light, opting instead to use the light from the navigator screen. The volume of the voices grew. He heard footsteps too; dozens of them. He focused desperately to try and make out the words.

"I'm tellin' ya. He had a rebel tattoo and a bionic leg."

Sembado's stomach turned hot and did a backflip. He could not swallow.

"Have you checked the vents yet?"

"No. Not yet. We were waiting for your team."

Sembado moved as stealthily as possible while he listened to the numerous footsteps trampling above him. He mistakenly kicked another loose fixture, and it clanged ahead of him loudly. He froze. The footsteps above stopped too. All at once he rushed to the ladder and sat poised for his next move. The hatch was jerked open and the light above nearly blinded Sembado. He stole himself for a moment, and lunged straight up, his padded shoulder turned out. He caught a handful of faces with his first attack, but the power of the leap was less than he had hoped. He landed in a pile of people and wheat, gripping the journal so tightly, he was afraid it would break. As the light's effect on his eyes faded, he began to see several shadows moving towards him. He kicked frantically at the closest ones, sending them flying in every direction. Suddenly, a single sensation broke through Sembado's anger and panic and turmoil: someone had pressed the end of a gun barrel hard against his forehead.

Part Two
The Eruption

Chapter Thirteen
A Visitor

Linx sat with his head in his hands. He struggled to make sense of his role in the now defunct plan that had unraveled before it could start. He exhaled and threw his head back. He was sitting in a living chamber turned prison cell. The Spring had captured his crew, albeit very politely, had placed him and the other men in a well-furnished home, and locked the door. The band of women was caring to Rita's injuries in a separate location.

The room was pleasant and well lit, and his crew sat around him on comfortable furniture, as if they were all just sitting at a social engagement that they were not allowed to leave. The informant, Kreymond, was curled up on the end of a sofa opposite Linx. He had undone his corn rows, and was anxiously combing his fingers through his kinky hair. It was still saturated from their misadventure in the pressurizing chamber, and lay across his head in clumped ropes. He jerked nervously when someone knocked on the door.

"No thank you, we have enough towels," shouted Linx sarcastically. He received only a few chuckles from Puolo and Kala.

"Step away from the door," the guard said. She did not sound humored. The sound of a clicking lock was followed by a quiet hiss as the chamber door was pushed open. A guard, in full Spring armor, swung inside and cleared the doorway officially. Puolo and Kala whispered to each other about the aesthetics of the guard's rifle. Linx rolled his eyes. Kreymond peeked over the back of the sofa timidly.

"Here, you can stay with your Elephant friends for now," said a second guard as she escorted Sembado into the room. Kreymond, Linx, and Sembado stared, mouths agape for a full ten seconds, the amount of time the guard needed to close and lock the door.

Kreymond responded first, laughing uncontrollably as he vaulted over the sofa. Linx also rose to greet Sembado, but wore his utter confusion on his face. Puolo and Kala greeted Sembado casually from their chairs.

Sembado collapsed into Kreymond and Linx's arms. He was sobbing uncontrollably. It took several minutes of Kreymond and Linx trading unbelievable comparisons of friendship to convince each other that neither was mistaken about Sembado's identity. By this time, Sembado could manage limited phrases through his tears.

"You've *got* to be kidding me," he said through several loud sniffles. "How on earth did you end up with him?" Sembado asked, indicating Kreymond and Linx simultaneously.

"You guys have really been friends that long?" Linx asked.

"Since, like, before primary school," Sembado said, squeezing Kreymond with a renewed embrace.

"How long have you been an Elephant?" Kreymond asked Sembado.

"Um, like almost a year," Sembado said, shrugging. "Right around when they announced the surface release," he added.

"Like that ever happened," Kreymond said, shaking his head.

"Well, kind of," Linx laughed.

"That's right around when Meligose went missing too," Kreymond said. "I haven't seen Mel either. Not for a couple months now, and…Sem! What happened to your leg?"

"Oh deeks. Oh, Krey, I forgot," Sembado started solemnly, "There's so much to tell you. You have no idea." He suggested moving to the sofa, and the three of them sat down.

"What is it?" Kreymond asked, looking back and forth at Sembado and Linx's somber expressions.

"Meligose is dead," Sembado said. He managed saying it with much less emotion than he thought he would.

"So is Jonah," Linx said flatly.

"What?" Sembado and Kreymond exclaimed in chorus.

"When?" Kreymond asked, tears welling in his eyes. His mouth contorted as he started to writhe against the sofa. He looked around aimlessly as he tried to keep from hyperventilating.

"A couple months ago," Sembado said as he scanned Linx's face for answers.

"Just the other day," Linx said. "He died saving my life."

"And Meligose died saving mine. I lost my leg in the same explosion that killed him," Sembado said. He reached for Kreymond who was still swaying in agony, and together he and Linx consoled their anguished friend. After listening to Kreymond's defeated sobs for too long, Sembado found himself quietly recounting his harrowing adventure from its start. He told Kreymond about how he followed his grandfather the day he was acting so weird at the Civillion so long ago. He described being inducted as an Elephant, his stint in prison with Mr. Feldman, confronting Fabian, and how they would not have escaped without Linx's help. He told the story of Mr. Feldman's betrayal, their escape to the surface, and finally losing his grandfather on the beach.

As Sembado's voice waivered, Linx carried on the story, telling of Meligose's arrival, of Gerard Hutch's attack, and Sembado's long recovery. He gave his account of Mr. Feldman's evolving role in their mission when he was captured on the island, learned of his son's murder, and swore his life to the Elephants' cause. Sembado and Kreymond both listened intently as Linx went on to explain how his personal opinion of Mr. Feldman grew and blossomed as he fulfilled his redemption. Linx faltered as he described his final moments in the attack submarine with Jonah, taking a long pause before explaining the development of the flash sphere and Jonah's ultimate demise. The unlikely trio sat in a quiet embrace for a long time while Puolo and Kala maintained respectful silence. After several quiet minutes Sembado spoke.

"So the Spring," he said. "They took the journal."

"No!" Linx said. He continued to shake his head and swear under his breath while Sembado described the journal and his mission to the rest of the crew.

"But they won't necessarily use it against, us will they?" asked Kreymond.

"Who knows," Linx said, standing to pace the room. "We've seen them shoot and kill penalty officers and they took us hostage. I have no idea what their endgame is."

"Hey!" Kala said. "Where's Kaluna? I thought you two came down here together'!"

"Oh deeks!" Sembado exclaimed, and he proceeded to describe his journey back down from the surface. His friends regarded his bionic leg with more and more reverence as he went along. Linx actually laughed out loud at Sembado's description of his battle with the penalty officers. Kreymond, however, seemed most concerned about the possibility of brainwave interference. Sembado finished by assuring Kala and Puolo that Kaluna was safe with Lahalo, and that she had begrudgingly stayed behind.

"Well I hope she doesn't come lookin' for ya," Puolo said with a smirk. "Last thing anyone needs is Lahalo running up against these warrior women. 'Cause I can tell you right now..." he paused for dramatic effect. "Ain't neitha' side backin' down from that fight." This elicited a strong laugh from Kala and Sembado.

***

Sembado was surprised to hear of the important role Kreymond and his uncle Markus had to play in their future plans, but the next several days were spent reliving their time apart. Kreymond had his own adventure to tell which included being confined to his family's living chamber for a month straight before his brother defected and took him to the surface. They ended up evacuating in a group submarine with their old 4D teammate Jean Paul and their favorite arena attendant Zetvez. Kreymond was describing the most frustrating details of being adrift with complacent Jean Paul. Apparently, even mild-mannered Zetvez had nearly come to blows with Jean Paul by the time they had been intercepted by Mahana's recon subs. Sembado was laughing so hard that the Spring watchwoman opened the door to investigate.

"May I remind you that you are here as prisoners," she said curtly. Before she could say anything else, a small squad of her compatriots approached from the corridor outside. Sembado recognized the woman at the front of the group as the one who had stopped him on his way to the J-vents. She walked into the room with a commanding pace, and outstretched her hand. She held Sembado's grandfather's journal.

"We have retrieved some very useful information from this book. We thank you and its author."

"My grandpa," said Sembado, taking the journal from her hands. His friends looked on as stoically as possible.

"He was a very well-principled man," said the woman sincerely. She looked into Sembado's eyes with her own pale blue ones. They were almost gray. "We had heard rumors of such a journal with the possibility to end this civil war, and it's very uncivil weapons."

"You mean to defeat the government? And Fabian?" Sembado asked.

"We intend to end the fighting," the woman corrected, narrowing her eyes. "We are interested in peace. We will pursue that singularly."

"The Spring wants to fight fire with fire then?" Sembado asked. He clutched the journal against his chest. Linx, Kreymond, and the others had slowly gathered by his side.

"No!" the woman snapped. No one in the room seemed to anticipate her shrill response. Kreymond took a half step back. The woman ran one hand through her short black hair. "The Spring intends to smother the fire. We are women, as you can see. And we are sick of the losses we've incurred. We are wives and mothers and sisters and daughters. We have among our ranks representatives from every social class, government agency, and the Elephants."

Sembado and the others exchanged looks of confusion.

"We've even seen a few islander faces join our movement," she said directly to Kala and Puolo. The two men gave each other a sideways glance. "Maybe even a friend of yours," she said directly to Sembado. "Our intention is to dominate this conflict, end it, and give everyone a say in the path forward."

"Everyone but Fabian you mean," Linx interjected.

"And Gerard Hutch," Sembado added angrily.

"We will deal with the criminally intent from any faction," the woman stated. "Now," she added curtly, "this is not a Q and A. I came here to give you back this most valuable artifact and say thank you. You will be assured that all but a few pages remain. Any missing information was deemed necessary to our previously stated objectives."

Sembado and Linx exchanged a quick glance.

"You're looking to defeat the orbs. Is that it?" Sembado said knowingly. The woman's pale eyes flared, and she silenced her entourage, who had started to whisper to each other in response to Sembado's blunt approach.

"The orbs are faster now," Linx added. "They're instantaneous."

"We have quite enough information of our own, thank you," the woman said. She was clearly annoyed at the proliferation of what she seemed to think were top secret details.

"But we can help you bring down Fabian!" Linx said loudly.

"That is enough!" the woman yelled, and without further discussion, she turned and left. Her guards followed quickly in her wake.

Chapter Fourteen
Shiny Things

Sembado and his friends immediately went to a nearby table to start pouring over what information was still available in the journal. Contrary to what the Spring Captain had said, quite a few pages had been removed from the journal. Every single page of Elephant related information had been sanitized out of the book. The only pages left intact were Sembado's grandfather's personal entries. Some were accounts of a certain day's trials and tribulations, others were creative outlets he had expressed, short stories, and socio-political essays. The others lost interest when Linx declared that there was no strategic value to the remaining pages. Kreymond left Sembado to read alone when he determined that what was left had become a more personal heirloom. Sembado scoured the pages. Each revealed more about his grandfather's passion for freedom, justice, and self-determination. With Grandfather dying so soon after Sembado became an Elephant, they had never had a chance to sit and share these kinds of ideas. These old pages represented every opportunity Sembado had to understand the old man's reasons for sparking a rebellion. One of the longer essays was titled *The Full Faith and Credit of the United States Government.* Another article expressed considerable doubt in the inherent value of money as well as the inherent respect and honor of leadership; the title was *Who Was the First King?* Sembado read through portions of these, but found them surprisingly angry and unfocused. He turned the next page to a short story titled *David's Last Day.* He read on eagerly, recognizing his great-uncle's name.

David's Last Day   *9 April 2071*
By: Hyron Klisk

This fictional account is based on all the phone calls my brother and I had. I loved him very much. This narrative is dedicated to all the older brothers who died for no reason fifty years ago today.

David walked briskly down a bustling city street with his good friend and coworker Alex trotting along next to him. The city beeped and chirped and rang at them as they hurried through it. Each of the young men was fresh out of the same engineering school, where they had become close allies. Now they were working their way up the ranks of a communication company's global headquarters.

David wore a bright smile across his freshly shaven face as he dodged taxis and limousines; Alex wore a stony grimace as he tried to keep up. Despite the fact that it was Friday, he was preparing to work a double shift that night, but David was only in for the morning. After a couple quick presentations, he was off to the airport and then to

Hawaii where he would meet his parents and younger brother whom he had not seen since his graduation several months ago. Work had kept him very busy as a fresh college graduate, but he had never had so much fun keeping up with the hustled pace of life that this megalopolis offered.

David and Alex had already braved three shoddy apartments together, and had each earned a promotion in their new employer's ever expanding empire.

The company, Communica, specialized in research and design for government telecommunication contracts, and had clients and investors all over the world. The two young engineers were helping spearhead efforts to find new usable telecom frequencies in an ever more crowded bandwidth.

David and Alex slowed to a casual strut as they crossed the street to trace the waterfront. The surface of the water reflected glimmers and sparkles from the brilliant sunrise. David admired the reflection of the clouds in the waves, for they stood out with contrast against the pail morning sky. Even in the rough reflection he could make out shapes of all kinds in the masses of white and blue.

"I can't believe they approved you for ten days," said Alex in a winded voice. "Not only was I denied this weekend off, but they put me on a double tonight. How do you always luck out?"

"I learned how to smile at people," replied David, giving his friend a sarcastic smirk. "You should try it sometime," he added.

Alex rolled his eyes, but remained silent for the next block. David continued to observe the vision of the sky mirrored in the harbor. A particular group of twinkling lights seemed to be moving unlike the rest of the random patterns of sun sparkle. They remained a part of the reflection as the clouds did. He furrowed his brow, and squinted his eyes to see better, but the water broke the vision into colorful chaos. It suddenly occurred to David to look into the patch of sky that he was seeing reflected. To his continued surprise, the cluster of shiny objects was actually there in the sky, back-dropped by the billowy, white clouds. His attention belonged wholly to the glimmering spots now. His pace had slowed to a complete stop.

"David! What are you doing, dude? We gotta get goin'," Alex called from up ahead.

This broke David's concentration only enough for him to point at the objects, a meager effort to communicate his curiosity to his friend. Alex came back to where David was standing, but only to lead him away by the arm. He did not have time for his funnier counterpart's silly antics. He was quickly irritated when David resisted his guidance, and pulled his arm back sharply. To Alex's surprise, it was David that lashed out next.

"Stop! Look. Those lights in the sky. Those shiny things. Are they moving this way?" More frustrated and annoyed than curious, Alex could not help seeing the dazzling lights.

"Are those airplanes?" he asked out loud.

"Can't be," replied David distractedly. *"There are dozens of them, and they're flying the wrong way for the airport."*

The gleaming lights were soon taking shape, and to the two young men's dismay, as well as that of several other pedestrians, that shape had wings.

Thirty large, loud airplanes soon reverberated their subdued hum off of the harbor, the buildings, and the awestruck bystanders that could not believe a flight of military-grade bombers was fast approaching their busy cityscape.

Some people started to make agitated or frightened comments, jumping to worst case scenario conclusions. The attacks that had happened a distant 20 years before suddenly seemed like yesterday. Others called friends and family on their cell phones, eager to share what they were witnessing. David and Alex just stood and stared.

The ever growing sound of the planes' engines was quickly starting to change pitch. To David's surprise, he began to hear an entirely different and unrecognizable noise which drown out the sound of the bombers altogether. At first he thought it was just him, but he stopped trying to unplug his ears when he realized others around him were looking all around for the source of this new, dominating hum.

It had now grown to a deafeningly loud level. It took all the other noises with it. It was not a ringing silence, for not even his heartbeat could be heard in his head. He looked back to the bombers to see them veer away to the south. Relief spread through his body, but stopped before it reached his head. What was this new noise and where did it come from? Just as his thoughts began to race again another strange sight caught his eyes. Something was climbing up out of the city. It was a sphere, electric blue and translucent. It was growing rapidly, accelerating every second. Soon, it's surface approached a large skyscraper. It transitioned past the building without incident. The blue dome simply materialized on the other side so that it engulfed everything it passed. David watched in horror as crowds of people raced in his direction; they were afraid of touching the blue hemisphere which was now expanding. David and Alex backed away quickly, but soon found themselves backed against the railing that traced the harbor walls. The mobs of people slowed as they encountered this same obstacle; some began to run away along the railings distance, but made little progress escaping the ever growing dome. The two young men stood close and clinched their fists as the dome would intersect the crowd in mere seconds. A rolling scream emanated from the front of the mob as the surface of the sphere passed through them. The gasps rolled right up to where David stood at the harbor railing. He grimaced and turned his head as the electric blue membrane passed through him harmlessly. The rolling scream was replaced by a hush as the crowd found itself unscathed. They turned as one to see the perimeter of the sphere grow out over the water. David craned his neck as he followed the surface of the dome up and over his head.

The crown of it shot up over a mile above the city as it grew ever larger. As the morning sun beat down through the dome, it cast a brilliant blue tint on everything; the city held one collective breath as it took in the new alien terrain that the blue light created. David looked away to the rest of the city and saw other domes growing into the one that encapsulated him. Multiple orbs grew and intersected, causing wondering dances of bright blue hues. He heard muffled voices around him and followed many pointing fingers out to the water where the edge of the dome, now a thousand feet away, had stopped.

Suddenly, from somewhere in the heart city, a column of red light shot up and collided with the center of the blue dome above. The two met with a flash of white, and then the blue dome started to fade to red from the top down. The blue shaded world below transitioned from a tranquil peace to an uneasy tension.

David's anxiety grew with every moment, and suddenly the dome began to retreat back toward the city. Unlike its ever accelerating growth, the shrinking process was slow and steady. It took several minutes for the dome to recede. As it did, David noticed a small wave forming where the sphere dipped below the water's surface. Many minutes later, the wave had approached the harbor wall, the receding sphere marching slowly behind it. David looked down to see the wave was actually schools and schools of fish which were now teeming against the harbor wall. The disturbing sight became worse as more of the creatures began fighting over the others. Many were pushed up onto the group so that they flailed helplessly in the open air.

"What would cause them to do that?" Alex whispered in David's ear. David's only response was to look up at the sphere. It was an untrusting glare. They watched as the dome crept closer to the frantic fish. The mass of scales was soon half out of the water, jumping off of each other in a fight to get away from the impending red terror. The dome soon reached the struggling fish. The crowd watched with anticipation which turned to horror as the surface of the sphere passed through the fish. Instead of passing through harmlessly as it had the first time, the sphere began dissolving the fish.

David watched in horror as the fish fought and squirmed until enough of their bodies had been dissolved that they died. They then lay motionless as the relentless red surface continued to devour them as their desperate brethren jostled their lifeless remains. The people in the crowd backed away in disgust and then fear as they realized the sphere was not going to stop with the fish. The sphere slowly dissolved through the handrail and crept across the pavement. Terrified realization began to overcome David as his thoughts raced to the minutes ahead when this dome would converge to wherever it had originated from.

Panic overtook the mob as it started to quicken its pace away from the shrinking dome. They moved faster and more frantically away from the red energy as it plodded determinedly behind them.

David took off as the crowd broke into a feverish sprint. He looked over his shoulder to see Alex sprinting right behind him. They quickly joined the ranks of the hundreds around him that were moving as one away from the shrinking sphere. David saw the colors and shapes around him, but none of it registered in his now frantic mind. He started to forget about Alex as he raced to stay ahead of those behind him. He moved along with the mob as it sprinted down the street.

The mass of now thousands moved faster with every passing moment. David was in the lead, and that was all he cared about. He was now tearing over a bridge, and to his right, he could see the edges of the sphere closing in; it was not stopping.

As he raced into an open intersection, other stampedes of people came in from his right, crashing violently with the crowd behind him. He tore on faster as a mounted police officer's horse raced by at a full gallop; it had no passenger. He wished he could have climbed on as he admired how quickly it put distance between itself and the hoard that followed. Everyone and everything in the city wanted desperately to not be last.

The masses began to converge at a large park in the center of this part of town. It was there. If David was more aware of his desperate surroundings, he would have noticed that the throng around him had abandoned shouting and yelling, and had adopted a call of heavy breathing and grunts as they bumped into each other.

Down the steps, over the fences, through the shrubs. The frantic mass of tens of thousands did not choose the most logical route, just the fastest as they fled away from the dome. People who fell and were hobbled continued to crawl and fight their way forward. Some threw themselves over the park's railings that led to perilous, twenty foot falls.

Thousands upon thousands of men, women, children, dogs, cats, rats, birds, and other beasts poured into the park. They were starting to pile up on each other so that some were not walking on the ground at all.

David was among the lucky few who had fought their way to the center of the park. There he saw it. A large metal cube, ten feet in three dimensions. He got right up to it. Maybe it would keep him safe. He had not even noticed he had just stepped on and broken another man's wrist; neither did the man. All that mattered was that he had made it. Several moments passed as the entire city emptied its streets and buildings into this park, and several other locations like. Each had its own metal cube. David hugged the cube tightly and closed his eyes, trying desperately to block out the screams that were erupting behind him, but soon it would be his turn.

Sembado's body felt numb, but his spirit felt heavy and burdened. All of the bitterness and anger his grandfather had ever expressed over the years was spilled out on the pages before him. He fought to breath as tears refused to well in his eyes. The sadness and pity he felt for the angry spirit trapped in the pages would not release itself. It dug into his insides and remained. He focused his balance as he rose slowly and soon found himself at the incinerator. He kissed the journal, spoke wordless thoughts to his grandfather's memory, and placed the tattered book inside the small compartment. The burners fired, heat emanated off of the enclosure, and Sembado sank to the floor as he said good-bye to all of the hate trapped inside.

Chapter Fifteen
We're on the Same Wavelength

"This video represents what we have learned so far from studying the dissolving weapons, be it the original slow-paced variety or the government's newly developed flash orbs." The instructor paused briefly to take a drink of water. She was briefing the newest class of covert Spring operatives on the science and function of their newest technological break-through.

Kaluna sat and listened tentatively. Her fourth day in the Spring's ranks had already found her in this special, new garrison. When Sembado had not returned or contacted her, she became worried and made the journey to the J-Vents herself. When a group of Spring patrollers had found her poking around the site of Sembado's recent capture, they apprehended her. Her admission of guilt and her knowledge of the journal had earned her a reputation with the women warriors; her abhorrence of the warring and loss that the men of the complex had caused had earned their trust. She was not sure that she did not believe her adamant disgust with her male counterparts, whether they were government, islander, or Elephant, but the convincing interview was satisfactory. Coupled with her

115

prolific espionage and battle prowess, it had earned her the position on the neutralizing force the Spring had created to execute the new anti-weapon. Because she had been assured of Sembado's safety, she decided to follow this neutralizing team as long as possible. After all, this information was the reason she and Sembado had come back down to the complex in the first place.

"The entire system of energized sphere technology, or EST, has two important components: wave length and power level. As you can see in this microscopic view, the damage is done through vibration. The energy in the orb vibrates living tissue cells at a frequency that pulls the membrane apart. Watch this skin sample closely. The natural bipolar forces on the phospholipid bilayer normally reject and attract the liquids on either side equally in order to maintain a balance in tension. This balance is overcome by the very special dissolving frequency when it is applied with enough power. The phosphates and the fats continue to reverberate until they are pulled apart. As each cell explodes, the contents are evaporated almost instantly by the heat generated by the orb." The instructor loaded a new video depicting a green-hewed orb.

"This is the basic healing EST. It obviously has a more popular function. Many doctors employ this frequency in order to heal broken bones, repair wounds, and to reduce scarring. You can see here that the frequency also vibrates the cell, but it has a greater effect on the interior cell functions. This is a higher frequency as evidenced by the apparent buzzing of the various cell structures. This frequency is meant to excite and promote cell functions. In doing so, it enables the cell to repair and reproduce at accelerated rates. The cell division you see is real-time; this video is not in fast-forward. I must note: as some of you prior nurses know, the healing EST must be administered carefully. If it is executed indefinitely then the healing and repair will become unencumbered growth. The cell will continue to divide and grow, causing tumor growth so prolific that it is visible to the naked eye. I do not enjoy this next clip, but it drives the point home." The instructor looked away from the screen as the room of young woman reacted with varying levels of repulsion. Kaluna curled her lip, but continued to watch the screen as the small rat that scurried around slowed under the weight of the tumor on its face. Soon the rat collapsed, emaciated, and a pool of red ooze began to emanate from below the growth.

"Notice the rat's body. See how it became visibly thin towards the end. The tumor growth was not created out of thin air. And remember, the EST cannot break the laws of mass and energy conservation. All that blood and tissue was pulled from the rest of the rat's body as the new cells continued to be excited. This frequency can be used to undo some of the damage already caused by the dissolving EST, but the two do not cancel each other out because one excites the cell membrane, while the other stimulates the inner cell functions." The instructor moved around more files on the presentation screen, opening another video with an orange colored EST.

"We are calling this the Klisk Frequency, after the man who found it for us," she began. Kaluna was caught off guard. Not by the mention of old Hyron, but by how emotionally she wanted to respond. She fought back a strong impulse to cry, and sat instead with tears quietly streaming down her face. She wiped them away as inconspicuously as possible.

"This is the frequency that we've been looking for. The government has had this technology for a very long time, and they have fought very hard to keep this information out of rebel hands. It would essentially neutralize any advantage the government's arsenal offers. According to the notes that accompanied the frequency's equation, this EST was actually developed first. The technology was to be used for deep space travel before the doomsday event. In this video, the Klisk EST affects both the cell membrane and the inner cell functions, and as the power on the sphere is turned up, all cell processes stop. Any transfer of energy, nutrients, or waste is held in suspension until the EST is deactivated. This does not kill the cell for lack of oxygen or nutrients because none of the processes that require those things are moving. The deep space function here would have been referred to as," the instructor paused to review a loose piece of paper in front of her. "Oh, here – suspended animation, meaning you could maintain a lifeform inside this EST for months, years, or even indefinitely. Additionally, this frequency has very interesting interactions with the other ESTs. As you can see in this first clip, we could get no growth to occur from the healing EST while the Klisk frequency was in place. Additionally, this energy equation seems to be the complimentary opposite to the dissolving sphere. Watch the outcome as the blue dissolving EST approaches the tissue already guarded by the orange Klisk sphere. The two energies literally cancel each other out. Now both ESTs still functioned after that experiment, but we had to reset and reenergize them." The instructor ended the video and closed down the presentation screen as her lecture turned into a logistics briefing.

"We are already underway in producing the new EST in a pendant. If you encounter a dissolving sphere you will simply activate your EST necklace and the threat is neutralized. Be aware, however, that you will shock your system momentarily as the Klisk frequency runs through your body. Now, it is our understanding that the government only just developed the new flash sphere in anticipation of the Klisk frequency being used against them. The idea being that the victim would not have time to respond and neutralize the rapidly collapsing EST. Know this: we are also working on addressing an auto-release function so that the pendant can anticipate the newer, faster flash sphere. We will not send you out against these things without proper protection. Our Spring leaders want you to embrace this new EST as a symbol for our mission statement. We want to neutralize threats and end suffering. That is it." The instructor paused as the young women around the class conferred positively about their new found electronic mascot. The instructor cleared her throat, returning order to the class. "That being said, be careful not to activate your pendant unless there is a credible threat. Without a dissolving sphere present for your protective EST to deactivate, you could potentially trap yourself in suspended animation until the pendant's power supply runs out of juice. Coincidentally, we will be taking advantage of that function as a prisoner containment system going forward with our operations."

The instructor had to pause again as the notion of suspended animation containment caused another round of excited chatter.

"Ladies, please. A little more concentration. We are almost done. Now, this is the last but most important warning. While there are very few drawbacks to the Klisk frequency, care does need to be taken when administering it, just like the healing frequency. While the Klisk frequency could theoretically be administered indefinitely, it must engulf the subject completely, or lethal hemorrhaging can occur. In this final video you will see what I mean. See how the cells just outside the sphere are attempting to pass nutrients to the suspended cells. The receiving cells are unable to absorb the nutrients and the giving cells are forced to erupt. It is much clearer here. See how the blood vessels are impeded by the Klisk boundary? The vessels burst and the subsequent bleeding is severe. The brain scans of these specimens indicated that this process, as you might expect, is incredibly painful. Now, in regards to prisoner containment: the prisoner's posture will be vital to safe and proper use of the Klisk EST. We will have the prisoner assume the fetal position before energizing the EST. Being spherical, this ensures that the EST is as small as possible while still maintaining the boundary layer completely around the subject. You *will* exercise maximum control in containment procedures. We have no interest in unnecessary pain or suffering. Well, that is all I have. Any questions? Good. Thank you, ladies. Please report to your command and good luck out there."

Kaluna lagged at her desk while the rest of the class got shuffled out of the room energetically.

"Not as excited to get out there as the rest, huh?"

Kaluna looked up to see another one of the students towering over her. She had choppy blonde hair and a decidedly unfeminine face.

"Yea, I guess not." Kaluna replied.

"You're new too, huh? My name's Rita." The blonde woman said, extending a rough hand.

"Yea. I'm Kaluna." Kaluna said.

"An islander in the Spring?" Rita asked, noticing Kaluna's husky accent. "I guess we're all getting sick of the fighting, huh?"

"Yes," Kaluna said resolutely.

"You two!" The instructor said, "Class is over. And I just got a message from Lerna. She wants to see both of you right now."

Kaluna and Rita exchanged confused looks, but exited the room expediently.

Rita, being slightly more familiar with the layout of the Spring's headquarters, led the way. They passed other classrooms, combat training sessions, and the infirmary. They moved into a secondary corridor which housed the armory and the executive office suite. Rita spoke her identification number into a speaker and they were buzzed in. A woman behind a desk stood and escorted them to a back office. She adjusted the pistol holster under her left arm as they walked. She opened the office door and directed them inside. Another woman sat behind a large glass desk. The desktop was cluttered with electronic files. The woman sat hunkered over one specific document, her head in her hands. When Kaluna and Rita entered the room, she minimized the document and sat up straight, her short black hair was mussed and wild from being held in her hands. It gave her a crazy appearance. Her look was amplified by here piercing, pale blue eyes; they were nearly gray.

"Good morning, ladies," she said. "I trust you two have become well acquainted."

"No ma'am," Rita responded. "We've only just met after our instruction." Lerna's look soured at the response from the two young women.

"I'm holding your collective of male counterparts together and you two don't know who each other is? You have both attested that you are down here on clandestine operations for the rebel leadership on the surface and you have not been introduced?" Kaluna and Rita exchanged looks of surprise. Lerna sighed as she threw her hands up. "You see? This is why men make such terrible leaders.

They only tell you what they think you need to know. Kaluna, Rita is down here on your uncle's orders."

"Your Mahana's niece?" Rita exclaimed.

"You two are killin' me," Lerna said, running her hands through her hair. "Look, this isn't why I called you in here. You both come from rebel factions, and I need you to prove your dedication to this cause. You are both very skilled and valuable to me, but I don't need you skipping out short-notice. This movement is about ending senseless violence. Both of you, like me – hell, like all of us – you've lost loved ones in this stupid fight. Now, we don't pick sides. Period. Good luck getting the men to agree to that; Government or Elephant. They're so busy fighting for what they *don't* want that they can't even tell you what it is that they *do* want. You know what I want? I want to be left alone. That's it, and I stayed out of this thing for a long time. Me and my sister knew it would get worse before it got better, but we didn't see this coming. And she didn't see the bullet coming either." Lerna paused and took a deep breath. Her eyes were not wet, but narrowed. "We went out of our way to avoid all this, and she ends up catching one of those blue orbs to the chest. Big one too. You know what I got out of it? I got to cradle her effin' legs – because everything else was gone. Before that it was just me and her – hell, I'm glad my parents died last year. They couldn't handle this crap. So listen. I got two hot targets for capture. You two will be joining me on the hunt – just the three of us – so you can prove your loyalty. Both targets have exhibited the kind of crap that we are fighting so hard to destroy: torture, betrayal, arrogance; neither one has any regard for the average citizen's health or wellbeing. One's from the government side, the other is an Elephant. They're both high profile characters with high profile behavior, and both of their peoples will know and understand why we picked them. So here it is: Sembado, Linx, and the others stay under the new EST until we capture these two."

Rita immediately bristled. Kaluna made fists so tight, her knuckles popped.

"Calm down," Lerna said. "You both just sat through the Klisk briefing. We will use the utmost care when administering the suspended animation. I haven't even put them under yet. A sign of goodwill. You help me get these two marks, put them under the new EST yourselves, and I'll be happy to negotiate what happens to your friends. No one else gets this offer. Ever." Lerna finished her proposition and leaned back in her chair, her hands behind her head.

Kaluna's stony gaze persisted. Her flaring nostrils were the only signs of movement. Rita looked from Lerna to Kaluna and back.

"Let's see the profiles," Rita said flatly.

Lerna waited a moment, seeing no indication of agreement from Kaluna. Kaluna let out a sigh and uncrossed her arms. Lerna leaned forward in her chair, tapped her glass desk screen, and highlighted two files. She rotated the photos and slid them across the screen to the two young women. The profiles slowed to a stop as they approached the screen's edge. Kaluna sighed deeply before breaking her glare-off with Lerna. She joined Rita in reviewing the bounty profiles in front of her. Both men's photos made her stomach turn over. One was Gerard Hutch. The other was Jean M'Gereg.

Chapter Sixteen
Lights Out

Sembado stood behind Kreymond. The evening's stress and confusion had more than compensated for the past few days' peaceful comradery. He watched his good friend with concern as Kreymond jumped and flinched at every guard and passerby. They were herded through a series of security checks, and stood in a bustling corridor as they waited for the next step. Linx was at the front of the line, and was continuing his defiant subversions toward their escort.

"Lean against that wall one more time," said the female guard.

"What's with the ruse?" Linx asked. "You guys keep us in a damn luxury suite, let us conspire for days, and then you want us to take you seriously just because you want to play soldier? This is *exactly* what I expected from a troop of wome – aaagh!" Linx's disobedient rant was abruptly interrupted when the female guard applied a shock stick directly to his neck. The others looked on submissively while Linx lay twitching on the floor. His jaw was clinched and contorted, his eyes glazed. The guard holstered the weapon with exasperation.

"Respect," The guard said. "that's all I want."

Sembado looked at the floor while he shook his head in disapproval at Linx's outburst. Kreymond's sobs were barely audible. Sembado quietly placed a hand on his friend's shoulder. Linx recovered from his correction and quietly stood back up. He remained silent for the remainder of the transportation. After standing quietly for a half hour, Sembado and his comrades were prodded forward into a chamber with a large mirror on one side; it was very obviously for one-way observation. They were ushered in and lined up against the wall: Linx, Puolo, Kreymond, Sembado, and Kala. They stood against the wall, some more nervous than others. Their escort entered the room. She dragged a metal chair behind her, and brought it to the center of the room. Sembado noticed that the chair had an extra brace welded in the front that stood out in color and shape from the rest of the frame. She stepped back from the chair, pointed at Linx, and then the chair. Linx looked around at his friends, he looked into the giant mirror on the wall, and then he looked at the female guard, but he did not move.

"Sit," she demanded.

He slowly moved forward and sat in the metal chair. The backs of his legs sat against the metal brace in an unnatural dangling fashion.

"Put your feet up on the ledge," the guard said.

Linx glared directly into her eyes as he complied. His knees sat up against his chest. The guard stepped forward, pulling an object from a pouch on her tactical vest. It dangled from her hand. She walked up to Linx and held the object over his head. He jerked his head back and then side to side to avoid the object in her hand.

"Oh, calm down. It goes around your neck," she said.

"Yea, I get it. That doesn't really help," he shot back.

She ignored him, dropping the small necklace around his head. He tried to pull his head back as if he could distance himself from the object. She stepped back and nodded to the mirrored wall.

"Wrap your arms around your knees," she said to Linx.

"Kiss my ass," he responded.

She shrugged her shoulders and nodded at the mirror again. An orange flash emanated from the medallion. It grew quickly and then stopped just as it had encapsulated Linx. Sembado lost his breath as he watched his brother in arms freeze under the influence of the orange orb. He clenched his fists and began to step forward.

"Easy now," said the guard. "He's fine. This is the frequency out of your grand-dad's journal. As soon as we turn it off, your friend will be his same awful and charming self. You will all undergo this treatment. It is completely harmless and can be undone so stop lookin' so pitiful and lemme grab another chair."

Soon it was Sembado's turn, but he tried a different tactic than Linx.

"Please," he said. It was not pleading, but calm curtesy. His experience with his grandfather's journal had resolved him to take a more peaceful spirit in his struggles.

"We have friends and information that can help. We don't have to do this separately."

The guard paused. Her face seemed annoyed. Not at Sembado directly, but that he was genuinely making her job more of a burden.

"Couldn't you just be a jerk like him?" she asked, indicating Linx's rigid form.

"Not even if I tried," Sembado said calmly.

The guard looked back at the mirror and then to Sembado.

"This is only temporary," she said. "Maybe we can talk when it's over." And with that, she placed the next pendant around Sembado's neck.

***

Tears welled in Kaluna's eyes as she watched Sembado crawl onto the chair to receive his suspended animation sentence. The look on his face was not worry, but also not stony resolve. She was surprised to see peaceful acceptance on his face as the pendant was fitted around his neck. She walked out of the observation room before his containment sphere was activated. Rita was waiting outside.

"The sooner we get Hutch and M'Gereg caught the sooner we get our guys free," Rita said.

"Then let's get it done," Kaluna responded.

Chapter Seventeen
The Weasel and the Badger

Kaluna and Rita arrived back at Lerna's office for their pre-mission briefing minutes later to find their new leader pouring over security footage on her desk-screen.

"Take a seat. We'll go over Hutch first," she said without looking up. She loaded a video file and rotated it to display for Kaluna and Rita. The video was taken over Lerna's shoulder as she interviewed a young lady. Kaluna and Rita recognized her as the guard who had just put Sembado and the others under the suspended animation spheres.

"That's Tizabeth Holren. Goes by Tiz. She's one of the many poor, young fools that was unfortunate enough to call Hutch her boyfriend," Lerna said. She then played the video and turned the volume up. They sat quietly while the recording of Tiz played.

"Gerard had disappeared for a couple weeks. We would go days without seeing each other sometimes, but not weeks. His mom wouldn't really see me – we don't get along that well – she just said he had gone on a mission that he couldn't tell me about – that happened sometimes

so I just stuck it out. Then he came to me – this was months ago, but I remember it so clearly because of how shaken he was. He never worries about anything, you know? He said he had been captured by rebels – I didn't know what he meant at the time – the fighting had just started, but the Elephants hadn't really gone public. Anyways, he said that he was escaping to the surface. A lot of people were. He said his mom and stepdad didn't know…"

"So this was after the Elephant's had captured him," Lerna said as she paused the video. "And then they took him to your people," she said to Kaluna. "He got away at some point after you escaped to the surface. He went to the surface too, but when Sembado recognized him, he came back."

Kaluna curled her lip at the thought of Hutch's surface visit and the attack that left Sembado without one leg. Lerna continued the video.

"He wanted to leave, but he came back right away. Anytime we talked, he would just complain about his parents and this whole situation. I didn't really get it at the time, but I think he was trying to tell me about the corruption: him and his mom and Mr. Fabian. But Gerard really is a terrible guy, and I think he only wanted to be comforted. He was so self-absorbed. If it wasn't his problem, he didn't care, but as soon as…"

"Sorry – we've all been there, but this isn't really mission essential," Lerna said as she clicked the video ahead.

"...and said she didn't even care. So his mom was so mad that she made him stay on the front line. Can you imagine? She's such a sea-cow. And Mr. Fabian too. What a creep. Last we spoke, Gerard was stationed where Red crosses over to Gold. I think maybe level 25 through 27, but that was just before we broke up so I'm not sure now."

"So there you go. Tiz isn't the brightest, as evidenced by her extended romance with Hutch, but she gets what we're doing, and since this video, she has really come into her own. In fact, as I understand it, you just watched her administer the Klisk pendants on your comrades.

"What about M'Gereg?" Kaluna asked.

"Yea, no more videos of old girlfriends I hope," Rita added.

"No video needed," Lerna said flatly. "I've known of Jean M'Gereg for a long time. He's the one and only reason the Spring's mission is focused on the Elephants as well as the Government. A few years ago, he lost his son – my brother-in-law, Andrel – on one of his stupid Elephant missions. My sister had no idea who or what the Elephants were until he died. Andrel had kept it a secret from her – for her protection, supposedly. And what does she get? A body delivered to her door step, and a cold shoulder from her bitter, old father-in-law. It took Tegea – my sister – the rest of her life to get over the heart break. And then she was killed by the same idiots – Elephant and Government – that killed her beloved. Poetic, huh? So M'Gereg had a debt to my sister, and now his debt's with me. And don't call it personal because, believe me, he's not the leader the Elephants deserve. He's certainly no Hyron Klisk. As for his whereabouts – we've got that covered. Let's focus on Hutch first – and then we'll go after Jean."

***

"Yea, Mahana is keeping order, but resources are running thin," Rita said to Kaluna. "He's having to run fishing vessels around the clock."

"Would you two focus. This is not a reunion tour," Lerna snapped. They were pausing at a corridor to allow the government soldiers they were tracking to get further ahead. "Your attention needs to be here, now, and with the Spring."

"Hey, Mahana would be more of an asset than you could believe," Kaluna said defiantly. "His goal is to liberate. That's all."

"We aren't having this discussion right now," Lerna responded. "Let's move forward."

They were just leaving the *Red Sector* and moving into the older *Gold Sector*. There was a commotion ahead.

"Maintenance closet – left," Rita said, and Lerna and Kaluna followed her lead. They tucked inside the closet.

"How long do you suggest we hide out here?" Lerna asked sarcastically.

"Would you stop?" Rita demanded as she crouched to the floor. "This mission is about earning trust, right? I used to work maintenance on this old sector. The utilities are laid out differently. The piping and air ducts follow the corridor." She moved a box of cleaning supplies to expose a floor hatch. "And there's access in every maintenance closet," she said as she lifted the hatch.

The three women were down the mechanical hatch in a minute with the lid closed above them. Rita led the way as they followed the utility line down the corridor. The pipes that crisscrossed the passageway made Rita and Lerna develop a duck-like gait while Kaluna's diminutive size allowed her to walk upright.

"*We can talk quietly, but there are vents every so often so keep it down,*" Rita whispered. "*There will be a vertical access shaft ahead. It will take us down to level 25.*"

They reached the vertical shaft. It was a small tube with ladder rungs attached to one side. Their gear had to be passed by hand in order to make the tight squeeze.

"We will assume Hutch is on patrol," Lerna said. "Kaluna, you go first since you can move quicker down here. Go ahead of us and sweep the halls. Listen for his voice or any mention of his name. We will move up behind you with the equipment."

Kaluna accepted the direction and trotted away as her larger counterparts shuffled their equipment through the tight passage. She ran along swiftly, happy to finally feel of special purpose since her near drowning. She had not attempted any real combat since her recovery. Her feet plodded along silently; even as she passed the floor vents the mechanical equipment around her made enough noise to cover her footsteps. She heard voices and hurried to them. There were two people walking along above her, and she slowly followed them as they walked and talked.

"I don't think so," said a man's voice. "He's definitely an Elephant. I heard he was the leader's grandson."

"Yea – the one with the bionic leg," said a second voice. "I heard he killed a couple of ours with it."

Kaluna's heart raced as she followed the two men.

"Yea, well that's why Fabian has us down here in *Gold*. I guess the old man had a secret book or something. Trust some old-timer to keep hard print around. I think Fabian wants the old man's apartment guarded in case the Elephants come back for the book."

"Yea – I heard Hutch bitchin' about it. I guess Fabian sent him down here for it already. Hutch was supposed to kill the old Elephant and get the book, but the old man nearly shot him."

Kaluna climbed over some low-lying pipes as she approached a corridor intersection.

"It's a book – how hard could it be to fin... Oh! Hey, Gerard."

Kaluna froze as a whiny voice scolded her chase.

"Yea – just a book! Why haven't we got it yet? I'll just pull one out of my ass!" the whiny voice shouted angrily.

"Sorry, Gerard. I just..." said the first man.

"Are we dating?! You call me Captain Hutch, goddeekit!" Hutch bellowed.

"Yes sir, Captain Hutch," the man said officially.

"Good! Now – you lead the way to the old man's apartment for another search. And *you*, follow behind me," Hutch ordered.

"Yes sir, Captain Hutch!" barked the second man.

Kaluna followed Hutch and his escorts until they arrived at Hyron's old living chamber. There was a floor vent just outside the door. She watched them disappear into the apartment before retracing her steps as quick as she could. She sprinted through the piping passage until she saw Lerna and Rita ahead in the duct. They quickened their awkward pace to meet her. She subdued her breathing as quickly as possible so that she could tell them what had happened.

"And he's right up ahead? That's perfect!" said Rita as she smacked Kaluna on the shoulder.

"Alright – let's find the nearest closet and climb out this damn tunnel," Lerna said as she ran her hand through her hair.

Kaluna led them to the floor vent just outside the apartment, and Rita pointed the way to the next exit point. They climbed out of a maintenance hatch nearby. Lerna handed out equipment as they huddled in the dark closet.

"Okay. Here's the plan. We'll toss in these smokes and knock them out," she said as she held up a metal canister. "When they go down, we will wrap Hutch up and activate a Klisk pendant. I have a little wheeled board to roll him out on. If we can wrestle him back into these maintenance shafts, we could sneak him out better, even if it is a little tight. Both of you take a respirator and a defense pendant. At any sign of an attack orb, these will deploy and deactivate the sphere before it can do any damage, but be careful – these offer no protection for conventional bullet wounds."

Kaluna and Rita followed Lerna's lead in fitting their pendants and respirators. Lerna then pulled out two collapsible assault rifles. She handed one to each of her soldiers.

"These are for emergency only," she said as Kaluna and Rita unfolded and shouldered the weapons. Lerna pulled out a hand gun for herself and opened the door. They quickly worked their way back to Hyron's old apartment where the door was left ajar. Lerna slowly extended her foot and pushed the door open further. She put her handgun in its holster under her left armpit so that she could pull the pin on the gas can. She nodded to Kaluna and Rita before pulling the pin and tossing the canister in the door. The can hissed loudly as it deployed its contents. Muffled shouting emanated from the apartment. Then three distinct thuds could be heard as each of their prey collapsed to the floor. They moved inside as the chamber smoke alert system responded. The smoke evacuation system cleared the air quickly, but Rita and Lerna had already wrestled Gerard Hutch's limp frame into the fetal position.

Kaluna watched the door, but found it hard to not be distracted by the slew of old Hyron's personal items that lay around. Any one of them would be a treasured surprise for Sembado.

Lerna and Rita hog-tied Hutch around an old closet rod and fitted the pendant around his neck. Lerna used the control to grow the sphere just large enough to contain Hutch, but left it small enough that the closet rod extended out like a handle on either end. Rita took the wheeled board off her back and laid it on the floor before she and Lerna hoisted Hutch up and onto the cart.

"Just like the pig he is," Rita chuckled though her respirator. Kaluna stood at the door and checked either direction.

"Clear," she said. She pivoted out the door while Lerna and Rita pushed Hutch along the floor behind her. Kaluna hurried back inside to collect whatever trinket she could get her hands on.

"Hey," Lerna snapped from the door. "Come on!"

Kaluna grabbed the first item she could, and turned back to the door. Lerna had her gun drawn. Before Kaluna could respond, Lerna shot. The bullet whizzed past Kaluna and struck one of the government agents behind her. She turned to see the man had come to and had his gun aimed right at her back. Lerna's shot hit him right in the heart, but as he shuddered and jerked to death, his gun fired. The single bullet passed right by Kaluna and struck Lerna in the torso. Her defensive pendant flashed around her as it reacted to the sphere-tipped bullet that had just deployed under her right breast. Rita rushed to catch Lerna before she collapsed.

"I guess the pendants work," Lerna said through gritted teeth.

"What do we do!?" Rita said in a panic.

"Put your pendant around her neck!" said Kaluna. Lerna gritted her teeth and growled.

"What? She said it wouldn't..." Rita started to say.

"It'll stop the bleeding!" Kaluna snapped. "She's useless right now anyway," she said, wrestling the pendant controller out of Lerna's pocket.

They heaved Lerna on top of Hutch and cranked her sphere out to engulf what parts of her Hutch's sphere didn't cover. Kaluna pulled one end of the cart while Rita pushed. They lowered Lerna and Hutch down into the maintenance shaft and closed the hatch just as a garrison of penalty officers arrived at the disheveled apartment down the hall.

Chapter Eighteen
The Council

Mahana sat with his great chin in his hand. He had just finished listening to the thirtieth complaint of the day. The steady flow of new citizens had ballooned the population of his floating village to tens of thousands. The network of boats and submarines stretched to a distance that strained his eyes, and a wave of democratic fervor had washed over those under his control. A general election was quickly held for council members, and Mahana sat and listened as the council, a body of thirty-eight men and women shouted over each other. Mahana was still the de facto leader and had cast the tie-breaking vote on what he considered far too many tied votes. The voting of the council was done for the day and each member was airing their grievances. Councilman thirty-one, a man named Astley, stood to air his constituents' complaint.

"Yes, thank you. Jarid Astley, district thirty-one. My constituents would like water rations increased." Mr. Astley's complaint was quickly shouted down by several other council members.

"Someone already said that, Astley!"

"Two people actually!"

"We are bringing a new desalinating craft on this weekend."

"And three more next week."

"Well, I'm sorry!" Mr. Astley responded dejectedly. "I can't hear everyone above all of the bickering."

"Okay. Dat's it," Mahana said. "We're done wit complaints for today. No, I know tirty-two trew tirty-eight still gotta go. We'll work backwards next time. I'm sorry. Meetin' adjourned," Mahana said. He squeezed the bridge of his nose while the council left his captain's quarters on *The Beluga*. One of the council hung back while the rest shuffled out. It was a woman named Jain. She was one of the only council that Mahana had befriended, and indeed, of whom he had grown quite fond. Jain walked around the back of his chair and placed her seemingly small hands on his massive shoulders. His great frame melted into her touch.

"You must stop taking these meetings to heart, Manny. After all, these are not personal complaints against you. That's just what we've come to call them," said Jain in her warm, smooth voice.

"I know it. Das not it, dough," said Mahana. "I think da council's a good idea. We just aren't gettin' anythin' done."

"Manny, dear," Jain said, moving her hand up to Mahana's face, "in the weeks that I've known you, you have seen your surface population grow by ten times and you have somehow managed to maintain services and food for all of…"

Mahana trapped her hand against his face with his own massive palm and slid it away.

"That isn't what dis was supposed to be. Dis ain't no permanent settlement," he said sharply, rising out of his chair and going to the window. "We were here as a distraction, but da complex is utta' chaos now. It's more of a distraction den we are. Dis has turned into a rescue haven, and it ain't gonna last. We need to leave for da mainland before dis giant raft collapses." He stood at the window and looked out over the expanse of vessels that surrounded his great ship. Jain came to his side and shared his vantage while they stood silently for a long time, and then Mahana spoke again. "Cause make no mistake, if dis ting gets any bigger it will collapse: food will get short, people'll get desperate, and den its ova'. It won't be an easy journey eas', but we need to get movin' sooner dan later."

Jain's eyes welled with tears as she looked out over the expanse of weary refugees. She pressed her eyes against her friend's great bicep.

"Will you propose it to da council, Jain? You know I can't," asked Mahana.

She pressed her face harder and sniffled loudly. When she pulled her face away, she had left an embarrassingly large wet spot on his sleeve.

"Oh dear," she said, wiping at it with her sleeve.

Mahana let out a long chuckle, and pulled her against him.

"Yes, Manny. I will propose it," she said quietly.

Chapter Nineteen
The Way Back

Kaluna and Rita remained crouched in the maintenance shaft below the apartment they had just left. They listened to the shuffle of dozens of penalty officers' feet as they swarmed the surrounding apartments, corridors, and stairwells. The rattling and hissing of the old mechanical equipment was enough to hide the sound of their movements, but the close quarters offered virtually no space to haul Hutch and Lerna at the same time. They had not moved Lerna or Hutch for an hour as the officer activity above had only continued to grow. They sat and rested, Rita offering what suggestions she could in an effort to solve their current dilemma.

"We could leave Hutch here and use the cart to roll Lerna back to a safer area." Rita whispered.

"Just leave him here?" Kaluna said. "What if they find him?"

"Better than them finding us. Besides, the half-life on that battery is a few days. By the time it wears off, we would be long gone and he wouldn't know what the hell had happened."

Kaluna reluctantly agreed and they spent several minutes readjusting their human cargo. They discovered that they could reach through the EST to push and shuffle the two rigid bodies, but only for a moment at a time. Once their hands crossed the boundary of the sphere, they lost the ability to move or clench their fingers. They could only use their stiff limbs to push and prod. Even those short intervals left their hands numb and senseless for several minutes. It took them nearly half an hour to arrange Lerna on the cart and deposit Hutch on the floor of the maintenance tunnel.

Reducing their load made a significant difference, and soon they were making good progress as they pushed their new leader down the narrow passage. Even at their speed, they estimated a journey of several hours; regular breaks became a necessity.

They slowed their pace as they approached the transition from *Gold Sector* to the newer portions of the complex. The alignment and configuration of the maintenance passage in the newer section was much more accommodating, but the transition from one district to the other included an awkward assembly of stairways and ladders. Kaluna and Rita stood and puzzled while they caught their breath.

"We can't carry her up those steps," said Kaluna. "We wouldn't be able to hold or grab her. Not with the EST activated."

Rita nodded slowly as she thought through the process herself.

"We could turn off the EST just long enough to get her up the steps," Rita suggested.

"And then turn it back on?" Kaluna asked.

"I guess so. I don't think her wound will bleed that much if we move quickly enough."

Kaluna considered the plan for over a minute before sighing deeply and pulling the EST control from her pocket. She looked over the controller carefully before pressing the button firmly. A buzz and a click sounded as the orange aura around Lerna disappeared. Her body immediately started responding. She breathed deeply with closed eyes. Suddenly her mouth began to contort; her lips curled sharply around her gums and she appeared to wretch.

"What should I do?" Kaluna asked quickly.

"I don't know!" said Rita. "Maybe it's just wearing off."

A gurgling noise emanated from the back of Lerna's throat. It slowly took on a pitch tone as it transitioned to a whine and then a louder, shriller cry. All at once her eyes shot open and she began to thrash. One hand gripped at her bullet wound while the other beat the grated floor with a closed fist. Soon, a steady stream of expletives was spewing from her mouth. Rita crouched and attempted to both console and silence her.

"Lerna. Lerna, shhh. We have to move you up these stairs, but we need you to keep it down. Lerna, please. Focus. We are going to lift you up these stairs and then put you back under the EST. Okay? Can you nod yes? Good!

Do you want a rag or something to bite? Here." Rita took a torn shirt sleeve from Kaluna and twisted it into a long, narrow knot. Lerna glared at her, but un-gritted her teeth just long enough for Rita to insert the rag in her mouth. She bit down with excruciating force; tears streamed down her face. Rita lifted Lerna under the arms while Kaluna grabbed her legs in a bear hug, and they began to haul her up the first half-flight of stairs. Rita lost her balance as she moved backwards up the steep incline and fell back on her rear. Lerna clinched her fists in pain, but returned her hands to her wound to maintain pressure. Rita recovered and they made it to the tiny landing above. Lerna jerked her head upwards to indicate that they not stop, and soon they were up the second half-flight. Kaluna ran down below to retrieve the cart while Rita cradled Lerna above. Kaluna returned with the cart and quickly carried it up their last obstacle: a five foot vertical ladder. She laid down in the opening with her hands outstretched, and Lerna reluctantly joined hands with her. The remaining effort was given by Rita who had Lerna over one shoulder as she ascended the short but challenging rungs. They reached the top and had just rolled Lerna onto the cart when she spit out the rag to speak.

"Turn this damn thing back on," she growled as she situated the pendant around her neck. Within moments, Kaluna had the EST activated and adjusted to Lerna's size, then she collapsed against Rita to rest.

**

146

Several hours of toil and effort found Rita and Kaluna pushing Lerna towards guards of the Spring territory. They quickly explained, at gun point, what had happened. Lerna was taken away to the medical team while Kaluna and Rita were left to recover.

***

Kaluna and Rita sat and ate in the dining facility. They had spent the day speculating over Lerna's health, and whether or not they would go back for Gerard Hutch. Kaluna was pressing Rita harder to join her in lobbying for their friends' freedom.

"Look, I know Linx can be a hot head, but Sembado will be reasonable with the Spring," Kaluna said while Rita ate quietly. "I think we should forget about Hutch. Even the girl in the video said Fabian doesn't care about him. We should try and get the guys to use old M'Gereg as a bargaining chip for Fabian. If they help detain and hold the old man, then Lerna should team with the Elephants against the government."

"And you think she'd agree to that, huh?"

Kaluna and Rita turned around quickly. Lerna was standing with a crutch; she had heavy bandages around her wound. "What?" she said. "You don't think one gun shot is gonna keep me from running this place, do ya?"

Kaluna and Rita were silent while Lerna gingerly situated herself across the table from them. Kaluna looked at Rita, but she suddenly seemed more interested in her food.

"Look," said Lerna.

"Can I say something?" Kaluna interrupted.

"Just a minute," Lerna said more firmly. "You'll get your chance."

Kaluna pursed her lips, but remained silent.

"I know I do things my way around here," Lerna said. "And I know I don't leave much room for input."

Kaluna fought back the urge to interject.

"But you two saved my life," Lerna said flatly. Rita looked up from her food, and Kaluna uncrossed her arms as Lerna continued, "Literally, saved my life." She sighed deeply. "You know, I criticize the Elephants a lot. For what they did to my sister. For what they did to my family. But these missions I'm going on. That I'm having my girls go on. They're the same thing. We're killin' people too. We're killin' Elephants, we're killin' pens, and I've lost some of mine in the process."

There was a long process in which Lerna looked away at the ceiling while Rita and Kaluna looked elsewhere.

"If you say Fabian needs to fall, then we will take him down," Lerna said as her eyes connected with Kaluna and then Rita. "And your friends are already scheduled to be released; by the end of the night. Poor bastards are gonna go through enough pain being thawed out. That part was worse than the gun shot," she said through the side of her mouth.

Kaluna and Rita exchanged looks of dumbfounded joy, and they embraced.

"It's time we start using the kind of cooperation we preach so much about," Lerna finished as she got up slowly. She was not prepared for Kaluna to throw her small frame around her, and released a low shout when Kaluna squeezed a little too hard.

Kaluna let her go and she and Rita sat back down.

"Oh, and one more thing," Lerna said as she turned back from leaving. "You're right about Fabian's love for Hutch. I sent a couple scouts back down those shafts. The poor bastard was still there. I let Tiz decide his fate."

Kaluna and Rita exchanged looks of curiosity.

"She finally let him go," Lerna said with a smile.

Chapter Twenty
The Chief Navigator

Mahana sat as his thoughts raced. His large brown palm was stretched across his mouth. The council had just finished voting to name him the Chief Navigator. The resolution and title meant that, while each of the council members were still the representative governors of their respective districts, Mahana alone had the role and responsibility of directing *The Surface Collective,* as they had come to call their floating settlement, to where it would sail to next.

"What's the matter, Manny?" Jain said, placing a hand on his broad shoulders. "Isn't this what you wanted?"

Mahana breathed out through his nose, and then dropped his hand from his mouth. He started to speak, but stopped.

"I jus' didn' tink it would happen so fast," he said. "Sudd'ly it's on me to say when. Can we just leave wit' all the fightin' goin' down dere? My lil' Luna and Sembado. I jus' don' know," he said, dropping his head as he finished.

"What would it take to get you to set off?" Jain asked. "We're struggling to maintain order and supplies. You said it first. We need to find a permanent alternative, and right now our only option is east." She sat down next to him so that they could see eye to eye. "So what needs to happen before you can say go?"

"I...I don' know. I guess I jus'," Mahana started to blubber.

"Manny, just say it!" Jain snapped.

He straightened his posture and looked her in the eyes.

"I need to know Kaluna's okay. My boy sent word dat she had arrived in my ol' village down dere, but now she's gone, and he don't know where to. I haven't heard from Sembado or Linx eitha'," Mahana said quickly.

Jain placed her wrinkled white hand on Mahana's saying, "Manny, I will help get the time you need, but you can't keep leading these people if your personal concerns are going to overshadow thousands of others."

"I know it," he said firmly.

"They need your undivided leadership," she added.

"I know it!" he said more loudly.

Jain pursed her lips and pulled her hand off of his.

"Don' do dat," said Mahana.

"How long do we need to prepare for sea?" asked Jain.

Mahana dropped his head back and sighed.

"Wit' yer council coverin' upkeep so tight? 'Bout a week," he said.

"One week?" she asked.

"One week," he repeated.

"Then we have a week to find out what has happened to your niece," said Jain strongly.

This time Mahana reached for *her* hand; he cupped it firmly.

Chapter Twenty-One
Pins and Needles

Sembado inhaled. His head pounded, and his body shook with chills. The mirrored wall in front of him showed the reflection of a blurry red ghost; his flushed skin almost blended into his fiery hair. He gasped for air, and then cried out in pain. His entire body was on fire. The pain of a sleeping limb crawled across every inch of his skin. His extremities were heavy and refused to move as the sharp, cold pain continued to pump through his body in waves.

Where'd she go?

The guard who had administered this new energy sphere just a moment before was nowhere to be seen.

Did she even turn it on? Is this all it did is make my body numb and sleepy?

A sudden zapping noise brought his attention to his side. Linx was just starting to stir. He curled his lip as the same discomfort started to crawl across his skin. Sembado

153

looked around to where Kreymond and the islanders had stood against the wall. They were no longer there. Another buzzing zap came from his other side. There sat Kreymond, Puolo, and Kala.

They weren't there a minute ago!

Kreymond was already whining through his numbing sensations. Puolo and Kala sat still. They were crystalized under humming, orange-hued spheres. Suddenly their spheres also dissolved and they began to return to consciousness.

She did activate them! How long have I been out?

Sembado gritted his teeth as he lifted his right leg off of the foot rest on his chair. It landed hard on the floor with little control. His arms too were difficult to manage. He was suddenly reminded of his recovery after losing his leg. *His leg.* He looked down to see that his bionic limb was still intact, but when he thought to move it off the chair, it did not respond to his cerebral command; he simply lifted his leg at the thigh. The heel of the prosthetic lost its grip on the chair and it banged to the floor. Sembado closed his eyes as a new wave of discomfort rolled through his weary frame. He breathed heavily as his stomach and other organs seemed to catch fire and then freeze. All around him his friends moaned and groaned through identical experiences. Sembado put the pads of his fingers on his eyes and pressed firmly. The pressure helped.

Sembado pulled his hands away to see Linx stand up as he started stretching his limbs. He brought one hand across his chest. There he discovered the pendant still hanging around his neck. He quickly ripped it off and threw it against the wall. Sembado removed his with a firm yank and was just about to throw it at the door when it swung open.

Kaluna stood in the opening. Rita and Lerna flanked her on either side. She wore a soft smile and her eyes welled with tears when they met Sembado's. Sembado's mouth fell open, he dropped the pendant, and suddenly his prosthetic responded. He stood up, teetering, and started to move towards Kaluna.

"Get away from her!" he said as he shifted his eyes to Lerna. "Stay away from her!" He lost his balance and stumbled against the mirrored wall.

"Sembado, no!" said Kaluna as she ran to help him. "It's okay. Stop!" She met him at the wall and they embraced. She turned his body so that his back was against the mirror and he was only looking at her. She held his face firmly as he searched her eyes for answers. He saw her guilt and regret, but mistook it for pain and sadness.

"What did they do to you?" he asked, but before he could look away at Lerna again, Kaluna turned his face back to hers.

"No. They did nothing. I helped them. I helped her. And now she is willing to work with you," Kaluna said quickly. Sembado continued to search her eyes, and before he could stop he was kissing her. It did not last long, but it was true and meaningful, and she did not pull away. As he pulled back from their embrace, he noticed that his friends had moved away from the door, and were crowded in the corner.

"I don't think they get it," said Lerna, and Sembado and Kaluna turned to see her walk away as she rolled her eyes. Rita watched her walk away before entering the room. Linx and the others still did not move.

"Kaluna's right," said Rita. "We've negotiated your release. Lerna wants to help us take down Fabian."

Linx and the others exchanged looks of excited surprise.

"But there's a catch," Kaluna said as she looked from Linx and the others to Sembado.

"What? What is it?" asked Linx.

"She wants us to help capture and hold Jean M'Gereg," Rita said as she crossed her arms.

"What?" Linx shouted. "Why in the depths would she want him?"

"It's a long story," said Kaluna as she leaned against Sembado.

"Well I'm not doin' a damn thing till I hear it," Linx said pointedly.

"It's this whole thing about M'Gereg, and her dead sister's husband dying on a mission for the Elephants," said Rita. "She wants to hold him accountable as an irresponsible leader."

Sembado looked into Kaluna's eyes while Linx continued to protest.

"We've all lost people in this fight," said Linx defiantly. "What makes her think she can pick and choose who gets punished? We don't need her help with Fabian. Kreymond can lead us straight to his uncle and the defected henches," he said smugly. Rita and Kaluna exchanged looks as Kreymond looked on bashfully.

"She doesn't want any other Elephants?" Sembado asked.

"Just M'Gereg," Kaluna responded.

"What does that matter?" Linx snapped. "We aren't gonna do it!"

"Deeks, Linx, would you calm down?" said Sembado. "We need all the help we can get."

"She might even let you lead the remaining Elephants," Kaluna said to Linx.

"We don't actually have to capture this guy," Rita said. "Just convince him to surrender and bring him in."

Linx laughed loudly as she finished the thought.

"You haven't met Jean, have you?" Sembado said with a dry smirk.

"They're right," Kaluna added. "But if we can convince the other Elephants to go along with it, then we might just be able to do it as peacefully as possible."

Sembado looked at Linx with raised eyebrows.

"Come on, man," Sembado said. "With Kreymond's inside lead, and the Elephants and Spring working together, Fabian's done. This is a very small sacrifice if you ask me."

Linx groaned deeply as he said, "This is all because her brother-in-law died on Jean's watch?"

"It haunted her sister for the rest of her life," Kaluna said.

"When was this? Did we know him? What was his name?" Linx demanded.

"Mmm, I don't remember," said Kaluna, shrugging.

"Well, we know it was Jean's son," Rita added.

Linx's eyes widened. He seemed to lose his breath as he fell into one of the nearby chairs.

"Linx, are you okay?" Rita asked. The others crowded around as Linx struggled to maintain his composure.

When he finally spoke, it was a barely audible whisper.

"It was Andrel."

Chapter Twenty-Two
Lost and Found

Lerna had transitioned from her crutch to a cane, and was awkwardly working her way through the cafeteria line. She stopped while a piece of fish was fetched from the steam oven. The person behind her bumped her tray with theirs. She looked up to see Linx.

"Sorry," he said solemnly.

"And I'm sorry for releasing you," she said as she took the plate of fish the line-server was handing her. "You look very upset with your freedom."

They continued to move down the line, grabbing assorted food items as they went.

"I'd skip that kelp bread if I were you," Lerna said.

"We have to talk," said Linx as he followed her to an empty table.

"About you helpin' me get Jean? Sounds good," Lerna said sharply.

"Lerna, I knew him too," Linx said.

"I know. That's why you're the perfect person to help me bring him in," said Lerna, taking a bite of her fish.

"I meant Andrel," Linx said quietly as he picked over his food.

Lerna stopped chewing, and studied her plate for a long time.

"I was wondering if you might have met him," she said, and when she looked up, she was surprised to see that he had tears dripping off his face and into his food. She looked down and then away. They sat in uncomfortable silence that was only broken by his loud sniffling.

Once Linx had collected himself, he spoke, saying, "I didn't just know of him. He was my mentor. He was my Elephant sponsor when I first joined, and I was there. I was there the day he died." Linx looked up at Lerna. His eyes were red and wet. "He was the first I had ever seen go," Linx added. "But he never said anything about his wife. That's kind of part of the deal."

Lerna and Linx stared at each other quietly for several moments. It was a look of mutual understanding and trust, something neither of them was used to.

"Tegea was *pretty* surprised to find her husband had died fighting a war she didn't even know was happening," said Lerna with a dry smirk.

"Was that her name?" Linx asked.

"Yea, Tegea Greka. That was before she became Tegea M'Gereg of course. I always thought that had a terrible ring to it. Anyway, she wasn't as surprised by Jean's reaction to Andrel, but it still hurt her very much," Lerna said as she went back to eating her fish.

"What did he do?" Linx asked.

"Nuffin'," Lerna mumbled through her mouthful of food. She chased the fish with some water and swallowed hard. "He did absolutely nothing. Stopped talking to her, even less than before. He was never a very kind man in my experience."

"Yea, that doesn't sound far off," Linx admitted. "He and Hyron had gone way back and all. The original Elephants, ya know? But Hyron was always the more human of the two."

"That's my whole point here," Lerna said as she wiped her mouth. "I've accepted that Fabian needs to fall, and I'm even open to an Elephant-Spring alliance. What I can't accept is Jean letting his old, cold hate fuel this fire any longer. He wasn't fit to lead back then and he isn't fit to lead now."

Linx considered the point as he continued to eat. When his mouth was clear, he responded.

"I can get the Elephants to agree to this. I'm certain of it. Getting Jean to step down might be a challenge, but it sounds like a necessity at this point. The Elephants and the Spring do not need to fight. We have one common goal now. With your new technology, we can reduce casualties, and with Kreymond's information, we can penetrate Fabian's ranks from the inside-out."

"Kreymond?" she asked. "The real timid one?"

"We are holding his older brother," said Linx. "A defected Pen – on the surface. He has contacts with one of Fabian's men. His uncle. A guy named Markus."

"Markus Dometica?" Lerna asked excitedly.

"We didn't get a last name," said Linx. "We just know he's a high-level penalty officer."

"Penalty officer?" Lerna said with a chuckle. "Dometica is Fabian's commander. He's like his number two!"

"Well, I've heard of Dometica," said Linx defensively. "I guess I'd never heard his first name. Like Fabian, you know?"

Lerna shook her head with a smirk.

"What? Like you know what J.L. Fabian stands for?" Linx asked accusingly.

"Jerdo Leopold," Lerna said without thinking.

"How do you know that?" Linx laughed. "I've never heard anyone else say that. *Jerdo Leopold?* No wonder he goes by his initials."

Lerna laughed and said, "He is terrible." Then the smile faded from her face. "Linx, he needs to go, and any of his loyalists too, but you know we can't just dissolve the government, right? Not in a place like this."

He solemnly nodded in agreement.

"I mean, maybe on the surface, you know? On land? People could run. They could hide, and find food. But that's one of the reasons they chose to make this place. People can't just sneak out; not normal people anyway – everyday people. They make all the food. Process all the water. The Spring has only just secured enough grow chambers to support our internal populace. I don't know how many the Elephants have."

Linx shrugged his shoulders and said, "Yea, I have no idea either, but I'm sure we could combine resources if I can find some connections."

Lerna agreed, saying, "I think our best bet would be to approach them openly. Let them see you. If you think that would work."

"I don't see why it wouldn't," Linx said. "I haven't had much contact with them since I've been gone. I don't have as reliable of a network as Mahana. Hey! What about the islanders? We should get them in on this too. Sembado said Mahana's son is their current leader. They like to keep their resources to themselves, but they might be willing to let us use their networks and connections. I'm sure if I could get Mahana's blessing, his son would give us whatever we needed."

"Yea, that's a good idea," Lerna said while nodding. "I don't have much experience with them. I just know they've pretty much stayed out of our way. They seem to have their own internal support for resources."

"You can say that again," Linx laughed. "They make surface runs on a near weekly basis. Just enough for themselves though, you know?"

"With all of our currently secured resources and Hyron's frequency, I don't think we would need much else but communication support from the islanders," Lerna responded.

"Well I think we should approach the Elephants first. It'll be a lot easier to sell this trouble to the islanders if they know we've already resolved the fight between your people and mine. So let's do this. Tonight," Linx said, extending his hand. "For Andrel," he added.

"For Andrel," Lerna said, and she shook his hand firmly.

Chapter Twenty-Three
Environmentally Friendly

Sembado was nearly skipping to dinner. He would be eating dinner with Kaluna for the first time in days, Linx and Lerna were going to win over the Elephants that night, and after dinner, Kaluna was joining him as he reconnected with his parents. The Spring had recently made a push for territory that included his family's living quarters. His home district also housed an electronics production module that the Spring and Elephants would need in order to mass produce the Klisk EST.

He entered the crowded dining facility by the food line. As he pushed and squeezed his way through the line of hungry people, he saw Kaluna waving from a table. She had collected enough food for both of them. Sembado sat down on the long bench next to her and embraced her with a sideways hug as she slid a tray of food towards him.

"They had those sea salt kale chips you like," she said.

"Thanks," said Sembado as he stuffed a handful of the crispy green wafers into his mouth. "Have you heard from Mahana yet?"

"No," she said solemnly. "We should really get back to Lahalo. I know they are staying in contact."

165

"We will. As soon as Lerna and Linx make peace between the Elephants and the Spring, we will go see Lahalo. By the way, are you nervous about meeting my family?"

"Why would I be nervous?" Kaluna asked. "It's not like we're dating."

Sembado fought to swallow his kale chips. His stomach turned hot, then his face followed suit.

"Well...I know. I just...I don't know," Sembado stuttered anxiously.

"Sembado, don't act like that," Kaluna said. "You don't have to worry about saying the wrong thing to me. We're friends. Best friends. And I know that can sometimes change between people, but for now let's just enjoy the fact that we're together and safe and that you still have a family to go back to."

"You're right," he said. Her calm, sensible words soothed his stomach immediately, but his face still felt very warm.

"Are you nervous about seeing your family?" she asked. "It's been a long time. And a lot *has* happened."

"I just want to know they're okay, you know?" Sembado said. "A lot has changed. I have changed. I've seen the surface."

"You are very different," Kaluna said. "Isn't it weird how going to the surface affects your view of this place?"

"I can't believe it," Sembado said as he nodded in agreement. "It all seems so dark, even with the lights on. It's so cramped; all of the ceilings and walls. I'm almost upset that I went at all. I wouldn't know what I'm missing, you know?"

"Well, don't you want to go back up?" Kaluna asked. Her tone was nearly incredulous.

"I mean, I've certainly thought about it. I guess I was just taking everything one step at a time. I haven't had time to slow down and think about what's next since we left *The Beluga*," he said.

"Well, I had always assumed we would go back up with Mahana and move East at some point. I sure don't plan on staying down here the rest of my life," she said firmly.

"Not for the rest of my life, no," Sembado said. "I guess I just didn't think about the sooner than later part. Even if this were to all clear up. If Fabian fell right away and Linx and Lerna were able to get peace and order restored, I don't know what I would do. I had a pretty simple life before all this, before I met you. I had an easy job. I lived with my parents. I played 4D – deeks, I forgot about 4D."

"I didn't mean to bring all that up. I'm sorry," she said, rubbing his back in comfort.

"That's the thing though. I don't really miss it," he said as he picked over a tuna egg roll. "Any of it. It all seems so unnecessary. The more I think about it, the more I can't really see a role for me to fulfill down here. I don't see a future. But up there, it's different. It's open and dangerous and the possibilities are endless. If we needed to run or even just wanted to run, we could. No running out of air.

This place was made to keep people happy. That was the life I lived. I don't want to be happy anymore. Well, you know what I mean. I want to have to try, to struggle. I want to find food, earn it, make it. Not have it allotted to me. Even here, it's handed out. The Spring. The Elephants. They want to give the power to the people so badly, but you can't do that down here. This place wasn't made for it."

Kaluna sat in silence as Sembado finished his rant. His passionate speech had grown just loud enough to draw the unwanted attention of those around him. He looked around as several people averted eye contact. He started eating with more purpose as he suddenly wanted to leave the dining hall.

"I guess that means you'll come back to the surface with me," Kaluna said with a smirk.

"Shut up," Sembado said, dropping his head sideways onto her shoulder.

***

Sembado and Kaluna made quick progress through the Spring's unchallenged territory. Sembado's bionic leg had become much more manageable thanks in large part to adjustments that the Spring's engineers had made. They passed regularly spaced watch parties; each acknowledged them courteously. Sembado's excitement grew increasingly difficult to contain as they approached his family's living chamber.

"That's the lift I used almost every day," Sembado said, pointing. "And that's where the Feldmans live...or lived," he added solemnly. He let out a deep sigh as they approached his old front door. "I don't know if I'm ready..."

Before they could do anything else, the door was flung open to reveal Sembado's mother. Her loud gasp was cut short as she covered her mouth with her hands. She inched forward as tears welled in her eyes. She looked into Sembado's eyes, and reached out to touch him. Removing her hands revealed that her mouth was open as she stuttered breathlessly. Sembado reached out to meet his mother's embrace, but as they touched, she fainted and collapsed into him.

"Oh deeks," Sembado said. "I think she was holding her breath." Kaluna helped Sembado shuffle his mother inside and they closed the door behind them.

"Deena?" a voice called from another room. "Was there someone at the door?" Sembado's father walked in and froze. "Sembado," he said, one hand grabbing his chest. "What happened?" he asked as he ran to his wife's side.

"She fainted," Sembado said as he helped his father carry his mother to the room.

Sembado and Kaluna sat with his mother while his father ran off to the bedroom. The commotion had awakened Sembado's brother, Herbert. He rubbed the sleep from his eyes as he walked into the room; he stopped short when he saw Sembado, his mother, and the dark stranger beside her.

"Holy ballasts! Wha…where?" Herbert blubbered as his father rushed past him with a wet rag.

Sembado's father folded the rag and put it on his wife's forehead. Kaluna rushed past Herbert, grabbed a pillow off of the sofa and returned to Sembado's mother's side.

"Thank you," Sembado's father said to Kaluna as he placed the pillow under his wife's head.

The extra jostling of her head stirred Sembado's mother, and she opened her eyes, blinking rapidly. As soon as her eyes focused on Sembado, she threw her arms around him, and pulled him in close. His father placed a hand on his back. Herbert came to sit next to Sembado too. Kaluna scooted out of the way to make room for the family.

Several minutes passed with nothing but loud sniffling filling the otherwise silent chamber. Finally, Sembado's mother broke the silence with the first of many questions.

"Where have you been? We thought you were dead!" she yelled through joyful tears. She had Sembado and his father help her to the sofa where she, Sembado, and Kaluna sat while Sembado's father and Herbert fetched fresh water and rations.

Sembado started at the beginning. He told of the Elephants, of Grandfather's legacy, and of how he came to get involved in the resistance.

"Yes, the government revealed dad's identity to us when they put our house on lock-down," Sembado's mother said. "They told us you were involved, but we didn't understand at the time."

Sembado explained what happened the night of the Elephant's kidnapping of Gerard Hutch, how he was left alone in the panic, and how he was taken to prison. His family sat with mouths agape and tears in their eyes as he described his stay in prison, rooming with Mr. Feldman, and being brought face to face with J. L. Fabian.

"He admitted all of that to you?" Sembado's father asked. He looked as personally betrayed as Sembado had when he had first accepted the government's true motives.

Herbert looked nearly delighted when Sembado described his fateful escape to rendezvous with Grandfather. Kaluna sat quietly as Sembado described experiencing the islander's refuge for the first time; the people, the food, and the music. He explained to his family how he had tried to return to them before leaving for the surface, but that Fabian's guards had already made it to their door.

His mother nearly fainted again when he described their escape from the complex, crashing through the containment net, and breaching to the surface. They were transfixed as he used vivid detail to tell them about the sky, the sun, and the fresh breeze. Their disbelief grew when he told them about the Hawaiian Islands and the settlement there. His mother grabbed Kaluna's hand when Sembado described Grandfather's great memorial service the islanders held on the beach. His mother pulled Kaluna in tighter once he explained her support in his recovery from Hutch's grenade attack. Sembado's father and brother marveled at his bionic limb which they had only

171

noticed for the first time. Kaluna joined his storytelling and the two of them described their nearly-fatal return to the complex, discovering the Spring, and reuniting with old friends. They were careful to avoid the details about confronting Fabian directly as Sembado's family had several questions from their story alone. Sembado spent nearly half an hour just convincing his father of the legitimacy of the Elephant's evidence against the government.

"Look, Dad," Sembado said calmly. "I don't pretend that they're perfect. The Elephants need more structure. More than just hate and revenge. That's why our friends are going to convince them to join with the Spring...tonight even. This is happening right now. The Elephants want justice, but the Spring want peace. If we can help them to merge that with the systematic order that the government has in place, then we might be able to strike a balance here."

His father looked into Sembado's eyes, then at his chest, and then back into his eyes. Everyone sat quietly, waiting for his response.

"But why do you need to be involved in this?" he responded. "There's so much at risk here – so much potential energy. No offense, Semmy, but what do you know about running the complex? It's a complicated place. Not just the mechanics and upkeep – feeding people and all – but the politics, the penalty officers. I mean, you're just a kid."

Sembado's stomach dropped. This was the last response he expected, and the truth of it sapped his confident calm instantaneously. Before he could respond, Kaluna interjected.

"Mr. Grey," she said in her quietly firm voice, "your son isn't going to run the government. He has no intention of making the decisions that you speak of."

Mrs. Grey still sat with her arm around Kaluna, and kept it there in support while her husband was forced to listen to the girl's reason. Herbert listened thoughtfully while Sembado discreetly took hold of Kaluna's hand.

"We want the men and women of your complex to continue doing the jobs they're good at. The workers, the growers, the technicians – they know their jobs and they do them well, but other things need to change. This war needs to stop, and the government's leaders need to be held accountable for their treason against the public. We have friends that are ready to make that happen. Your son means more to these people than you know. At times he has been the only one to know justice, true justice, and has pursued it singularly. He isn't fighting for himself – he isn't fighting for Hyron's vengeance. He fights for unity. He and I have become the single link between the Elephants, the Spring, and the islanders. We will help our friends join these three factions against a murderous, tyrannical villain."

"Fabian has fought to keep law and order afloat here!" exclaimed Mr. Grey. "He is not a villain!"

Sembado clenched his free hand and pounded it on the couch.

"Deeks, Dad! Open your eyes! I have spoken with this man face to face. He is out for blood, not order. He thinks he *is* the law. It is his weapon – not his tool. They killed millions before – hundreds of millions – all in the name of law and order. He is prepared to do that again!"

"Is that what you think happened?" his father asked loudly. "You think they killed them off for peace?"

"Dad, you haven't seen what I've seen," Sembado said with a sigh. "You don't know why…"

"I do know!" his father shouted as he stood to pace the room. "Do you think I'm some kind of fool? Some happy idiot? Do you think your grandpa's rebel friends have a monopoly on secrets? What do you think I did, working for the science department? I know about these secret letters – these secret reports. I know the event was planned!" he shouted. His words echoed through the chamber.

Everyone sat and stared. Sembado's stomach became hot and his leg twitched. His father ran his fingers through his hair; he clenched his fists as they were tangled in handfuls of his thinning locks. They all sat in quiet tension as he let out a series of heavy sighs.

"Your grandpa had it all wrong," Mr. Grey said quietly. "It wasn't for law and order, and it wasn't to regain control. That was just an added bonus."

Sembado breathed deeply as he fought to maintain his composure. Despite the Spring's adjustments to his leg, he could feel it humming in reaction to his emotional state.

"It was for our future," Mr. Grey said more quietly. "There were just too many people, and there was no end in sight. All of the reports that I've read. The research that was done for years – for decades – all pointed to the same thing. People weren't willing to change their habits – their intake. We needed an incentive for everything. It used to be money. But even when we were presented with the evidence, the challenge wasn't how to slow down, but instead, how can we continue without changing. We were even trying to take people to Mars to ease overpopulation. When the event happened, there were almost eight billion people on the planet. By this time, there would have been closer to eleven. We were racing through fossil fuels, but struggling to bring wind and solar online. Do you know why? Because the profits weren't there. Developments in information and technology were outpacing the general population's understanding of it. The expectations of luxury were on the rise worldwide. Bigger houses. Acres of super-chilled server farms to support people's computing needs."

Mr. Grey paused for a drink of water, but no one interrupted him. Sembado was captivated by his father's passion and the revelations he shared. His father cleared his throat before he continued.

"But this place was supposed to be different. The complexes were not just meant to house people. They were meant to be invisible to the environment. Zero net heat transfer and zero impact on ocean temperatures. One-hundred percent renewable energy from solar, wind, and tides. The entire submarine industry was augmented to comply. Sonar was eliminated for its impact on wildlife. Material science grew by leaps and bounds to create thin but sturdy viewing shields which were coupled with traditional radar to accommodate navigation. These complexes marked the first time in recorded history that man allowed his progress, luxury, and profits to take a back seat to something – anything else. And in order for all of this to succeed, to function as designed, and for the surface to return to its homeostasis, then all of those extra people had to go. If there wasn't enough room up there, then there certainly wouldn't have been enough room in these close quarters."

Sembado and Kaluna accepted the presented facts and the horror behind them much more easily than Mrs. Grey or Herbert. Sembado's mother and brother had been very well protected from exposure to the unfortunate truth of their surroundings.

"It's taken these last seventy years just to bring the impact of the previous hundred to a firm stop," Mr. Grey added with lighter tone. "It was a very exciting time for us in the science department, until this civil war broke out. We were just starting to track the very first positive trends: steady climate patterns lasting decades, ocean levels haven't risen in ten years, and our satellite images have shown a healthy surge of reforestation around the globe."

Sembado contemplated his father's words quietly as he took a break for more water. He let out a sigh before he continued.

"So I know what happened, Sembado. And I know why. I am not happy for what had to be done, but I will not say I am not thankful to be here, to be alive, and to be part of the next evolution of man. The government has been burdened with a heavy task. I just don't know if your friends understand what they are getting into."

The room remained quiet while Sembado thought on his response. His father had never addressed him as an equal and with such candid honesty. These were compelling truths, and he understood the difficult decision that his father had described, but the past had little to do with the treacherous conflict he and his friends were planning to bring to an end.

"Dad, I understand what you've explained," Sembado said calmly. "I get that the environment is a valuable resource and that it comes first. I do think that the government enjoyed the advantage of complete and utter control that came after the event, but I believe you that the sacrifice was maybe a necessary evil. The bigger picture is that all of the remaining people have a planet to continue to live on instead of having to suffer through some ecological system failure, but..."

Sembado paused as he pondered his next statement. Kaluna squeezed his hand to show her support. His father waited respectfully. Mrs. Grey and Herbert continued to wrestle with their new realities, and they hung on Sembado's every word as he continued his rebuttal.

"What's happened in the past is done," Sembado said resolutely. "Me and my friends aren't interested in holding Fabian accountable for some difficult decision made almost a hundred years ago. We want him to be held accountable for his corruption and greed. I understand if people are forced to sacrifice and forfeit their luxuries and privileges for the greater good, but that has nothing to do with the basic dignity and liberty and justice they deserve. That should be universal whether we live on the surface, under water, or on the Moon!" Sembado finished his statement more strongly than he thought he would. His father did not seem offended, but pensive.

"I promise you," Sembado said as he looked into his father's eyes, "your priorities are not his. He wants power and control, not peace and quiet. He doesn't care about anything except maintaining his tight grip on what he has. And mark my words: he will cling to his status so desperately that something will break. It might even be him."

Mrs. Grey and Herbert carefully observed Mr. Grey's reaction as Sembado explained away any remaining philosophical conflict.

"I am ready to live this life you have described, dad," Sembado said. He looked down at his and Kaluna's entwined fingers as he pulled her hand closer to his lap. "I want to go back to the surface. I want to live on the land and live for the land. I want to practice the stewardship you envision for our future. Kaluna and I will do it together, but not until the people here in the complex are free of this tyrant."

Mr. Grey held his hands flat together in front of his mouth. He breathed slowly and silently. His wife and younger son sat quietly, studying the floor. Sembado and Kaluna studied each other's knuckles.

"I have to say," Mr. Grey said through his fingers, "I'm not surprised. You have always more curious than your friends. You have always more curious than *my* friends. The surface. The sky. Why we're here. If you hadn't found your way to your grandfather's Elephants, then it would have been something else. It was only a matter of time, and even in complete and utter peace, they would not have been able to keep you pacified forever. Not with their virtual reality and not with their submarine races. You would have grown tired of it."

Sembado looked up from his and Kaluna's hands to exchange a heartfelt gaze with his teary-eyed father. Sembado's eyes were also beginning to moisten. His relationship with his father had always been polite but distant, and this was the most sincere exchange they had ever had.

"I think you're right," Sembado said. "And as soon as we get some kind of security plan in place, Kaluna and I will go to the surface so her uncle can take us East to the mainland."

While Kaluna squeezed Sembado's right hand, his mother grabbed his left and pulled him into her shoulder.

She wept into his long red hair, and whispered to him how proud she was.

Chapter Twenty-Four
Well Played

"There are a few that I think will resist aside from Jean," Linx said to Lerna as they stepped quickly behind the Spring guards ahead. "My brother has always enjoyed ruining any of my plans, but there will be several more that will see the value of this alliance."

"We are approaching the edge of our territory," said the lead guard.

"I will lead," said Linx. "Let them see my face."

The guards exchanged looks with Lerna who gave them a firm nod. They parted the corridor. Linx paused a moment, biting his lip, and stepped forward. Lerna and her guards followed a safe distance behind him.

Linx walked only three corridors into the Elephant's territory before shots were fired just past his head. He collapsed to the ground with his hands over his head while Lerna and her guards retreated to cover.

"Wait!" Linx yelled. Another stream of gunfire ricocheted off the walls behind which Lerna and her guards sheltered.

"Run to us!" a voice ahead shouted. "Run to us, brother!"

Linx stood, but did not move forward or back.

"Linx, what are you doing?" the voice shouted. "Run!"

"No!" Linx yelled back. "They're with me! Now hold your fire!"

The silence to follow was long and tense. Linx's hands started to tremble and he focused on his breathing to avoid holding his breath.

"Linx are you okay?" Lerna called from behind him. Before he could respond another order was shouted from ahead.

"Tell them to lay down their weapons and join you out in the open!" the voice shouted, and then there was silence.

"Did you hear them?" Linx called back to Lerna and her guards. There was more silence. "Lerna!" Linx shouted.

"Yes! We heard them," Lerna replied sharply. A moment later, she and her guards slid their rifles out into view. Then they too came out from around their corner.

"Here they are," Linx shouted ahead. "Don't shoot!"

He led Lerna and her guards forward. The rifles of the Elephants could be seen poking around the corners ahead. They slowly moved out from their cross-corridors as Linx and his companions approached. A handful of Elephant troops ran to retrieve the Spring's abandoned rifles while the squad leader removed his face shield to address Linx. His bright blue eyes stood out against his pale face and thick black whiskers. Linx recognized him as his old training partner, Rohn. Linx threw himself forward, and the two shared a loving embrace.

"Man, it's been a long time," Linx said happily.

"Yes. Too long," Rohn added. "I heard you made it to the surface. Why on Earth would you come back down? Just to run with our enemy?" He glared at Lerna and her guards.

"I came back for Fabian," Linx said. "I have an insider ready to take him out, but we don't stand a chance unless the Elephants and the Spring come together. We're here to broker an alliance." Lerna and Rohn exchanged a cautious stare.

"Elephants," Rohn ordered, not breaking eye contact with Lerna. "Escort Linx and our new friends to a more comfortable location."

The group walked down several corridors and climbed many flights of stairs. Rohn had the procession double back three times in an attempt to hide the coordinates of their destination. They passed a set of sentinels that guarded an open doorway. Beyond it, there was another door with more watchmen. Rohn waved ahead and the door was opened just before they reached it.

The opened door revealed a recovery center. Men, women, and children huddled around small piles of belongings. They slept on cramped cots while volunteers walked the rows, handing out rations. A double door to the side of the room revealed an identical scene in the adjacent room, and another beyond that.

The Elephant escorts peeled off one by one as they were greeted by family and friends. Soon just Linx, Lerna, and her guards marched behind Rohn as he moved into the next room. There, men and women toiled over large piles of supplies. The supplies were being organized and sorted. Some were put onto shelves while others were prepared for immediate distribution. A few weapons lay about, but the piles were mostly nonedible, personal items: toothpaste, toilet paper, and clothing. The workers gawked and sneered at the Spring women and their proudly decorated armor. Rohn led them on further through more chambers with more functions until they finally arrived in the Elephants' lead logistics room. A group of older men sat around a large table. An even larger screen hung on the wall. It cycled through various sectors and floors of the complex; each new image showed the territory and faction control. The men around the table puffed and fussed as the Spring warriors shuffled in.

"Rohn! What's the meaning of this!" one of the men protested.

"Is that Linx Waverly?" another asked.

"Son of a bitch," said the gruffest voice of all. Everyone became quiet as Jean M'Gereg stood up from the table and eyed Lerna knowingly. His labored breathing was made worse when he stood, and he braced himself on the table in front of him.

"It's been a long time, Jean," Lerna said stoically.

"Not long enough," M'Gereg said bitterly as he plopped back down in his chair. "What are you doing with our boy Linx?"

"I brought her here myself," said Linx. "They've cracked the code from Hyron's journal."

"That journal was private property!" Jean shouted. "And they shouldn't have gone snoopin' in other people's…"

"Oh, shut up, ya old blowhard!" Lerna snapped. "And let him finish his damn proposal!"

A hush fell over the room as the other Elephants waited for his retort, but old Jean M'Gereg remained silent while Linx continued.

"These are powerful weapons we have access to now. And I have brought an insider back from the surface; a friend of Sembado's. His name is Kreymond, and he is going to put us in contact with his uncle – one of Fabian's lead men – Markus Dometica." The Elephants, including Rohn, exchanged looks of interest. "We have the in, we have the weapons, but we need the people," Linx said. "For those of you who don't know, this is Lerna Greka. She is the Spring's commander and she wants to help us take down Fabian. The plan is to join territories, resources, and forces in order to turn the tide against the government. With the addition of our inside guy, we think we could topple Fabian within the week."

The Elephant leaders talked excitedly with one another, but Jean was not convinced.

"The Spring has more territory, more food, and more guns than the Elephants. Why in the blue depths would you want to partner with us?" Jean said bitterly.

"I want the fighting to stop," Lerna said firmly.

"That's the answer I expected from a damn woman," Jean said mockingly.

"And I want you!" Lerna growled through gritted teeth.

"What the hell did you say to me?" Jean snapped back.

"In exchange for this alliance, access to the anti-weapon code, and all of the other resources the Spring is willing to share, they want to see M'Gereg detained and kept from a leadership role of any kind," Linx said quickly.

The table of old men exploded into argument while Jean and Lerna exchanged particularly choice insults. Linx put his hands on his head while Rohn covered his mouth in a poor attempt to hide his raucous laughter.

"Some plan there, Linxy," he said as he elbowed his friend in the side. "Just march in here and tell M'Gereg to personally surrender. Well played."

"We've got to work this out," Linx responded. "We can't take Fabian down with just the Elephants and Islanders."

"Islanders?" Rohn said loudly; the shouting at the table was reaching a dull roar. "They haven't been with us for weeks. It's not the same without Mahana. His son thinks everything he's done for us is a mistake, and he refuses to send his people to fight for us. I can't blame him really. He's just watchin' out for his own."

***

M'Gereg's frail condition left little room for a struggle, and he was eventually cornered and detained. He refused almost all care and feeding for several days before a medical team administered an I.V. drip. Some of the other Elephants resisted, but Rohn and Linx were able to convince most of them that they were fighting an uphill battle, and soon news of the alliance spread quickly.

Families were reunited across previously divided sectors, and celebrations were had all across the allies' combined territory. But Kaluna was quite distraught to hear of her cousin's unwillingness to continue his father's legacy of goodwill, and she and Sembado used their new found freedom of travel to pay Lahalo a visit.

They found Lahalo in his quarters where he received them with his typical, mischievous attitude.

"Mahalo, great peacemaker's, and congratulations on forgin' such a stunnin' alliance. Fabian'll be shakin' in his flipper's fa-sure!" he said with a great chuckle.

"It'd be an even better alliance if they still had Mahana's support!" Kaluna snapped, refusing to sit down while Sembado fidgeted nervously. "Now that the fighting has stopped between the rebel factions, I will assume you will lend support in defeating the government!"

"That sounds like somethin' you'd assume," Lahalo said lightly. "Problem is, Mahana can't offer support if he's not here. He's got bigger fish fryin' up top, and I'm runnin' things down here."

"Does he know that you're disgracing him by refusing the strength of our people to those in need?" Kaluna snapped.

"Look, little cuz," Lahalo said as the smile quickly faded from his face. "You gotta stop this. This place is mine now, and if you come up in her runnin' your mouth again, I'm gonna send ya packin'. Mahana's leavin' soon. Real soon. He sent word down the other day. You know what's holdin' him up?"

Kaluna responded by glaring.

"You," Lahalo said. "He's about sunk with people up there, and he's holdin' up the whole damn show cause of you."

Kaluna slowly sat down as her anger subsided.

"As soon as you got here, I sent word back to him to let him know that you're okay. But that's all you get from me. I'm not sorry if ya think I'm a disgrace, but I am sorry for every time Mahana's big ass heart has spoken for our whole damn family. Once he hears you're okay, he's gonna leave. That's what he told me. So if ya plan on takin' ginga' here back to da surface, ya'll betta hurry up and bag ya head tanka'."

Kaluna starred at Lahalo strongly, but it was not a glare. They exchanged the look for a long time before she stood and said, "Good bye. I'll miss you."

"Don't lie, cuz," Lahalo said with a great chuckle. "It doesn't suit ya well."

Chapter Twenty-Five
Friend of a Friend

Sembado moved quickly along the corridor, using his leg to make up time. He slowed his hurried pace as he approached Lerna's chambers. She, Kaluna, Linx, and Kreymond were just coming out. Kaluna tossed him a small handgun.

"Keep it hidden," Lerna called from the front of the line. Sembado followed behind quickly as they made their way out of the Spring headquarters, and into the complex beyond.

They made quick progress through the Spring and Elephants' combined territory. Along the way, they passed several lively gatherings as some of the citizens in these sectors were still celebrating the new alliance. Many cheered as they saw Linx and Lerna marching side by side. The two new comrades' friendship had become a symbol of the alliance, with one local artist combining the Elephant and Spring emblems to form a popular, new sign of their union.

The friendly, happy faces became sparser as Sembado and the others approached the extents of their allies' control. Lerna slowed the team to a stop as she checked her wrist-mounted navigator. They sheltered in place in an abandoned housing unit while she and Linx divined their location in respect to the current government- controlled territory.

"We're already out of our safe zone," Lerna said to the group. "Are you sure the coordinates are correct?" she asked Kreymond directly.

"He told my brother he would be there every day at the same time, in case someone wanted to find him," Kreymond responded.

"We've got a ways to go," Linx added. "Keep your faces concealed from cameras as much as possible. Sembado, I think you should lead the way. That leg is the quietest weapon we have."

Sembado agreed grudgingly, saying, "Fine, but I want Kreymond in the middle. Not at the end. No offense, buddy, but you're kind of the most vulnerable."

"None taken," Kreymond laughed.

"Sembado, me, Kreymond, Kaluna, Linx," Lerna said flatly. "Now, sync your nav-units one more time and let's move."

Sembado led the team back out into the corridor where they continued forward. Twice they held back around a corner while a government patrol ahead marched passed. Their progress slowed as the frequency of penalty officer sightings increased. Sembado was scanning the corridor ahead for movement when Kreymond called from behind.

"Turn right here," he hissed. Sembado lurched to a stop, turning quickly and pressing off of his bionic leg harder than intended. The goofy stumble sent him forward quickly, and he collided with another body. He grabbed the person to keep them from falling, and when he had regained his balance, he realized he was bear-hugging a Penalty officer. He let go and the man fell onto his back. Lerna pushed past Sembado and subdued the officer, putting her gun to his temple, while Linx turned to secure their rear.

"*Wait! Wait! Wait!*" Kreymond whispered harshly as he moved forward. "That's him."

The man smiled, despite having Lerna's gun still pressed against his head.

"How ya been, little Matroid?" the officer asked. Lerna slowly pulled her gun away, and she and Kreymond helped the officer to his feet. He gave Kreymond a brief embrace. "Let's get out of the open," the officer said, indicating for the team to follow him to a nearby chamber. They filed inside quickly while the officer stood watch at the door. Soon he was pulling the door shut behind them.

"Lerna," Kreymond said as they situated themselves, "this is Coney Benton." The penalty officer gave a flamboyant bow. Linx smirked. Lerna was not amused. Coney straightened himself up, and adopted a slightly more serious face, but the corners of his mouth still threatened a smile.

"Alright then," said Coney, "we've got a lot of work to do, and Markus is running out of viable time."

"Then Markus should have come himself so that we don't have to waste our time playing this telephone game,"

Lerna snapped. Her outburst did little to contain Coney's mischievous grin.

"Well, I'm sure he regrets disappointing you so much," he responded playfully.

"Alright, that's enough," said a deep voice from the back of the chamber.

Sembado and his team turned quickly, drawing their weapons on the voice's owner.

A large frame sat in the shadows of the room. It did not move when they drew their weapons.

"Please. Let's not do this. Like Coney said, we've got a lot of business to attend to," said the voice.

"Ladies and gentlemen," Coney piped in, "I give you Markus Dometica!"

Markus stood, his height only amplified by the low-ceilinged space. He moved out of the dimly lit corner to approach the group where they stood.

Kreymond moved forward first, and attempted to shake his uncle's hand. Markus responded with a disapproving look, and pulled Kreymond into a great bear hug.

"It's good to see you alive," said Markus. "Let's try and keep it that way."

Kreymond's muffled response was lost in his uncle's embrace. Markus released Kreymond, and offered his greetings to the group.

He extended his large, dark hand to Lerna, who had only just lowered her weapon. She holstered her gun and shook his hand, looking up into his eyes; he was a whole head taller than her. Markus introduced himself to each person in turn, paying special attention to Sembado once he heard his name.

"Sembado Grey," he said with hid deep, booming voice. "I've heard almost as much about you as I have about your granddad. I've been meaning to pick my nephew's brain about his infamous friend, but I didn't want to implicate him in your shenanigans."

Sembado returned the courteous smile, but said nothing. Markus ended the pleasantries quickly as he reiterated the role that timeliness played in their plan.

"I wasn't going to join Coney today, but news of your treaty has spread quickly. While I congratulate you on a peace well deserved, Fabian is getting worse by the day. He's executed nearly a quarter of our elite guard in just the past week. We need to end this now."

Sembado and his friends exchanged looks of nervous excitement while Markus returned to his chair to fetch some paper documents.

"We've been using paper for some time now," Markus said as he shuffled through the papers. "It's the only way to avoid Fabian's many eyes."

"If you and your men are ready for him to fall," Sembado said, drawing everyone's attention, "then why does he have so many loyalists? Isn't everyone as ready to be rid of him as you?"

"That's a bright question, Grey," Markus said with a chuckle. "You'd think that we'd have declared a mutiny by now, yes? Problem is, Fabian has spent the last fifteen or so years meticulously constructing a web of lies and deceit. He has secretly blackmailed nearly every elite guardsman and most regular penalty officers too. I am ashamed to admit that I have stood by his side for most of those years and turned a blind eye as he carefully destroyed countless families. He literally uses their own love against them." Markus paused as he found the paper he sought, and handed it to Lerna.

"This is a list of officers I have made successful contact with," Markus said. "They will help us turn the tide."

"But still," said Sembado, "if there are so many of his men that would like nothing more than to see their family's safety secured, then why would they all continue to play his game?"

"You really don't miss anything, do you?" Markus asked as he nodded in approval. The smile slipped from his face as he prepared to answer Sembado's question. "That is the worst part," Markus said solemnly. "Every single officer thinks that they are the only one he is blackmailing. The man is a political genius, albeit evil. He has never mentioned one man's threat in front of another. He has them all scared to death that if they ask anyone else about their plight, then he will kill their loved ones. And as far as my outreach, Sembado, it's taken me this long to recruit the few that I have because of my high profile within the security world. I can't just walk around asking every penalty officer if they're caught in his web. It's taken me years to earn his trust, and at this point, I think he would still have me executed without a second thought. He has truly gone mad."

Before Sembado could respond, a loud banging sounded on the door.

"*Elite guard! Open up!*" a muffled voice called.

Everyone in the room froze.

"*Elite guard! Open up now!*" the voice repeated.

Markus pulled his side arm from his holster and pointed it toward Sembado and his friends.

"Do not move or mention my nephew," he commanded bitterly.

He unlocked the door, and a team of eight heavily armed officers stormed in. They each took one of Sembado's party into custody, forcing them to their knees with their hands above their heads. One last officer stepped in slowly. He was more decorated than the rest. He observed the room slowly.

"Commander Dometica, what is the meaning of this?" he said with a sharp, nasally voice.

"Well, Colonel Woodren," Markus said slowly, "Officer Benton here promised to lead me to these rebel leaders. He seemed to be under the delusion that I would like to conspire with them."

A look of horror spread across Coney's face as he realized what Markus was implying.

"Sir, please," Coney said with desperation. He grimaced as the nearest elite guardsman kicked the back of his leg so that he too fell to his knees. Coney locked eyes with Sembado, and flashed him a devious smile when no one else was looking.

"Frankly, Colonel, I am very disappointed that your men hadn't sniffed this traitor out sooner. Do you really think I have the time to attend to this kind of thing myself? I've got a damn complex to win back. I don't need to occupy myself with every slinking eel in security's ranks."

"My deepest apologies commander," the colonel said shamefully. "I will have my men double their efforts in detecting defectors."

"A lot of good that will do," Markus replied. "And what of your contraband team? Are they on vacation? Look at this pile of papers. Do your men even know what paper is, Woodren?"

The colonel said nothing. The guardsmen stood silently too.

"That was not a rhetorical question, Woodren!" Markus bellowed suddenly. His rumbling volume made everyone in the room, guard and captive, jump. "Do your men know what paper is?" He asked pointedly.

"Yes, commander, my men know what paper is," Colonel Woodren replied contemptuously. "We just don't see it that often."

"Well, Colonel, here's a whole pile. Do you see *it*?" Markus replied viciously.

"Yes, Commander," Colonel Woodren replied flatly.

"Good," Markus barked. "Now have your *elite* guard escort these captives straight to the Director. I have a feeling Fabian would like to see them in person."

"Yes, Commander!" Colonel Woodren replied.

Sembado watched his friends struggle against the guards as they were stood up and marched out of the room. Markus stood by the door as they exited, staring at each one knowingly. Lerna was being led out ahead of Sembado and she lashed out as she passed Markus, spitting in his face. He quickly backhanded her before the guard jostled her out of the room. Sembado was the last to be escorted out, and just caught sight of Markus breaking into a smile as he wiped Lerna's spit from his face.

They were marched out of the disputed territory quickly. Soon they were being paraded past every station of society under the government's control: men, women, and children booed and mocked them as they walked by. Penalty officers congratulated the elite guardsmen as they passed, patting them on the back and cheering.

Sembado began to recognize his surroundings as he and his friends were turned into one of the corridors that led to the Civillion. They were brought straight through the great gathering space, and Sembado balked at how dead the Civillion seemed inside. The life and energy had been sucked out of it; there were no barters shouting, there was no music playing, and the only smell of food came from a government food line that was assembled to one end of the space. Tofu spread and reconstituted fish were the most distinct aromas. Most of the stores had been abandoned or closed. The submarine showrooms were dark and empty, his favorite restaurants shuttered, and Jean M'Gereg's old antiquity shop, Terranean Memories, looked to have suffered a fire. The iron-framed courtyard that sat beside it had once supported a thick skin of green ivy vines. Sembado had had his first interaction with the Elephants there when he accidently discovered a secret note of his grandfathers. The courtyard was now in blackened ruins, with only a few shocks of green where the resilient ivy attempted a recovery. Sembado thought back to all of his memories in the large, round space. He looked up to see that even the great, glass dome of a ceiling looked murky and dull compared to its once sparkling glory.

The team was shuffled through the north end of the Civillion and the high ceiling quickly gave way to the tight corridors again. Sembado recognized their route as the one that had led him to his stay in the penitentiary. Linx appeared to have come to the same conclusion as he started to fidget and twist in his captor's arms. The surroundings became less and less domestic as Sembado and his friends were led into the official government chambers. They were led through the same processing center that Sembado had once gone through, but this time it was very meagerly staffed. Where a field of dozens of data processors once sat, there were now no more than ten. Colonel Woodren led the procession straight past the required layers of bureaucracy; Markus brought up the rear. The group was divided in two as the elite guard forced the captives into separate elevators. Despite his attempts to shove his way closer to Kaluna, Sembado was forced into the other elevator. They were only able to exchange a single fleeting glance. Her eyes and expression were unequivocally poised.

The elevators dropped away as they passed countless floors of what Sembado knew where holding cell levels. After only a short moment, the elevator was already coming to a stop. They were forced out into the waiting chamber where the other elevator was emptying too. The group shuffled down a narrow corridor where a single elevator waited. Again they split into smaller groups, but this time they had to take turns. Sembado made a more determined effort and soon found himself squeezed next to Kaluna in the cramped lift.

Are you okay? He breathed into her ear. He didn't think she heard him until she gave him a delayed head nod.

The elevator doors opened and they were prodded down the ornate hallway. The fine finishes haunted Sembado from his experience less than a year before. It had been a long time since he last spoke to Fabian, and now he felt wise and hearty in a way that he could never have imagined.

By the time they had been led to Fabian's office door, the other half of the group had caught up to them. They waited for the rich wooden door to be opened; the sign on it read:

J. L. FABIAN – DIRECTOR OF SECURITY

Chapter Twenty-Six
Growing Pains

"Come in. Come in," Fabian said as the captives were ushered into his office. "Commander Dometica, what time do you have?"

"Sir?" Markus said.

"I said what time is it, Markus?" Fabian repeated pointedly.

"It's 17:28, sir," Markus replied obediently.

"Then let the record show that at 5:28 pm on July 9th, 2085, we finally captured the leaders of these silly rebel bastards," Fabian laughed. "I'm serious, dammit! Write that down!"

Colonel Woodren tapped away on his communication device feverishly as he did his master's bidding.

Markus ordered the elite guard to present Sembado and his friends to Fabian, and they were marched up in front of his desk. The immense glass wall behind him showed a crystalline blue visage of the deep ocean beyond it. Several large sharks circled by the monstrous lens as bubbles glided upwards along its surface.

Fabian flashed a wicked smile at Sembado and each of his friends as they passed. The smile was quickly replaced by a curled sneer as his eyes fell upon Coney.

"Commander Dometica," Fabian said without breaking eye contact with Coney.

"Sir?" Markus responded.

"This is the man that was caught abetting our guests?"

"Yes sir," said Markus.

"And why is he still alive?" Fabian asked in poorly dramatized confusion.

Markus quickly stepped up to the penalty officer nearest to Coney, pulled the officer's shock stick from its holster, and applied the full voltage to Coney's neck. Fabian grinned wildly as Coney convulsed under Markus's continued application of the electric wand. Markus relented only when Coney had stopped making noise. The young man lay in a shivering heap as Fabian grinned madly.

"Sir," Markus said while forcefully measuring his breathing, "I would like to note that I had to sniff out this traitor myself, and that our esteemed colleague, Colonel Woodren, has not been conducting the *'Patriot and Propoganda'* program as effectively as promised."

"Director, this could not be any further from the truth," Colonel Woodren protested immediately.

"In addition," Markus said over his subordinate's appeal, "the amount of information our mutineer carried is enough to cause irreversible damage. If we cannot expect to intercept a low level informant's messages simply because they are transcribed on paper, then I highly suspect our forces are not ready or willing to resist the physical onslaught of our enemies' newly forged alliance."

"Surely you can't believe this, Jerdo..." Colonel Woodren stopped his feeble plea short as he realized his mistake. All expression faded from Fabian's face as his eyes slowly drifted to meet Colonel Woodren's. His emotionless glare almost dared the Colonel to look away.

"Colonel Woodren," Fabian said flatly.

"Yes sir," Woodren replied submissively, the remaining color washing out of his already sallow face.

"Have your men detain you," Fabian said as the fire in his eyes reignited.

"Sir?" Woodren replied.

"Are you deaf?" Markus shouted at the surrounding officers. "The Director gave you an order! Take the Colonel's weapon and detain him!"

The surrounding officers went to work obediently. While one wrestled the Colonel's sidearm away from him, two more forced his arms behind his back. Colonel Woodren continued to grovel as one of the officers forcefully removed him from Fabian's chamber.

Fabian redirected his look of disgust from the Colonel to Sembado and his friends. He picked out Lerna, who was ushered up to his desk.

"So you're the great leader of the Spring, huh? What a stupid name," Fabian said coldly. "You really think that women hold that great of power over men that you would stop these idiots of mine and the Elephants from fighting?

What a concept, a *woman's* concept. And you didn't even use your *real* assets to do it?" he said with a smirk. "You tried to do it by force. Men have been fighting for thousands of years. Wars have been fought almost constantly for the entire history of man, and you thought you were special because you didn't like it? Do you really think you're the only woman to ever wish that their men would give all this up?"

"No," Lerna said defiantly, "I'm just the first one to actually do somethin' about it!"

"And look where it got ya, sweetie," Fabian snapped. "All that fighting and toil and loss and a stupid name, and now you're here. You really showed me," he finished sarcastically.

"At least they're free now," Lerna shot back.

"Is that what the Elephants sold you on? Freedom? For what? Do you think any of these morons you call friends really know what to do with it? Do you think their lives would change for the better if they knew the truth? You can't possibly think they're safer now than they were before these fools started stirrin' up trouble."

Lerna stood and seethed as Fabian shifted his loathsome gaze to Sembado. Sembado was brought forward so that Fabian could look him up and down.

"Something's different about you," he said, making sure to exaggerate his surprise at Sembado's bionic leg. "Oh my! I had heard the news, but I didn't realize Gerard had done such a number on you. *And* he killed the traitor, Feldman's boy, too? Hmm, maybe that little shit was more valuable than I thought. Perhaps I shouldn't've killed him after she turned him loose," Fabian said with a whisper, thumbing to Lerna secretly as if she could not see or hear him.

Sembado observed Fabian coolly. The man before him was clearly deranged, and Sembado pitied his deep-seeded psychoses. He basked in the warm comfort of his indifference as any hate, anger, or loathing for Fabian seemed to wash against him without notice. His dull and dignified response seemed to strike a nerve with Fabian who lashed out in a desperate attempt to unsettle Sembado.

"Not as fiery as you used to be," Fabian said to Sembado. "The last time you were in here, you spat in my face, and now you want to act calm and collected? What if I ordered my guards to hold your little girlfriend here? Hold her still, while I dissolved her fingers one at a time," he snarled, pointing to Kaluna. "Is that shocking enough?"

Sembado's pensive reflection turned to a stony resolve and he defiantly glared Fabian down.

"That would be your mistake, not mine," Sembado growled with flared nostrils.

"Well that was too easy!" Fabian exclaimed. "See what weakness women bring to the fold?" he asked Lerna soothingly. "It really isn't fair."

"You've chosen the wrong women to use as threats," Sembado said. "These two are tougher than the rest of us combined."

"How inspiring," Fabian said. "And what of the thousands of women that float with your allies on the surface? Or the hundreds of thousands more that are still trapped down here in the complex?"

Sembado communicated his confusion with a furrowed brow.

"Or the hundreds of thousands of men and children that join them," Fabian continued darkly. "You are all here because you know the truth of this place, and how the underwater populations came to be."

Fabian paused while he took a drink from the glass on his desk. The dramatic lighting in his office cast dark shadows on his eyes, lips, and chin. The sharks that swam outside his window flashed the reflection of the light with their black, lifeless eyes.

"You all know that my predecessors eradicated millions," Fabian said. "Hundreds of millions of random civilians for the greater good. The greater good. Earth could live on so that our grandchildren would have a viable planet of their own. What a majestic dream. What a terrible decision to have to make; and yet, here we are, part of the surviving few. We are those grandchildren."

Sembado chewed on the inside of his cheeks to keep from shouting back at Fabian and his twisted interpretation of the truth.

"Yes," Fabian continued. "They were so noble in their righteousness. But now I am in control. I *am* the control."

Sembado's leg twitched, jostling his hip ever so slightly as he continued to repel his enemy's psychological assault.

"So if they were willing to kill all of those people to protect the planet and our future," Fabian said as he leaned back in his chair, "what makes you think I won't do the same for my complex?"

Sembado's leg stopped twitching as he focused on Fabian's last words. His mind raced as he processed the implications of such a threat. His body became numb, his prosthetic felt like a distant and foreign force as the words sunk in.

"By the stupid looks on your stupid faces I would wager you hadn't considered that," Fabian said with a twisted grin. "Thousands, maybe a million of those beautiful, blue spheres planted all over the complex. The whole damn complex. By my understanding, a good portion of them have even been smuggled into your friends' floating fortress up top," he said, pointing upward. "And I can set them off at a moment's notice," he said maniacally. "How does that soothe your nerves?"

Fabian's words faded as his verbal assault continued. Sembado teetered in place. His thoughts became a firestorm of turmoil as he clung desperately to whatever rational considerations his waning consciousness could muster. His grip on his sanity weakened and was ripped away as he fell further into the dark and troubled potential that lay deep in the chambers of his mind. His bionic leg began to hum; the searing heat it emanated fueled Sembado's already rapid descent into his animalistic drive. A single statement cut through his rage, and pulled him back to reality. Fabian's voice echoed deep in the recesses of Sembado's soul.

"Bring me the girl," the voice said.

Sembado's leg recoiled just before it pushed back down against the nearest guard's kneecap. The guard's armored leg buckled backwards in an explosion of bone and blood. The back of Sembado's fist caught the guard's face just as it fell into position.

Sembado then rocked onto the powered limb, and it rotated his body with incredible speed, bringing his real leg into the chest of the guard that held Kaluna. The guard took flight, and collided into Markus without warning. Kaluna fell to the floor, and the rest of the chamber erupted into chaos. Linx held one guard so that Lerna could kick him repeatedly while Kreymond threw every improvised weapon he could find. Over the commotion, Fabian could be heard shouting, "Don't shoot. You'll hit the window! Shock batons and presets only!"

Sembado kicked an approaching guard square in the chest, and the man ricocheted off the window and collapsed to the floor; the sea creatures outside scattered from his impact. Sembado continued to march forward toward Fabian, who squared his shoulders and stood his ground as he produced an electric baton from under his desk.

Sembado approached with his right foot, planted it, and brought up the left leg up to kick. Fabian dodged the blow, and Sembado blasted the desk away to the left. The desk slid across the floor and rammed Markus against the wall just as he climbed to his feet.

Sembado recovered from his misstep, and approached Fabian a second time. Fabian whipped the shock stick masterfully with one hand, adjusting it to its highest setting. The tip glowed and crackled. He locked his wild eyes with Sembado's and they began to pace closer to each other. Without warning, Sembado's leg propelled him forward. He aimed his outstretched hands at the arm Fabian was holding the weapon with. As he made contact, he locked one hand around Fabian's wrist, the other grasped at his throat. Sembado's impact moved his foe backward, but Fabian used the momentum to throw Sembado to one side. As he pushed Sembado away, Fabian lashed out with the shock stick, striking the bionic leg with the deadly wand. Sembado fell to the floor, and fought to recover. His leg had been rendered inoperable. He backed away on his hands, and pushed off with his right leg, dragging the heavy prosthetic as he went.

Kaluna was quickly resuscitating Coney, whom she had dragged off to one side of the room. He had just come to when a new team of elite guardsmen stormed the office. Fabian bellowed his moratorium on firearms to the arriving officers. The six men stopped and drew their shock batons as they surveyed the state of affairs in the room. Kreymond helped Sembado to his feet. Three guards lay at Linx and Lerna's feet; both held fully functional shock sticks. Kaluna supported a foggy-headed Coney. Markus was wearily pushing the desk away from himself. The guards spread into an arc shape as they attempted to contain the room. They reached Coney and Kaluna first, and the closest guard expressed his confusion with Coney's position.

"He's with them you idiot!" Fabian shouted. "Kill them! Kill them all!"

All six guards activated their weapons at once. The synchronized crackle and buzz made the hairs on Sembado's neck stand up. Kreymond helped him limp towards Lerna and Linx.

"I think it can be reset," Sembado said to Kreymond. Lerna and Linx stood guard while Kreymond quickly tinkered with the controls on Sembado's prosthetic.

The group of guards had broken into groups, and four of them were quickly approaching Sembado and his friends.

"I got it," Kreymond said, "but it's going to take another minute to reboot."

Lerna and Linx had their shock sticks extended at arm's length as the new guards approached. Kreymond was weaponless, but did his best to step between Sembado and the approaching officers.

Suddenly, a disengaged shock stick landed on the floor and rolled to a stop between Kreymond's feet. He and Sembado looked up to see Markus approaching them. He tossed a second baton to Sembado, and activated a third for himself. Disorder filled the room as everyone realized the totality of Markus' betrayal.

The remaining two guards that approached Coney and Kaluna also stopped short. They embraced Coney briefly, and then turned on their fellow guardsmen, shielding Kaluna with their advance.

"Dometica!" Fabian screamed. "I'll have your head. Kill them! Kill the traitors! This is mutiny!"

The four guardsmen that approached Sembado's group doubled their pace, but were soon waylaid by Kaluna, Coney, and his friends.

Markus and Kreymond stayed back to protect Sembado while Lerna and Linx joined in Coney's advance. Sembado's leg had nearly rebooted when he heard Fabian approaching from the rear.

He turned just in time to see Fabian bring down his electric baton with a heavy, overhand swing. Kreymond hit and deflected the strike just in time, giving Markus a chance to turn and face Fabian instead.

"Is this what you want?" Fabian asked coldly. He backed away from Markus as they took turns swinging at the space between them. "You want this, don't you? You want everything I have!"

Markus remained silent, but the tortured scowl on his face told a story of its own. He fought through a terrible mixture of broken loyalty and indiscriminate justice as his once great leader spouted on like a lunatic.

"You want my power? My position? You would be nothing without me!" Fabian shrieked, grabbing his discarded drinking glass from the floor and hurling it straight at Markus's face. Markus moved aside and Sembado stepped up, batting the glass away with his baton. It shattered into a thousand sparkling bits that rained back onto Fabian's twisted face. He turned away, but still caught the broken shards on half his face and one eye. He howled in pain as he locked his one good eye on Sembado. Crimson beads formed across his face, and wept from the other firmly closed eye. Fabian bobbed his head as he focused the vision in his injured eye. He blinked it open to reveal a hideous, red orb with a black dot in the center. He backed away cautiously as he took in his expanded threat: Markus and Kreymond flanked his sides as Sembado approached straight on. As he backed away, Fabian nearly tripped over the scattered clutter underfoot. He glanced down just long enough to identify a piece of the debris as an abandoned machine pistol.

***

Kaluna worked her way across the room with caution. While the loyalty of half the room was in question, she could only move forward assuming the young men that led her attack formation were allies. Coney and the two mutineers advanced toward the four loyalists that stood pinned against Linx and Lerna.

Kaluna picked up a spare shock stick off the ground as she followed her fierce supporters. Coney and his friends wasted no time engaging the loyalists as Lerna and Linx had grown visibly fatigued of keeping them at bay. As Kaluna locked her grip on the baton, she caught sight of Sembado approaching a disgruntled and bloody Fabian; Kreymond and Markus were on either side. Fabian was just retrieving a small automatic handgun he had nearly tripped over. Kaluna's eyes widened and her heart beat out of her chest as she watched Fabian cast his baton aside and ready his newly acquired weapon.

The struggle between the loyalists and mutineers was quickly devolving into a physical shoving match, and several bodies were jostled into Kaluna; she was nearly knocked to the floor. She desperately pushed off and away from those around her as she struggled to move closer to Sembado.

Fabian was backed all the way up against his giant glass wall. His face and shirt were drenched in the blood that streamed from his mangled face. He pointed the gun haphazardly as blood worked its way into his good eye. Sembado and his allies continued to press their containment until Fabian focused the pistol's sights on Kreymond.

Then, without warning, Markus produced a small, harpoon-like item from his waist line. He pressed a button, and the object glowed with a green light. He drew it back and whipped it at Fabian. The thing flew end over end; it left a green blur in its wake. With a solid and sickening crunch the weapon stuck deep into Fabian's chest. He grasped at it with one hand; the spastic reflexes in the other hand caused him to squeeze off a stray round. The room shuddered from the loud bang, and for a moment, the fighting stopped. Each person, loyalist and revolutionary stood aghast as Fabian struggled to pull the barbed knife out of his chest.

He used his free hand to yank at the handle of the weapon; blood leaked out around it. He shouted in surprise as an electric orb began growing out of his chest. He looked up to Markus with utter shock and betrayal pained across his face. His shock turned to confusion as the translucent shell grew larger.

It was Sembado who gave Markus the next confused look as the orb had taken on a discernable green hue instead of the terrible blue one he anticipated. Markus averted his eyes in shame. Sembado watched in disgust as Fabian actually laughed away the attack, but soon the green orb had grown nearly large enough to encompass Fabian's entire torso. The jade sphere stopped expanding when it spanned from his navel to his chin.

"This is your big plan?" he asked Markus, waving the gun in his hand flamboyantly. "To stab me in the chest and immediately heal the wound?" Markus stared Fabian down silently. Bitter resentment welled in his eyes.

Sembado stood with his shock stick at the ready, but was transfixed by the progress the sphere was making. The blood flow around Fabian's puncture wound ceased instantly; the tissue fused and healed before Sembado's eyes. Unfortunately for Fabian, the skin and muscle were being repaired around the hand of the weapon.

"What the hell," Fabian exclaimed, digging at the bright, new tissue that grew across his wound. "Why...why isn't it stopping?"

Markus remained silent, and as Sembado realized the nature of the weapon, Markus's stoic glare took on a darker, icy appearance.

Fabian cried out as he scratched and tore away layers of the freshly healed skin with his free hand, but reaching inside the powerful green sphere proved to be disastrous. As his fingers continued to dig into the healing flesh, it pulled them in deeper. His scar tissue quickly grew to consume his hand, trapping it against his chest. Fabian's anguish emboldened his otherwise stunned guards into action. Their fresh attack pressed Sembado's allies closer to where Fabian toiled.

Kaluna moved to Sembado's side where their triumph turned to terror. Their nemesis had a head-sized mass growing off of his sternum. Fabian's face was noticeably paler; it had become gaunt and jagged. He flailed his free arm with less and less vigor as his machine pistol grew increasingly heavy for his now atrophied limb. Sembado struggled to not look away as the grotesque mass continued to swell; its surface was purple and veiny.

The elite loyalists reached a frenzied panic as their leader collapsed to his knees under the weight of his deadly tumor. Sembado had just turned to help quell their final attempts when Kaluna cried out and took hold of his arm. She gave him a great tug as a raucous string of noise came from behind him. She pulled him onto one foot and pushed him away; in the shuffle he lost his footing, fell, and hit the floor on his back. He looked up and he took in a heart-stopping sight: Fabian's collapsing reflexes had pulled the trigger of the machine pistol, emptying its full load.

Sembado climbed to his feet and dove toward Kaluna as the rest of the room had taken cover. He took her limp frame in his arms; her body was riddled with bullet holes. He cradled her petite but muscular frame in his lap as he began to weep. Through his tears, he searched for any of the telltale signs of the blue horror that might be trapped inside her. His tears fell on her golden brown face as the vision of a blue orb finally broke through his blurry vision. His stomach fell away from his heart as he frantically wiped the moisture from his face. To his mild relief, the blue orb was actually growing out of his own leg – the bionic one.

The orb-tipped projectile was just visible through the framework and wires of his prosthetic. The material around the sphere started to smoke and shot sparks as the sphere began to grow. His prosthetic started to grow hot against his skin. He looked around desperately for a tool to dig out the projectile. He grabbed the closest item, a deactivated shock stick, and tried to use it to pry apart the components that retained the bullet. He forced the end of the baton into the mechanics of the leg, but it sparked in his face and blew the weapon from his hand. The resulting sparks sent waves of heat and anger throughout his body. The leg jerked violently, and it jostled Kaluna's motionless, bloody body that lay on top. Sembado closed his eyes from the pain, and concentrated to calm his nerves and leg movement.

When Sembado opened his eyes, the room around him had taken on a sudden and eerie shade of blue. The walls, the floor, his friends, and Fabian's engorged corpse were all filtered in a deep, electric blue.

It was only after observing himself and Kaluna that Sembado realized that the electric potential in the shock stick and his leg had coupled to power the orb to an obsene size. Its diameter had stopped at about six feet, and sat waiting.

Sembado abandoned his current preoccupation to tend to Kaluna's desperate state. While he could still find breath and a pulse, blood spilled from at least a dozen entry and exit wounds.

Outside the orb, Lerna and Markus had rallied the others to incapacitate or detain the remaining loyalists. They now watched in dismay as the giant blue orb slowly receded around Sembado and Kaluna.

Sembado concentrated on keeping Kaluna as still as possible. He sneered bitterly at the irony of his situation.

If I only had a green healing sphere for Kaluna instead of being trapped in this stupid blue one. If I would have just left it alone it, would have dissolved in the leg harmlessly.

"I'm so sorry," he whispered to Kaluna. "I love you so much." He kissed her flawless face, and sobbed over her dying body as the orb closed in around them.

"Sembado!" Lerna yelled.

He looked up just as she tossed her defensive pendant to him. He extended his hand as far as he could, and caught the pendant just inside the surface of the collapsing sphere. He placed the pendant on Kaluna's chest, closed his eyes tight, and pressed the button. After a moment, he opened his eyes to see the room still bathed in the same awful blue light. He pressed the pendant's button over and over, but nothing happened. He looked through the blue shell to Lerna.

"It's not working!" Sembado screamed. "It's not working!"

"The dissolving sphere may be too big!" Lerna said back. "It should respond when the blue sphere gets smaller."

"Gets smaller?" Sembado shouted. "Do you know how these things work?"

Sembado frantically adjusted Kaluna's body and himself to make them as compact as possible. The blue sphere's relentless collapse continued. Sembado strained to quiet his mind as the powerful electric charge surging through his leg sent a barrage of meaningless signals back to his brain. The adjustments the Spring had made to his leg did little to defend the feedback coming from the bullet's mighty power source. As he calmed himself, Sembado prepared for the end as the sphere began devouring Kaluna's outstretched braid, leaving nothing behind of her hair but an acrid stench.

Sembado closed his eyes one last time, thinking on all of the great memories he had had with the young woman that lay dying in his arms. A light pressed through his eyelids. A numbing sensation crept across his legs, his lap, and his stomach. He opened his eyes just in time to see a bright, orange light approach his face before his mind went black.

Part Three
Beyond the Surface

Chapter Twenty-Seven
Difficult Decisions

Mahana stood at the back of *The Beluga*. The mass of smaller boats that were lined up behind his ship stretched out of sight. It had taken nearly a week to devise all of the logistics required for the impending voyage, but the navigational authority bestowed to Mahana relieved the council from their usual bickering over the less significant details. Instead, Mahana had declared an order and pattern for each councilperson to dictate to their constituency.

The sun was out and a nice breeze was blowing across the deck. Mahana laid against the old pipe handrail that outlined the ship as the vessels behind it continued to align and reorder.

"It certainly is a beautiful day," Jain said, approaching from behind him. "I think we can take this as a good sign of what's to come." Mahana nodded in agreement as Jain joined him at his side. "Tomorrow's the big day," she said, using his large arm for support as she leaned against him. "How are you feeling? About Lahalo's message, I mean."

"Well, I'm happy to hear 'bout Kaluna and Sembado, if dat's what ya mean," Mahana said with a quick chuckle;

tears welled in his eyes. He paused as he concentrated on not letting the wetness in his eyes develop further. Jain squeezed his big arm with both of hers. "He's really takin' dis leadaship ting to heart," Mahana added. "I'd be a fool to be surprised at how little he's willin' to do for udda people, and yet here I am…surprised."

"But he is taking care of *his* people," Jain said.

"His people, my people, our people," Mahana said defiantly. "I taught him betta den dat. It's just people. Especially now! Wit Fabian gone, it doesn't have to be us and dem anymore. I just wish Lahalo would have more love in his heart."

"Manny," she said, stroking his arm, "if you keep expecting the whole world to have as much love in their hearts as you do, then you better get used to disappointment."

"I'm not talkin' 'bout the rest of the world," Mahana said; the tears returned to his eyes. "I'm talking 'bout my son."

Chapter Twenty-Eight
Democracy is Complex

Sembado's eyes burned as light flooded back into them. The uncomfortable and familiar feeling of every cell in his body recovering from being frozen in time was more fleeting than before. He sat motionless as his brain synapses started to fire again. The movement in his lap brought his vision downward. His heart started pumping faster as he processed the sight of Lerna applying a healing wand to Kaluna's assortment of injuries. As the feeling returned to his limbs, he gingerly supported Kaluna's head and neck. He leaned her up and forward so that Lerna could tend to the exit wounds on her back. Sembado did not speak. No one in the room spoke; they were all watching Lerna work feverishly to restore Kaluna's composition.

Sembado cradled Kaluna back after the work was done. He stroked her face, waiting for some kind of response; her breathing was faint and slow.

"She is healed," Lerna said softly, "but she has lost a bit of blood, and we can't fix that here."

"As long as she is safe," said Sembado.

"She will be," Lerna replied as she stood up. Behind her, Linx and Coney were speaking heatedly, while Kreymond clung to Markus in a desperate embrace. The other insurgents were guarding the loyalist prisoners. They observed cautiously as the disagreement between Linx and Markus grew to a shouting match.

"This isn't what he planned, and he is not here to take over!" Coney shouted.

"He was Fabian's number two," Linx shot back. "What did you think was going to happen?"

"I already told you," Markus said as he tried to comfort Kreymond, "I did not expect my subordinate colonel to interfere tonight. That was not part of the plan. And by the way, that colonel, along with almost every other penalty officer, was not privy to this operation! While the vast majority of them will be more than relieved to know that Fabian's control has come to an end, that still leaves all of his loyally corrupt goons to flush out from an otherwise dependable security force."

"Sounds like the perfect job for their new leader!" Linx said loudly. Before Markus could respond, Lerna interrupted both he and Linx.

"Are you two fricking kidding me?" she snapped venomously. "Fabian's bloated pile of guts over there is still hot, and you two are already bitchin' like a couple of my worst recruits! This is not why we did this! Linx, shut the hell up, now! And Markus, we have a complex to secure, and like it or not, you are the most qualified to make that happen. We will send out word of the truce tonight. We can deal with Fabian's loyalists as they come. That is, if they're even brave enough to come forward. But first thing's first, we need to help Sembado get Kaluna to the nearest medical unit."

***

Sembado sat in Markus's recently acquired medical facility. The entire medical staff was quite happy to learn of the coup; they had all been working twenty-four hour shifts since the conflict started. Sembado held Kaluna's small nutrient pouch while she drank its green contents through a straw. Both of her arms lay sore and bruised across her lap; the blood transfusion was a success. Sembado had tried desperately to volunteer his own, but learned that he did not have the correct type. Instead, he had to sit, quietly fidgeting, while Kreymond and Rita each had two pints of their own blood pumped directly into Kaluna's gray forearms.

Kaluna made a sour face after finishing the last of the thick green liquid. While some fruits had been added for sweetness, it was mostly fortified kelp. The nutritional supplement served as a make-shift celebration for the two friends as word of the new-found peace treaty was spreading through the complex like wild fire. Lerna was able to get Linx and Markus to broker a three-headed allegiance between their separate factions.

The three unlikely allies spent the entire day locked in Markus's chambers as they poured over the high-level government operations and procedures that Fabian had hijacked and redlined each page as they went. Markus relied heavily on his strong network of revolutionaries to sustain the daily upkeep of the complex as the organizational deliberations slipped into a second, third, and fourth day. Sembado and Kaluna stopped in shortly, but were waylaid by the steady stream of experts and specialists that was called in for insight and opinion.

During their brief visit, Sembado was able to gleam the general intentions of his friends' freshly crafted democratic composition. Markus's existing government structure would offer law and order to the newly formed pact, while the Spring's significance was peace and civility, and the Elephants' contribution was transparency. Representatives from the two rebel factions would provide oversight to the governmental hierarchy, while for the first time in the history of the complex, the citizens would be allowed to vote. Not only would the voting stand for elected officials, but choices on nearly every operation, rule, or law would be left up to the citizen masses. Ironically, this new function would utilize the same system, network, and servers that a popularized government broadcast once used to count viewers' preference for a television program's character development and plot outcome. Now, each and every adult citizen was going to be afforded daily input on the subjects and matters about which they were most concerned.

In a show of negotiated triumph, Lerna was able to get Linx to agree to be the interim security chief as Markus was voted into a community tribunal position to help oversee the judgement of Fabian's followers. Sembado was especially entertained to learn that Linx's first move as the head of the penalty officers was to reform the prison system to a more progressive rehabilitation program, and to remove any and all remaining food troughs from the penitentiary's feeding chambers.

Linx sent word of the treaty to the surface, and Mahana wasted no time in releasing all of Markus's informants. Among them was Kreymond's older brother. Their joyful reunion was marked by more victory when the new leadership announced that Sembado and Kreymond's old virtual reality administrator, Zetvez, was to be the new director of four dimensional training and development. He would oversee an overhaul of the 4D system which would allow guests to use small, aerial drones to explore the surface ahead of their own ascent. Zetvez chose Kreymond to co-captain the program.

Chapter Twenty-Nine
A Day Late

The most difficult and complicated task the new government faced was maintaining control and order over the rush of citizens that were interested in experiencing the surface. Teams of penalty officers were set at the exits around the clock to maintain a safe outflow.

Sembado's final visit to see his family placed him at just the wrong time to vacate the complex. He and Kaluna waited for seven hours in a hot, crowded line just to gain access to his parents' submarine. Mr. and Mrs. Grey had been kind enough to gift the submarine, its full tank of fuel, and all the supplies inside to Sembado and Kaluna for their voyage beyond the surface. They still planned to rendezvous with Mahana first, but the spare submarine would ensure them more freedom and potential privacy.

Sembado and Kaluna shuffled forward slowly as their position toward the front of the line progressed. They had become quite familiar with the smells and sounds of the people around them; one particular baby boy had been whimpering nonstop for two and a half hours. Sembado readjusted the heavy bag that hung over his shoulder; it was laden with food. Kaluna had established a comfortable head rest in the crook of Sembado's other arm, and was beginning to doze sporadically. Her repetitive breathing had created a hot, humid point near his armpit, but he endured the discomfort stoically. Kaluna had become much more affectionate since her latest attack, and Sembado was enjoying every minute that he could. His feelings for her had grown from protective to amorous since they departed *The Beluga*, and he was elated to see her finally reciprocate his sentiments. They continued their cuddled embrace as they reached the depressurizing chamber. Four penalty officers stood at the entrance of the chamber, and wearily regulated the flow of citizens. Their expressions were tired, but content. One of the officers was even maintaining a steady stream of humorous commentary and jokes as he ushered the long line of weary citizens. His encouraging antics were lost on some; the whimpering baby boy behind Sembado and Kaluna made sure to express his extreme dissatisfaction. Luckily, Sembado and Kaluna were the last ones admitted to the chamber for the next round of evacuation, and the heavy steel door sealed out the child's screaming quite effectively.

Sembado helped Kaluna climb into his parents' submarine as the chamber's other occupants loaded into their own. They quickly sealed and prepared the submarine for launch before Sembado used their few extra minutes to familiarize Kaluna with the vessel's various features. The submarine was posh compared to the standard line; the craft was a luxury purchase made only after his father had secured a sizable promotion. Kaluna laughed at the unnecessary nature of many of the amenities, but was quite taken with the heated seats. She averted her attention from the elaborate dashboard just long enough to bend her face down to where Sembado sat in the primary's seat. She observed his face, his messy red hair, and his thin, pale lips. She initiated what was to be a very long kiss, but the evacuation sirens outside signaled the imminent air purge. She smirked at Sembado's disappointment as she strapped into the secondary's seat.

"Do you think Lahalo's estimate of surface dwellers was accurate?" Sembado asked as he watched green sea water being pumped up the face of the submarine.

"Who knows," Kaluna responded, "he tends to exaggerate. But on the other hand, Mahana does tend to put himself in those awkward situations."

"I guess we'll find out," Sembado said wryly.

The chamber finished filling with water, and the great hatch was opened. With the Greys' submarine docked in the back of the chamber, Sembado and Kaluna had to wait patiently while the other vessels slowly vacated the space. Sembado followed the onboard guidance system as it led him out of the chamber and into regimented traffic. As he worked his way out and away from the complex, the OGS's now defunct navigation module continued to warn him that he was approaching restricted territory. Kaluna grew weary of the incessant beeping, and she turned the navigation system off.

They continued their ascent slowly. The congested lines of people inside had translated to slow and precarious traffic all the way to the surface. Hundreds of submarines were climbing slowly through a large hole in the containment net. As Sembado and Kaluna took their turn passing through the great rend, they saw teams of workers disassembling the surrounding steel mesh so that more citizens could pass through.

Once he had navigated through the opening, Sembado made a deliberate detour to the East as he worked their submarine away from the congestion and crowding. He leveled out approximately ten meters below the waves. The dense mass of submarines floating on the surface imposed endless shadows below, but sharp rays of sunlight intermittently pierced the floating network of crafts.

"I guess Lahalo wasn't exaggerating *that* much," Sembado said as he scanned the sparkling ocean ceiling ahead.

"But I think most of these people are just getting to the surface," Kaluna responded. "These can't all be *The Beluga*'s followers."

"Mahana was supposed to be staying here above the complex, wasn't he?" Sembado asked.

"Well, I didn't think he was going to leave without us," said Kaluna. "He probably left a rendezvous beacon. We can scan for its message with the radio system. He tends to use the same familiar access codes." She pressed a series of commands on the dashboard display, but could not locate any nearby beacons.

"The beacons work better in surface to surface contact," Kaluna said as she pressed through the radio's settings. "Can you just bring us up to the surface?"

"As soon as I can get out from under all these damn people," Sembado said cynically. He accelerated the submarine sharply; the force pushed him and Kaluna back in their seats. They cruised along quickly, and soon the surface above held significantly fewer vessels. He brought the nose of the submarine up and within moments, their viewing shield was glistening with sun-kissed beads of salt water. As the tinted viewing shield adjusted to the bright daylight outside, contacting *The Beluga* lost priority to smelling and breathing fresh air. They both waited for the other to be ready before cracking the seal on the side door. With a determined nod from Kaluna, Sembado pushed the door up and swung it outward.

Sembado's ears immediately popped. The new, crisp tone allowed the crashing of the waves to resonate beautifully; the familiar smell of the briny air filled his nose and throat. He used his bionic leg to kick the door completely open. The view of the Pacific swells disappearing and reappearing was sickening and beautiful.

Sembado and Kaluna stood together in the hatchway and took in the views of the magnificent blue sky. It was filled with large, puffy, white clouds. The morning sun sat low in the Eastern sky; they had waited in line all night. The two friends shared a firm embrace for several minutes before a noise from inside the submarine interrupted them. Kaluna ducked her head inside to investigate.

"It's the recording!" she said happily.

Sembado pulled the hatch closed while Kaluna reset and adjusted the recording. They sat excitedly while the message finished loading. As the loading screen reached eighty-five percent, Kaluna reached out and grabbed Sembado's hand. The message started right after loading.

Dis is Mahana Kalani. Its uhh...four o'clock on July da tenf. Dis message is for my sweet Kaluna. *Clears throat* Kaluna, baby girl, I'm so sorry we hadta leave. We got so many people wid us now, and dey are hungry for land. We gonna head due east at full speed, but I'm sure you can catch us up. I'll try 'n leave more messages as we go. Sembado, if ya listenin' brudda, take care of my niece, or it'll be your tailfin. *Chuckles* I love ya'll so much. Shoots!

"I guess we better get movin' then," Sembado said, priming the submarine back into its travel functions.

Chapter Thirty
The Love Boat

"He said straight east," Kaluna said. "So don't let this number move," she added while pointing to one of the two coordinates on the dashboard.

"I know how it works," Sembado laughed. "They're the same coordinates underwater." He dropped the nose of the submarine underwater so that he could turn into their heading more easily. He turned it around quickly and accelerated eastward. As he came back up to cruise on the surface, he adjusted his heading until one coordinate stayed fixed just above seventeen; the other one had just dropped below one hundred forty-one. Sembado brought the submarine up to its full surface speed before checking the gauges and engaging the auto-captain; they were cruising along at forty-two knots.

"We could be going much faster down below," Sembado noted with a furrowed brow, "but we'd have to be down quite a ways."

"Yeah, but we're still going a lot faster than Mahana's group can manage," Kaluna said. "I'd prefer to enjoy the sun and fresh air while we go."

"Fine with me," Sembado said, leaning back to grab some food from the bag his mother had given him. From it, he produced two bottles of water, and a large puffed grain cake. It was wrapped in crispy kelp leaves.

"Thanks," Kaluna said, taking her share. "I will be happy to have some surface food again. I think it will take a while before I have a kelp craving."

"Yeah?" Sembado shrugged. "I get why *you* say that, but I don't think I could go without kelp chips."

Kaluna made a funny face as she finished chewing her current bite.

"I just can't get into it, but it'll do for now," she said. Sembado chuckled and then yawned loudly.

"Deeks, I just realized how tired I am. I think we've been up for almost twenty-four hours," he said as he stretched and yawned once more. "Well, I have," he added with a smirk. "You got to sleep while we waited in line." He checked the auto-captain one last time, and then got out of his chair to move to the back of the main compartment.

"Yeah right," Kaluna said, throwing a bit of her rice cake at him. "My eyes were closed, but I couldn't sleep with that baby whining the whole time!" Sembado laughed as he picked up the food scrap and ate it.

"Who's being whiny?" Sembado said with raised eyebrows. He slid one of the convertible chairs around in the back, adjusting it to its sleeping configuration. He opened a storage drawer in the back to reveal some sleeping accessories his parents had provided: two small pillows and a light blanket. Kaluna continued to protest as she moved her way to where he was in the back.

"I hope you don't mean me," she said shaking her head. "You're the one looking to take a nap, ya big baby!" She sat down next to him.

"Nap nothing," Sembado said as he stretched out on his back, and kicked off his shoes. "I want to sleep!" She shook her head as she fought back a smile. Sembado yawned one more time and put his hands behind his head. He was careful to shuffle to his side so that a small space remained on the bed for Kaluna.

She continued to stare at him with a humored, pursed sneer as she set down her food, and took off her own shoes. Her expression softened as she undid her hair ties and let her loose hair fall about her shoulders; a short, intricate braid rested behind her right ear.

Despite his eyes being heavy and tired, Sembado's heart and stomach were quite alert as he watched the morning sunlight cast shadows on Kaluna's already tan skin. Her honey colored cheeks were high and tight across her delicate facial structure. Her green eyes danced as she took in his hazel ones and his fiery orange mane. She leaned closer as they continued to search through each other's gaze. She paused briefly near his face before closing her eyes and taking his thin lips into her own full-lipped kiss. He closed his own eyes as she lowered the rest of her body against his. She brought her legs up onto the cramped bed to lie alongside him as they continued their loving exchange. She laid her hands across his chest, and he lazily engulfed her in his gangly arms. They broke their kiss just long enough to exchange a happy look and a smile. Sembado's goofy grin made Kaluna giggle, but she gave him another long, passionate kiss anyway.

Sembado's attentive kiss became slack for a brief moment as his head drifted sleepily back against the pillow. He shuddered and jerked as he realized he was dozing off.

"I'm sorry," he said longingly. "You know that I'd like for this to continue. I'm just so tired."

"Sembado, its fine," she said with a soft smile. "Go to sleep."

"Okay, but I just want you to know," he started to say.

"Sembado. Stop. Go to sleep," she said emphatically. She kissed him one more time before cuddling up beside him and resting her head in his arms. He took her advice quite literally, and was sound asleep in minutes. Kaluna carefully arranged the small blanket as far across their legs as possible. It was long enough for her to tuck under her chin, but it stopped at his chest. She continued to snuggle against his chest as she too drifted off into a content slumber.

***

Sembado slept for a solid five hours before stirring. He opened his eyes to see Kaluna in one of the front seats. She had slowed the submarine down to one-quarter speed.

Sembado rubbed his eyes as he looked beyond her silhouette to the movement in front of the submarine.

"What's going on?" he yawned. "What's that up ahead?"

"It's a pod of dolphins," Kaluna said without looking back. "I only slowed down a minute ago. I just wanted to watch them for a bit."

"What time is it?" Sembado asked.

"Just before noon," Kaluna answered. "Come watch them jump!" Sembado sat and stretched broadly. He kicked the tangled blanket off his feet, stood up, and teetered up to the front. He absentmindedly brushed Kaluna's hair as he sat down in the other front seat. He briefly reviewed the dashboard as he sat:

12 knots | 17° 14' 23" N | 138° 2' 43" W

He looked up from the console just in time to see a dolphin explode out of the water. It did a graceful somersault right before it dipped back below the water. Two more flew into the air right behind it. A wonder-filled grin spread across his face as he watched the acrobatic display. The porpoises zipped in and out of the submarine's path as they jumped, spun, and dove. Sembado and Kaluna continued to enjoy the spectacle as they cruised into the early afternoon.

Chapter Thirty-One
S.O.S.

Sembado and Kaluna took turns scanning for beacons as their journey stretched into the next day. They slept in shifts so that they would not miss a potential recording. Kaluna expected Mahana to be setting as many of the small radio buoys loose as possible, but the ocean currents could be sending the small floating transponders elsewhere.

It was approaching midnight when Sembado looked back at Kaluna longingly as she slept soundly in the rear. He turned back to face the front of the submarine, and ahead in the sky, the most beautiful starry exhibition was blooming in the night. He looked down to check the instruments:

41 knots | 17° 14' 25" N | 130° 39' 12" W

Sembado furrowed his eyebrow. At the rate they were going compared to *The Beluga*, they should have caught up by now. The mass of secondary boats should have provided even more visibility. He looked back up at the beautiful, twinkling points of light. He gasped as one shot

240

across the sky like a rocket; it left a long trail behind it. Just as it fizzled out, another followed it. Sembado's mouth fell open as the shooting stars continued to cascade across the sky. He sat in utter silence as the spectacle continued for several minutes. Just as the meteor shower was reaching its climax, the alarm on the scanner went off; it startled Sembado out of his daze. He immediately went to action, sending the radio into receiving mode so that the message could be processed. Behind him, Kaluna was already stirring from her rest. She appeared at his side, groggily rubbing her face.

"We get something?" she asked sleepily.

"Yeah, it's taking a while to load though," Sembado responded. Sembado directed Kaluna's attention to the last couple shooting stars as the file finished loading. They both listened carefully as the audio file began to play back, noticing immediately how different the tone was.

Dis Mahana. It's real late on da twelf. Tings aren't lookin' good and dey gettin' worse. Movin' dis many people mighta been a mistake, but we've come too far to turn back. Kaluna, Sembado, if ya'll are followin' us and hear dis, keep movin' eas'. We're tracking into da mornin' sun pretty good, but we're goin slow, and my fisherman can't keep up on da feedin'. We got a lot of mouds to feed. We should be able to hold out to da coast dough. God be wid us. Shoots.

Kaluna's tired state did little to emotionally prepare her to hear her uncle in such distress. She slumped down in the seat next to Sembado; tears were streaming down here face. Sembado looked away, and pretended to adjust the settings on the console.

"Is that the only one we've received?" Kaluna asked between sniffles.

"So far," Sembado said quietly. Kaluna dropped her head back against her seat. They sat in silence while the submarine skipped across the surface of the sea.

"What are we doing?" Kaluna whispered. "What does he expect us to do? Catch up with him? Then what? We can starve alongside them?"

"Kaluna, please," Sembado said as he took her hand in his. "We will do whatever we can. That's all we can do. He expects nothing more than that. Come on." She squeezed his hand in response.

"He said the twelfth," Kaluna noted. "That was just over a day ago. Could they be that far ahead of us?"

"I don't see how," Sembado replied. "With such a big fleet, we should have spotted something by now."

They both looked out to scan the open ocean as if they might see *The Beluga's* fleet right over the next heaving swell. The waning gibbous moon shined white over the pitch black sea water; its bright reflection danced along a million little mirrors below.

"We're going as fast as we can," Sembado said as he continued to scan the distance. "We're bound to catch up eventually."

Both Sembado and Kaluna refused to sleep the rest of the night. They sat poised at the dashboard until the black, star-filled sky started to give way to indigo, blue, then green. Wispy clouds on the eastern horizon hung in the early morning sunset like a grand, ghostly signature. The green hued heavens quickly succumbed to orange; a fiery red-orange. It painted the skyline in one bold, defiant stroke. Then the sun came; a white hot pin prick that seemed to jump over the end of the earth in an instant. It spread into a dazzling line, and then to a brilliant orb.

The captivating sunrise was suddenly interrupted by the sound that Sembado and Kaluna had been so desperately anticipating: a new rendezvous beacon. Sembado and Kaluna blinked tears out of their strained, bloodshot eyes as they struggled to interpret the data streaming across the screen. The message loaded within a minute; Sembado and Kaluna were sitting on the edge of their seats as the next distress call was translated into its audio format. While the audio clip started playing, nothing but static could be heard for the first fifteen seconds. Then, Mahana's troubled voice broke through the silence; his grief was palpable.

Heyo... It's...uhhh...jus' afta' dark on the tirteent... We had to send all our helty people off ahead wit da smaller crafts. Dey lookin' for da shore ahead 'o us. Da Beluga is real heavy wit da sick and is now servin' as da medical quarters. We've had to have da smaller ships break off to

cover deir own food too. We're all real hungry.
I've lost plenty o' weight myself. * Chuckles*
Long silence
We jus' found out we been off course for tree days.
Our coord'nates is twenty-sev'n poin' tree four
wes', and a hundred twenty-six point eight nort.
But it's all for da bes'! Kaluna, baby girl, don't go
straight eas'! I repeat! Don't go straight eas'. Da
coast is closer da furtha' nort ya go. Start heading
norteas' as soon as ya can. We settin' course for
an old village called San D'ego. God be wid us.
Love ya. Shoots.

Sembado's eyes widened as he processed what he had just heard Mahana say. He looked down at the instruments:

43 knots | 17° 14' 3" N | 126° 51' 23" W

Kaluna was already scrambling to calculate an intercept. She punched the screen feverishly with her finger; Sembado waited patiently while Kaluna worked on the navigational calculations.

"If they're going as fast as I think they are," Kaluna said breathlessly, "then we could run into them at…thirty point forty-four and one nineteen point sixty-one." She continued to manipulate the computations vigorously. "But that means…it will take another twenty-four hours at full speed to do it." She dropped her shoulders as she realized the unlikely scenario she was proposing.

"Well let's get to it then," Sembado said passionately, and he took the controls back from the auto-captain. He turned to the Northeast at full speed; the submarine skipped and crashed through a few random waves before he straightened it out.

"A little bit more," Kaluna said, and Sembado adjusted their course to the North until she was satisfied.

Sembado's unflinching decision emboldened Kaluna with hope, and she kissed him quickly before retiring to bed for more energy. Sembado stoically sat in the primary seat for the next several hours. He waited for Kaluna to stir before he went back to the bathroom compartment to relieve himself. He exited the bathroom to see Kaluna feverishly working through a new transmission.

"We got another one," she said, excitedly looking back over her shoulder. Sembado trotted to the front and sat down just as the message started.

Midday on da fourteent...we're runnin' low on everyting. Ain't got any more toiletries, and most of da toilets ain't workin' anyway. Dis heat ain't helpin' wit da smell eitha'... We can barely feed da kids anymore. Still alive an' kickin' dough. Headin' norteast. Shoots.

"Ugh, this is killing me!" Kaluna snapped as the audio feed cut to an end. "Why did he leave himself so vulnerable?"

"Luna, calm down," Sembado said softly. "We are doing everything we *can*."

Before Kaluna could protest further, Sembado leaned over and kissed her firmly on the mouth. She pulled away, stared him sternly in the eye, and then returned with an even more passionate kiss. She grabbed him by the head, her fingers tangled in his red hair, and pulled him closer. They entangled further as they fell to the floor of the submarine. The passionate embrace continued for nearly a half hour; Sembado was the first to surrender.

"I really need some water," he said breathlessly. He was careful to stand up the right way, painfully embarrassed of his visible arousal. He climbed into the primary captain chair where he gulped down an entire quart of water in one go. Kaluna straightened herself too, and joined him in the front, where they continued to cruise in silence for the rest of the late morning.

Chapter Thirty-Two
San Clemente!

Sembado smiled as the salty ocean mist teased his olfactory senses; it made his nose tickle and the tip of his tongue dance. He stood watch on the wing of the submarine as it bobbed up and down in the waves. A storm had just passed, but its choppy swells remained behind. Kaluna was tied off in the water, and bathed in the briny sea. Sembado had gone first, and while he had eliminated the greasy film off of his forehead and back, his body now smelled strongly of the sea. Kaluna called for his assistance and he pulled her in gently. She held onto the wing while Sembado untangled her garments and passed them down to her. He desperately pretended to not notice that her naked body was on full display just below the clear Pacific water; it was not easy. The sun cast delightful shadows on her golden shoulders and collarbones. Her supple figure trembled in and out of focus under the mere twelve inches of water that separated it from Sembado's view. Her curves were modest yet ample. Sembado fought to avert his gaze just in time for Kaluna to reach for his hand. He helped her onto the wing, and they dried in the sun for a short while before continuing their pursuit.

"Do you think our break put us behind much?" Kaluna asked as they brought the submarine back up to full speed.

"I think we can make it up," Sembado replied. "I don't think my dad even knew this submarine was built with that supplemental solar array. It's increased our top speed by twenty percent over the last twelve hours. Look at it! We're well over fifty knots. This is ridiculous!"

"Well I'm glad we could stop. That salt water isn't very refreshing, but I think it'll hold us over until we can have a proper bath. I felt disgusting," said Kaluna.

"Well, you don't look disgusting," Sembado said, wishing it had sounded more complimentary. "I mean…"

"I knew what you meant," Kaluna laughed. "Thanks for the effort."

"It could be worse," Sembado joked. "We could both be horribly sunburned."

"No," Kaluna replied. "You would be sunburned. I would just get darker."

Sembado rolled his eyes dramatically, and said, "Yeah, that's fair. Pick on the pale guy."

"Oh stop," Kaluna said. "You make fun of me for being so quiet."

"I make observations about you being quiet," Sembado said. "I am *not* making fun of you!"

"Alright, alright," Kaluna said. "*Sorry.*"

Their journey continued into the night without interruption. Sembado woke at three in the morning to Kaluna beating on the dashboard. The submarine was stopped; it tossed to and fro in the slow Pacific waves.

Sembado rushed to the front to comfort Kaluna as her frustrations reached their peak.

"What's going on?" he asked. "What's the matter?"

"The effing batteries are dying," Kaluna snapped. "Even with your stupid solar array."

"Well it's the middle of the night," Sembado said innocently. "I don't think the solar…"

"I'm not stupid, Sembado! I know how they work!" she snapped.

"I know that!" he said regretfully. "Deeks, I'm sorry. There must be a short somewhere that is causing it to drain. The batteries weren't going to last forever, but the solar arrays should have at least helped recharge them."

"Not with you pushing it over fifty!" Kaluna snapped. "Wow, that's incredible! I can't believe this," she mocked.

"Hey, come on," Sembado reasoned. "We can figure this out. Worst case scenario is waiting for first light. That's only three hours from now. We aren't going to miss them in three hours. Not at the pace we've been going."

Kaluna brooded silently while Sembado made a feint effort at resuscitating the dashboard.

"Do you remember what the last coordinates were before it shut down?" Sembado asked.

"Umm, twenty-something…eight?" Kaluna said sadly. "Twenty-eight and one hundred twenty-something. It might have just been one-twenty. I don't know!"

"Okay," Sembado said. "So twenty-eight and one-twenty are close to our rendezvous point! Really close! I think we're only about two hours away, three max."

"So that's six hours total, Sembado!" Kaluna said. "Three waiting for sun up, and three to get there. That's assuming the damn sub starts up right at sunrise! They could move up to one-hundred twenty miles in six hours!"

"But Mahana said they were going slower than he hoped, and that line of boats is probably a hundred miles long by now. That'll increase our chance of running into someone. And I already told you that we've been making faster progress than we thought thanks to the solar array."

"Oh, shove your solar array," Kaluna snapped. "We'll wait for the damn sun to come up!" As she got up and went to the back, she yelled over her shoulder, "Don't follow me!"

Sembado sat, dejected, and watched the moon as it moved slowly across the sky. He chewed on his nails until his fingertips were red and tender.

I don't know why she's so mad at me. It was both our faults. Neither one of us knew how the deekin' solar array worked. I'll make it up…I'll have this thing moving before she even wakes up.

Sembado struggled through calculations in his head until the night sky started to hint of dawn. He deactivated all of the unnecessary features including the dashboard display. As the first morning light crept across the horizon, Sembado balanced the solar power between forward progress and charging the battery. Before long, he had the submarine moving along at a steady pace, and was able to work up the top speed while Kaluna slept soundly in the rear. He discovered the maximum he could maintain while continuing to trickle-charge the main power supply. However, as the battery's charge increased, he was able to adjust the balance on the solar load to charge more, and within the hour, he had the submarine skipping across the waves. Without the dashboard he was not exactly sure of his speed, but he knew it was in excess of twenty knots. The lack of amenities meant he had to steer manually, but he had already developed a pattern with the waves, and he made steady progress as the sun climbed higher in the sky. He thought of waking Kaluna.

No— I'll wait. The further I get, the happier she'll be.

The morning faded to early afternoon, and the sun started to make its decent down the other side of the sky. An uneasy feeling grew in Sembado's stomach as he realized he should have seen at least some of Mahana's extraneous flotilla by this time of the day. He sheepishly looked over his shoulder at Kaluna before flipping on the dashboard accessories; he was quite distraught by their readings.

28 knots | 32° 46' 21" N | 119° 37' 10" W

Sembado, you idiot! You passed the rendezvous point completely! You might have seen something on the radar if you had any of the accessories turned on. You should have just woke her up. She's going to be so angry.

Sembado slowed the submarine to a stop while he prepared himself for the verbal attack that was soon to come. He tried to practice what he would say, but just as he approached Kaluna in her resting place, she stirred and opened her eyes.

"Wh…why is it so bright out?" she said sleepily. Her indignation grew as she became more alert. "What time is it? Why did you let me sleep so long? We're going to miss them!"

Sembado stood quietly, with his shoulders dropped in disappointment. His body language did little to sooth Kaluna's fiery reaction.

"Sembado!" she shouted. "Why aren't we moving? What is the matter?"

"I went too far," Sembado said softly.

"What?" she asked.

"I went too far, for too long. We passed the rendezvous point. I never saw anyone."

"What?" she snapped indignantly. "Why didn't you stop? You didn't see *anything* on the radar?"

"I…I had the accessories turned off to conserve power," Sembado said quietly. "I didn't want a repeat of yesterday. I took it slow with the solar panel and everything."

"Well, not *that* slow!" Kaluna said as she peered up to the dashboard. "Does that say thirty-two and three quarters? Sembado, we were supposed to stop at twenty-eight!"

"I know…I…I was trying to make it up to you, okay!" he snapped; he fought to keep the tears in his eyes from welling over their lids. "You acted disgusted with me this morning. I was just trying to fix it."

Kaluna sighed deeply as she crossed her arms. She dropped her head and sighed again.

"And you didn't see anything?" she asked without looking up.

"No," Sembado said. "I've been looking in every direction."

"Well you aren't going to see more than a couple miles away," Kaluna said. "Not this close to the water."

She stepped past him as she moved to the front of the submarine. Sembado stayed where he was; he stared at the floor.

"Have you tried scanning the radar since we stopped?" Kaluna called back to him.

"I haven't done anything since we stopped," Sembado said as he hesitantly moved to Kaluna's side. "Kaluna, I'm *really* sorry. Seriously."

"I know. I get it," she said firmly. "Let's just figure this out, okay?"

Sembado sat down beside her and helped get the submarine up and running again. He settled into his seat as Kaluna brought the sub up to speed and gained her bearings as best as possible. Suddenly, she powered the sub back down; she was transfixed on the horizon. She let the submarine drift carelessly for a full minute without saying anything.

"Kaluna, what are you doing?" Sembado asked. She did not respond. "Kaluna!" he said loudly.

"Well, don't you see it?" she asked.

"See what?" he asked, scanning the horizon in vain.

"Land!" Kaluna replied.

Sembado remained awestruck as Kaluna slowly piloted the submarine closer to the land mass. A long ridge of mountains grew taller as they approached; it seemed to stretch off in either direction.

"Do you think this is the Sandego place that Mahana mentioned in his message?" Sembado asked as he continued to gawk at the beautifully colored landscape. The falling sun was just starting to paint the greens and browns red and gold.

"He said San Diego," Kaluna replied with precise diction. "And no. San Diego is supposed to be on the mainland. This is an island."

"How do you know?" Sembado asked, finally breaking his gaze from the scenery. "It looks big enough to be the mainland to me."

"What do you mean, how do I know?" Kaluna shot back. "I'm from an island. I know what they look like from the water. Watch as we pass the North side here. See? You can see the water wrap around that point. The mainland will be bigger; almost infinite."

Sembado turned a furrowed brow back to the mass of earth as they passed closely around its northern most point.

He could see strange, horned creatures scaling the steep slopes that led to the mountain ridge. Their black and brown hides appeared almost red in the setting sun. Some of the larger animals had thick black hair around their necks, and longer, more elegant horns sprouting from their pointed heads. Sembado marveled at the funny animals as they pulled away from the island.

Kaluna increased their speed as they moved back into open water, but within the hour, they were staring at another land mass; she steered straight toward it.

"I'm guessing that's an island too?" Sembado asked.

"I'm guessing so too," Kaluna replied.

"Then why are you headed straight for it?" Sembado inquired.

"Because the sun is about to go down, and I don't want to spend another night in this damn submarine," Kaluna said firmly.

"Oh," Sembado said quietly.

"Oh, stop!" Kaluna said sharply. "Would you get over it? I didn't mean because of you. Don't you want some fresh air and firm ground?"

"Sounds good to me," Sembado said lightly. "We *are* running low on food and water."

"We'll find something there," Kaluna said. "Do we have any weapons with us?"

"My dad only packed us one shock stick," Sembado responded. "But I also have an old knife of my grandfather's. Do you think we'll run into any people?"

Kaluna squinted at the approaching shoreline where an orange dot flickered on the beach; a large bonfire was being stoked to life.

"I think we already have," Kaluna said.

Chapter Thirty-Three
Nina from Catalina

They watched cautiously as long-shadowed silhouettes appeared in front of the fire. One of the figures stood motionless and stoic while the others jumped in the air and waved their arms. The figures moved away from their fire as they congregated to the point where Kaluna would soon beach the submarine. The bright blaze backlit the inhabitants with an ominous glow, but the dying light of the sun painted warm and happy colors across their young and friendly faces. There was only one adult, a tall white man that stood back near the fire. The children waded into the water around the submarine as it skidded to an abrupt stop. They made loud and excited noises as they admired all of the interesting details of the submarine's exterior. Their tattered clothes stuck to their wet bodies as they climbed back out of the water. They adjusted the large leaves and other natural materials that supplemented the worn garments. The man remained stationary, staring out past the submarine. He leaned on a large walking stick; a large machete hung overtly on his hip. The sling of an assault rifle pulled tightly across his bare chest; its barrel was just visible over his shoulder.

One of the more boisterous children returned to the water to bang on the front viewing shield of the submarine.

"Come on out!" She shouted loudly. She put her hand to the window to block the glare and peered around the cockpit excitedly.

Sembado slid his knife into its sheath and attached it to his pants. Kaluna holstered the shock stick. They pushed the door open to find that the girl had moved around to greet them.

"Well come on out already," she said in a bright and husky voice. She grabbed Sembado's hand and jumped up and down. "My name's Nina. Nina from Catalina! Well come on out!"

"Nina, come out of the water," the man commanded from the beach; he still had not moved.

Sembado jumped down with a splash before turning and helping Kaluna out of the submarine. Nina tried to help them out of the water. She pulled on both of their hands as she toiled backward with gritted teeth; several were missing. The sand stuck to their wet legs; Nina's unnecessary kicking sent it up to their waists.

"I sure like your sink-boat," Nina said loudly as the other children gathered closer. They seemed to feed off of Nina's energy; they marveled at Sembado's bionic limb.

"Are you a mermaid?" one asked.

"Do you speak English?" asked another.

"Why is your hair orange?" asked Nina.

"What's your name?" asked a girl.

"My name's Fresno. What's yours?" asked a boy.

"Shut up, Fresno. I asked first," said the girl.

"You shut up!" yelled Fresno.

"Children!" bellowed the man. "Leave them alone and come warm yourselves. You're soaking! Nina! Now!"

The man stood with his arms crossed as the children obediently complied with his orders. They circled the fire, and dried their ragged outfits. The man glared at Sembado and Kaluna. They stood just outside the water; the breaking waves washed their foamy reaches around their feet.

"You should come up," the man called. "It's getting dark." He reached down to his feet to pick up a pile of something and threw it out to them haphazardly. Sembado and Kaluna sidestepped its trajectory, and a giant corkscrew and rope landed just feet away. They looked back up to see the man standing with his arms crossed again. Sembado struggled to dig the screw into the sand while Kaluna tied the rope off to the submarine. When they had finished, they moved slowly up the beach where the fire was roaring. They stood near the man as the children huddled in a giggling mob, and passed around pieces of roasted fruit.

"My name's Barton," the man said as he continued to watch the water. "Are you two alone?"

"Yes," Sembado replied. "We were trying to meet a large fleet on its way to Sandego."

"San Diego," Kaluna corrected.

"Well, you're a little ways north," said Barton.

"We know," Kaluna added. "We got off course."

259

"I'll help you with directions," Barton said. "But we can't let you stay long. I'll give you three days."

"We only need one," Kaluna said.

"We'll take two," Sembado said firmly. "Thank you very much."

For the first time since Sembado and Kaluna's arrival, Barton turned his attention away from the water. He watched the children finish their fruit as they started to play and dance around the fire. They made big loops around the pile of burning logs. Each time one of them would try and stop to talk to Sembado and Kaluna, Barton would send them back to the fire. Barton let the fire die down before he filed the children up the hill at the end of the beach. He had Sembado and Kaluna follow at the rear of the line. Little Nina shuffled slowly until she was at the back with them. She held Sembado's hand until they arrived back at their village.

Chapter Thirty-Four
An Offer You Can't Refuse

The next morning proved to be an exciting one in Barton's village. The inhabitants were friendly and curious about the details of Sembado and Kaluna's journey, their origins, and their 'sink-boat.' The village was of modest size with a population of a few dozen.

Sembado and Kaluna joined Barton and some of the other men and women on a fishing trip in the late morning. Each person did their part; some carried pots, some baskets, and a few struggled with one large, intricate net. They walked along a grassy path that ran halfway up the nearby mountain ridge until they came back to the small bay from the night before. Sembado and Kaluna's submarine lay canted to one side several yards from the water.

"Don't worry," said Barton. "High tide will return your sink-boat to the waves."

They walked the nets out to the shallows and cast them down into the water. Small bits of flaked fruit were tossed out over the net, and soon an entire school of fish was teeming around the feed. It took the entire team to pull the laden net onto the dry, sandy beach. The fish were rinsed and placed in the baskets before being hauled back to the village. Sembado and Kaluna stayed back with Barton, two others, and the collection of pots. Barton led the team back into the trees and up a long mountain path to a fresh water stream. There, they filled the pots with the cool water, and took a break.

"We sure could make use of that sink-boat of yours," Barton said, wiping his brow. "Anything we could trade ya for it?" He and his followers exchanged several awkward looks with each other, Sembado, and Kaluna

"I'd love to help you," said Sembado carefully, "but we need it to reach the mainland."

"We could go with you, and come back with it," Barton said matter-of-factly.

"It sounds like you've thought this through," said Kaluna.

"We are *the* largest village on this island," Barton said. "But we're not alone. We've always been very diligent in our population control. Who can have children and when – that kind of thing. Our elders always made sure we were responsible with our resources, but I'm afraid some of the more...aggressive folks on Catalina don't share our principles. We've been here for as many generations as you all have been underwater. Our elders told us how the big blue storm fried all the electronics. The computers... The engines."

Barton's villagers looked down at their feet as his story weighed heavily on their pride. Sembado and Kaluna exchanged a look. His was pity. Hers was suspicion.

"Your sink-boat is the first vehicle I've ever seen in operation," Barton continued. "If I had something like that I could make runs to the mainland for more supplies. We wouldn't have to worry about challenging our neighbors' territory anymore. If they got worse, why, I could even ferry my people across the channel. Move 'em off Catalina for good."

Sembado could tell Barton's plea was honest and forthright. He already assumed that he would be forfeiting the submarine to the villagers; the only question was at what cost.

"You have to understand that we will need to discuss our situation privately," Sembado said in as genuine a tone as he could manage.

"Yes!" Barton said enthusiastically. "Yes, of course."

Sembado and Kaluna wasted no time in arranging their private exchange: as Barton and his people walked ahead with their pots of water, Sembado and Kaluna fell back with theirs.

"I really have no idea what you think you're doing," Kaluna snapped as soon as the others were out of earshot. "I'm sorry, but this is not the time to be playing charity case. I want to get out of here as soon as possible!"

"Why?" Sembado asked sharply. "I think these are genuinely good people! It's not like we'll need the submarine once we get to the mainland. Mahana will have plenty of spares, and I don't expect us to be hitting the high seas anytime soon anyway. Do you?"

"I just don't think it's a good idea to be promising our only lifeline right now," Kaluna responded. "What could they possibly have that is more valuable than our submarine?"

"Give me a day to find out and I'll tell you!" Sembado snapped. "Just calm down, would ya?"

Sembado led the way as they made double-time progress back through the trees and brush. They caught up with Barton and his people just as they reached the village. Sembado and Kaluna stepped into the ring of huts and shelters to see a large mat of woven sticks suspended over a large fire. The morning's catch of fish was sizzling in a beautiful array of fillets. The men and women who tended the grill chatted happily as they fought off the children's peckish advances; they rotated golden brown vegetables around the base of the coals.

The gathering fell into an orderly procession as man, woman, and child lined up for their portion of the feast. Sembado and Kaluna joined Barton on a nicely sculpted log as the others worked their ways into different corners of the fire-centered gathering.

Sembado marveled at the amount of flavor the humble cooking treatment had afforded the fresh fish. Its smoked, crispy skin gave way to moist, flaky flesh. The roasted vegetables had been seasoned with some kind of salty mineral.

"I trust you were able to discuss my offer?" Barton asked quietly. His voice was barely audible over the popping fire and laughing children. Sembado's full mouth made him unable to respond. Kaluna responded instead.

"You mean your request?" she asked. "You never offered anything."

Barton considered Kaluna's words earnestly, despite Sembado's obvious discomfort.

"I believe you're right," Barton said lightly. "I am afraid I have little that would be of genuine value to you, except for one item." He looked into the fire as he weighed his words. "It was truly a sacred artifact to my predecessors, but I think it was more sentimental than anything."

While Barton's theatrical presentation was well executed, even Sembado had a difficult time expressing genuine interest. Barton, seeing that his performance was falling flat, decided to cut to the chase.

"I have a map," he said.

Sembado and Kaluna were careful not to openly laugh at Barton's offer. By the time he had made the final pitch, several of his fellow leaders were eavesdropping for the answer.

"I understand why you want the submarine," Sembado said calmly. "But a map is of little value to us if we have the coordinates we need. I appreciate what you are trying to do, and we may consider another offer, but this isn't really what we need."

Despite the fact that several villagers bristled at the blunt response, Barton remained calm and poised.

"You're right," he said with a benign smile. "This was a silly offer for a people as advanced as yourselves. I will consider what other resources we have that would be suitable to you, and we can speak again later. For now, let's enjoy this feast and a little music." He motioned to a few others and they disappeared into a nearby hovel. They returned with three small drums and a pair of highly polished sticks.

The grilling mats for the fish were removed from the fire, and the flames were stoked higher as the sun dropped behind the surrounding canopy. As darkness fell, the smaller children climbed up into their mothers' laps. Several individuals refused the responsibility of the music, and the drums were passed around until all three were finally claimed. The polished sticks were given to one of the elders. The older villager began clinking out a bright, high beat with the sticks. When they were done with a simple beat, the drummers would echo the pattern. Each round became more and more complex until the drummers could no longer keep up, at which point the villagers erupted in laughter. The drummers were just starting to take turns performing their own solos when a small container began making its way through the crowd. Each grown villager lifted it to their lips before passing it on; the children did not partake. It arrived in Sembado's hands, and he looked down at the reflective surface of the liquid inside. The bright colors of the fire danced across its wavering surface.

"Drink it," Barton said as he motioned for Sembado to tip the container to his lips. Sembado looked to Kaluna for approval. She shrugged her shoulders as she eyed the mysterious liquid.

Sembado lifted the container to his mouth. He could smell the fruity, pungent smell of alcohol. He parted his lips as the bowl met them. The liquid was warm and sweet and strong, but it fell smoothly down his throat without incident. He passed the bowl to Kaluna who also took a healthy draw of the aromatic liquor. The circle of adults became increasingly relaxed, and soon some of the older teenagers were sneaking into the line for their own share of the communal libations.

Sembado and Kaluna continued to take their turns with the bowl, but they had not noticed that it was passing their seats with an increased frequency. Sembado's head became heavy and light all at once. He was suddenly aware that if he closed his eyes as often as he would like, his head began to swim and bob in a way that he did not like. Kaluna became increasingly still next to him; her head hung loosely against his shoulder. He watched the fire flicker and dance in smooth, pallid streaks. His breathing grew increasingly labored, and he began to refuse the bowl as it passed. Kaluna's face smeared down Sembado's chest and into his lap just as he fell backwards off of his log perch.

Chapter Thirty-Five
Up a Creek

A firm pressure pulled across Sembado's forehead and squeezed tightly at his temples. He clenched his closed eyes and contorted his open mouth in pain as he let out a low moan. He breathed loudly through his mouth while a bright light shined painfully into his eyes through their closed lids. Another wave of pain pulsed through his head; it took his breath away. He closed his mouth; the roof and tongue were exceptionally dry. Another pain pulse washed over his head. He turned his head away from the light and opened his eyes. A dark mass faded into focus; Kaluna was sitting next to him. She sat cross-legged; her chin rested on her chest as her head hung slack. A pile of vomit lay in front of her. Sembado closed his eyes again as the pain returned. The knots in his stomach would have offered more discomfort, but the agonizing pain in his head was his singular focus. The pain was too much, and Sembado tried desperately to fall back to sleep. He tried to bring his hand up to rest his head on, but that's when he realized an irritating tension on his wrists. He let his head drop lazily to observe his wrists. He stared stupidly for a full minute as he took in the sight of his raw, pink wrists wrapped together with a length of fibrous twine. With his head hanging loosely, he was able to doze in and out of sleep, and for a long while, he ignored his wrists as he concentrated on losing the pain in his dreams. His immediate dream state was accompanied by the mental illusion that he was suddenly falling from a great height. His reaction shocked his body back awake with a violent twitch. He reached to brace his painful head with his hands, but instead smacked himself square in the face with his bound fists. His nose burned and his eyes watered; he released another long moan. Sembado's bionic leg seemed to react by suddenly kicking at random as if it was trying to walk in place.

A shadowy figure blocked the sun from Sembado's eyes for just a moment before a large vessel of water was thrown right into his face and lap. Sembado gasped and coughed awake; his eyes were suddenly open. He looked around wildly as the pain in his head was temporarily overruled by the cold, wet sensation that covered his entire body. Barton and three other men stood over him; two more resuscitated Kaluna in a similar fashion.

"You should really watch how much you drink," Barton said, shaking his head. "You gotta know when to stop." One of his followers chuckled softly while the others continued to sneer.

Sembado's body began to shiver as the water that soaked his clothes began to evaporate in the late morning sunlight. His splitting headache fought back violently for his attention. He looked around timidly as his eyes adjusted to the light. He and Kaluna had been stripped of their clothes and accessories; their wearables had been replaced by the same modest, make-shift garments of the villagers. Barton and his followers each wore various pieces of Sembado's outfit. Barton had even claimed Sembado's cerebral transceiver for his prosthetic. He wore it around his neck like a prized trinket. The village leader squatted down to face Sembado. As Barton crouched, Sembado's bionic leg received the wireless signal from Barton's neural message, and retracted as well.

"You people are all the same," Barton said, ignoring Sembado's spastic leg. "There have only been a few of you over the years. Maybe only once a decade, but it's always the same. You laugh at our plight – at our meager lifestyle. Because we don't have the technology you do – no electricity. What? We aren't as good as you?" Barton stood up, still not noticing how Sembado's bionic limb mimicked his every movement. Barton's followers stood at his side with their arms crossed as he continued his rant. "Heaven forbid we don't have to struggle for day. Heaven forbid you offer us help without something in exchange. We have nothing, you have everything, and you still want something from us? What's a matter with you people?"

Sembado failed to make sense of Barton's words as his head and stomach continued to vie for his discomfort. He turned his dazed gaze to Kaluna. She was recoiled into a shivering fetal position; her clothes had retained more water than Sembado's and her position was shaded from the sun.

"So now I have a *real* offer for ya," Barton said bitterly. "How's about this? How about we load up you and your girl here in your fancy sink-boat, take you to the mainland, and dump your arrogant, self-righteous asses on those deadly shores?" The men that stood with Barton nodded in agreement and chuckled darkly as he continued. "How's that? Sparing your miserable lives. How's that? Is that a good enough trade?"

The men smacked Barton on the back and encouraged him further. He glared at Sembado angrily before spitting on him and kicking dirt toward his face. Sembado's bionic leg responded to Barton's direction again, jerking out simultaneously with Barton's own foot.

"He's kickin' back at you!" one of the men said.

"Little bastard!" cried another.

Barton lashed out again, but swung his foot directly at Sembado's ribs instead of the ground. Sembado braced himself feebly as the powerful prosthetic jerked again. Before Barton's attack could connect, Sembado's prosthetic struck just behind Barton's other heel, causing him to topple to the ground. Sembado's bionic leg continued its errant behavior as Barton's own legs scrambled to get beneath him. He swore wildly as his medulla oblongata was unexpectedly assaulted by the electromagnetic feedback from the powerful prosthetic. He thrashed angrily at his followers as they tried in vain to stand him up and untangle his kicking legs from Sembado's.

Sembado covered his head as best as he could with his bound hands as Barton's flailing tantrum continued. He noticed the familiar heat developing where the prosthetic met the remainder of his leg.

When Barton's men finally pulled him away, he seemed to be experiencing a heated discomfort of his own. He grasped at the back of his neck desperately with both hands. He quickly made a sour face and retracted his hands.

"The damn necklace is burning my skin!" Barton yelled. He ripped the transceiver from his neck and whipped it angrily at Sembado.

It hit Sembado in the chest with a sorry thump. He moaned through the discomfort as his hangover continued to dominate his thoughts.

"Forget it, man," said one of the men, holding Barton back. "They'll be gone soon, but they ain't goin' anywhere right now."

Barton's men pushed and prodded him away until they were out of sight and his angry ramblings had faded. Sembado breathed deeply for a moment as he tried to collect his thoughts. To his left, Kaluna had crawled to a seated position, but still sat shivering. She looked at Sembado with pained and tired eyes; her wet hair was stuck to her face. Sembado shuffled toward her on his rear, but he struggled to push his prosthetic across the ground. He looked down at his lap where the wearable transceiver lay blinking. He grabbed it with his bound hands; the straps dangled from either side. He tucked his chin against his chest, each move was excruciating to his head. With his chin still tucked; he reached above his head and draped the straps and receiver just below the knot at the base of his head. He struggled to flop and readjust the straps to get them to lay flat on either side of his neck. When the assembly was finally in position he pulled his hands back under his chin to carefully click and connect the fastener. A few basic test functions confirmed that the leg was receiving and preforming appropriately

Sembado used his newfound mobility to quickly move across the ground to where Kaluna sat shivering. He sat cross-legged next to her, lifted his arms over her head and dropped them around her shoulders. She made a feeble attempt to help hoist herself into his lap. She laid her head against his chest and wept. Luckily, the sun had moved from behind a few trees and their position, was now bathed in warm, bright light. Before long, their skin was mostly dry, and the moisture trapped between them started to warm slightly.

With Kaluna's consent, Sembado moved her off his lap so that he could stand and stretch. He collected her in his arms and quickly moved into the heavy brush. In a moment, they were out of sight.

***

Kaluna walked beside Sembado while they stumbled through the undergrowth on the hillside. They had been away from their captors for several hours. Sembado observed their elongating shadows on the bare dirt path he walked. The sun was still high in the sky, but it had moved to the east side of the island.

"I think it's about three," he whispered to Kaluna.

"I'm hungry," she replied. "And we really need to find some water."

They continued down the small game trail until it hooked around a large rock embankment. A strange noise could be heard just past the rock. They approached it cautiously so that Sembado could peer around the next corner. He carefully approached the edge of the rock as the noise became louder.

"Water!" he exclaimed as he moved forward quickly. He and Kaluna looked at the small, clear creek as it fell down the hill to a series of pools below. Its origins were up the ridge and out of sight. They kneeled at the creek and gulped mouthfuls of the cool, refreshing liquid. Kaluna dabbed her brow and forehead. Sembado pressed his wet fingertips against his eyes. They used small river stones to beat and fray the stranded cord that bound their wrists. When their hands were free, they rested on the smooth, weathered rocks that lined the babbling brook and let the sun warm their skin. Sembado continued to take more drinks of water as the liquid already in his stomach settled and passed.

"I don't know if it's just our situation or what," he said, nearly smiling, "but this water tastes so much better than the desalinated stuff from the complex."

"It's not you," Kaluna replied. "The spring water on my island was beyond compare. It just can't be recreated."

Sembado took in the clean taste once more as he looked around from their high vantage. They were high enough on the island's mountain to see the water, but their view of the submarine was blocked by a rock outcropping just down the slope.

"How about we move down the creek to those rocks so we can get a peek at the sub," Sembado said. "We may be able to make a run for it."

Kaluna nodded silently, and they moved slowly down the rocky incline. They reached the large boulders and paused to relieve themselves. Sembado went first and then stood watch while Kaluna took her turn. When they were both finished, they carefully peered over the ledge together.

The curved bay stretched out to the left and right; the submarine bobbed in the shallows right in the middle. Right in front of it, an entire camp of make-shift tents had been assembled on the beach. The fire circle blazed brightly as the villagers stoked it with more brush and driftwood.

"Ah, deek it!" Sembado snapped. "We aren't going anywhere while they guard the damn submarine!"

"Well, I don't know," Kaluna said quietly. "I would wait until nighttime, and then get down into the water. If we can get in the shallows out to either side, then we might be able to get a better approach from the water."

"I think they might underestimate us just enough for that to actually work," Sembado said.

"Then let's move away from the creek a little bit, and find somewhere to bed down," Kaluna replied. "Maybe something to eat too. I think I left most of my dinner back in that clearing."

They found another rock escarpment further to the north; it offered them a view of the submarine as well as cover from above and below. Kaluna used some broken branches from the surrounding bushes to make a packed and cushy pad to lie on. Sembado allowed her to rest while he searched for something to eat. Nearly an hour of searching had proven difficult, and Sembado returned with a sparse handful of some dark berries and yellow roots.

"I really had no idea what to look for," he said sheepishly as he handed Kaluna his findings. "I saw a couple small animals, but they were too quick."

"We can't cook anything without a fire anyway," she yawned. She started chewing on the roots as Sembado stretched out his body next to hers.

"We should keep hydrating as much as possible," Sembado said. "But we need to get some better sleep as well."

Kaluna agreed with a head nod. She struggled to hide her reaction to the bitter roots, but continued to chew them voraciously.

"I can take the first watch," Sembado said. "No offense, but you look tired."

Kaluna rolled her eyes weakly, but snuggled up against Sembado and closed her eyes.

"Wake me up in two hours," she said.

"Yeah, I'll be sure to set my watch," Sembado replied sarcastically.

She smacked him lightly and nestled in closer.

***

"Kaluna," Sembado whispered; he barely breathed her name. "Luna, wake up."

Kaluna stirred slowly at first, and then more quickly as she noticed the darkness.

"Why is it so dark?" she asked. "Haven't you learned your lesson of letting me…"

"Shut up," Sembado hissed. "Shhh. They're on the move."

They laid motionless and listened to the sounds of the night. Not far away, the small creek was still splashing over its smooth stones. Critters of all types could be heard rustling and chirping. Then came the noise of men; they stomped and shuffled and argued. Sembado and Kaluna held their breath as the noise of broken sticks and stumbling feet bounced around their rocky retreat. Light from the moon and the stars cast shadows on the walls of their hideout. Lumbering figures danced across the rocks as they marched by.

"That one right there is broken too," said one of the voices.

"Where?" replied another indignantly.

"Well, don't you see it?" said the first voice.

"That? That could've been a pig!"

"A pig? Don't be stupid! Don't you see the line of broken twigs? It damn near goes in a straight line. Ain't no pig gonna walk a line like that! I think they've been here and we need to tell Barton."

"Barton ain't gonna wanna hear some dumb shit like this! Now hurry up. I wanna get back to that fire!"

"You're such a lazy ass, do you know that? They could be right around the corner, and you'd have no idea because your head is so far up your ass."

"Screw you! Keep running your mouth. I dare you!"

"No, screw you! These ocean dwellers seem pretty crafty to me. You didn't get as good a look at that guy's crazy metal leg like me. He about broke Barton's ankle without even tryin'. So watch him catch you, and put it right up your ass…right next to your head."

"Dude, back off, or I'm gonna put my foot up *your* ass."

Sembado and Kaluna breathed silently and listened helplessly as the men drew closer.

"Hey man, don't push me! We aren't doin' this again."

"Then back off!"

"I'm goin' back down to the fire. This is stupid. Hey! I said don't frickin' shove me!"

The scuffle quickly devolved into a fist fight, and the two men were soon knocking each other into Sembado and Kaluna's hideout. Sembado and Kaluna sprang up just as the men fell into their space. Kaluna shot past them while Sembado planted one heavy kick into the closer man. They both shouted out as they ricocheted into the nearby wall and cracked their heads. Their yelling and confusion echoed loudly in the rock enclosure. Sembado and Kaluna could hear the men arguing about who kicked whom. Their feud was now being reverberated off of the surrounding rock formations. Sembado and Kaluna ran nearly one hundred yards before ducking behind a tree.

They watched as a series of torches was lit at the beach bonfire. The line of small orange dots moved away from the beach and into the trees below as the men's dispute continued to broadcast to the villagers below.

"This might be our chance," Kaluna whispered in Sembado's ear. "We should make a break for it!"

Without hesitating, Sembado grabbed her hand and started barreling down the hill. He kept the line of torches visible in his right periphery as they ran a full out sprint to the bottom. Kaluna called out in protest as his prosthetic boosted him ahead of her. He stopped just long enough for her to climb onto his back. His strides quickened at the base of the hillside, but Kaluna jumped off his back as his pace slowed in the loose sand. They raced across the open beach, kicking the dry powder up into the shower of moon beams that fell from the cloudy sky above. Sembado's lungs burned, but he did not relent; the line of torches was suddenly back at the beach line. The procession broke into angry commotion as they recognized Sembado and Kaluna tearing across the moonlit shoreline. Kaluna reached the water first. She jumped through the shallows as best she could before having to wade the last few feet. Sembado followed up behind, just dodging a volley of fire-hardened wooden spears. His bionic prosthetic propelled him across the twenty foot distance with a single, powerful push. He landed next to Kaluna with a splash, and flung open the submarine door for her. Kaluna had just enough time to scream and duck before Barton's calloused foot shot out of the submarine doorway and struck Sembado square in the face.

Chapter Thirty-Six
Thanks for Coming Out

Hot, salty fluid dripped down the back of Sembado's throat. He slowly drifted back to consciousness, and swallowed the large amount of blood that had pooled in his mouth. He gagged on the thick, metallic-flavored liquid, and spat and retched the blood onto his legs and the floor of the submarine. He gasped for air, immediately aware that his nose was not working.

Sembado squinted through bruised and swollen eyes and took in his surroundings. Barton sat in the secondary chair while Kaluna piloted the submarine across open water; he pointed a crude shank at her face while looking back to Sembado.

"Rise and shine there, ginger!" He laughed as the morning light silhouetted his tangled hair; he had Kaluna steering straight toward the sun. Six of his men sat hunkered and crouched around Sembado; they all chuckled at Barton's mockery.

"I gotta admit," Barton added. "I was kinda surprised you made a run for it. I mean, it's not like we tied you up real good. I just didn't expect some pampered, techie folks like you to have the gonads, that's all."

281

Barton returned his attention to Kaluna. He reviewed the dials and buttons on the dashboard with her. She repeated each function and use obediently.

"Don't be tellin' me no lies now," Barton said, prodding her neck with the tip of his knife. "Else I'll find out and then I won't be so nice. Neither will my boys."

Kaluna stared stoically out the front viewing shield while Barton's men hooted and hollered in response to Barton's threat. They cat-called at Kaluna and threatened her with their various special talents.

"Alright," Barton called. "That's enough! I'm tryin' to actually learn somethin' up here, you dogs."

Sembado continued to spit and purge as much blood from his mouth as he could. He gagged again when a large piece of dried blood slid from his nostrils down the back of his throat. He spit it out on the floor, causing Barton's men to protest and swear.

"Oh, it's just a little blood!" yelled Barton. "Would you guys shut the hell up and keep him under control. Watch that leg of his too. He broke a couple of Mario's ribs with it."

Barton had Kaluna perform a limited amount of subaquatic maneuvers to show the submarine's true potential. Despite the fact that she was just below the surface, the demeanor of Barton's men changed in an instant. They each observed the surrounding water with a look of confused and impatient anxiety. Sembado yawned dramatically and the corners of his jaw popped painfully. The loud and sudden noise startled the men. They looked around quickly to see the source of the noise before returning to their uneasy viewing of Kaluna's artful piloting. After ten minutes of underwater exhibition Barton commanded Kaluna to bring the sub back to the surface.

"And it just...eats electricity?" Barton asked. He eyed the men in the back to confirm his terminology.

"Well those shiny panels on the roof make electricity out of the sunlight," Kaluna said patiently. "It isn't alive. It doesn't eat anything. It's a machine."

"Don't back talk me, bitch," said Barton, brandishing the knife. "I think it's a pretty honest question. How am I supposed to know what kind of unnatural nonsense you people have cooked up? You live underwater for, God's sake. You think that's normal?"

Sembado had taken to gingerly prodding his various facial injuries. His nose was an unfamiliar lump of tender cartilage, his eyes were puffy and hot. They only stopped hurting if he shut them and sat very still, but as soon as he did that, the motion of the submarine started to make him nauseous.

"Hey," Barton called back to his men. "We've got sight of the shore. We'll slow down to dump these two and then we'll move north to check out that long beach that old Duncan told us about. We'll stay away from the beach to avoid trouble. These two aren't worth running into any of them green police so keep a low profile, dammit."

Barton's men acknowledged his orders and started to prep themselves to deposit Sembado and Kaluna into the shallow, coastal waters. They hyped each other up and cheered as Barton took full control of the submarine for the first time. He ushered Kaluna to the back where his men subdued and groped her. One of them held Sembado's head up by his hair. He pulled harder until Sembado obediently stood. They opened the submarine door, and Barton turned until their course was parallel with the shore. The submarine skipped along the waves at twenty knots. One of the men marshaled Sembado to the open door by his hair; another shoved a piece of paper in Sembado's waistband.

"Your map, as promised," he laughed.
Sembado looked out into the bright water; it hurt his eyes to squint into the glare. He braced himself in the door of the submarine and tried to judge the speed of the water as it rushed by. Before he could completely gain his bearing, Barton yelled something and one of the men planted his foot on Sembado's rear and gave it a great shove.

Sembado flopped forward with both arms spread and belly flopped into the rushing waves. His face and stomach skipped painfully off the water and he flailed and thrashed until his feet found the ocean floor. He stood up, gasping, just in time to see Kaluna leaving the submarine under her own power. She seemed to have left one of the men with a bruise or two.

Sembado moved to shallower water where he braced his hands on his knees and finished the terrible cycle of hacking and vomiting until his throat was clear and his stomach was empty. By the time he had finished, Kaluna had reached him, and she helped him out of the water and onto the upper part of the beach. The shoreline was rocky and treeless. Kaluna took Sembado to the base of the hill that truncated the beach. She found a larger shrub and settled him into its shade. She rocked him quietly as they watched their submarine disappear around the next point. Tears of pain and toil and despair filled Sembado's swollen eyes; the salty drops burned his cracked bruises. Kaluna continued to comfort Sembado until he nodded off into a deep and noisy sleep.

***

Kaluna walked the beach, never losing sight of Sembado. She collected a number of familiar looking plants, and was even able to trap a handful of small crabs. She returned to Sembado's resting place to find that he was awake and crying again; he held a piece of paper in his hands.

"Where'd you get that?" she asked as she deposited the fruits of her labor at his feet.

Sembado did not answer immediately, but handed the piece of paper to her.

"They shoved it in my pants before kicking me off the sub," he said flatly.

Kaluna looked down at the paper. It was a faded, wrinkled map, but not like the technical ones she had reviewed with Mahana. This one was almost cartoon like with a colorful heading that read *Southern California.* It was covered with silly letters that spelled out words like *Hollywood*, *LAX*, and *Orange County*. There was even a little character that looked like the sun wearing sunglasses. Toward the bottom of the map, she saw the words *San Diego* in bright letters.

"Well, see," Kaluna said encouragingly. "There's San Diego right there."

"Oh, Kaluna, stop!" Sembado said as he started to break down again. "That's a child's map. Some kind of old gimmick for little kids. We can't navigate with that."

"Well it tells us this much," Kaluna said firmly as she traced the map. "All we have to do is follow the coast south and we will get to San Diego sooner or later. It can't be that far. But we aren't going anywhere until we get you cleaned up and healthy."

Sembado gave her a pitiful look, but did not protest further. He just sat and pouted while she tried in vain to feed him the stringy plants and raw crab meat.

Chapter Thirty-Seven
Slightly Buzzed

Sembado breathed in the salty sea breeze through his nose for the first time in the two days they had been on land. The air was still tingly as it squeezed through his swollen nostrils. His ears prickled; a faint buzzing filled them. He tried to pop his ears, but the buzzing persisted. Kaluna shook her head as she approached with drift wood for a fire.

"Would you stop already?" she said in disbelief. "The swelling is going down. You'll breathe through your nose when it's ready."

"Do you hear that?" Sembado responded, ignoring her advice. "That buzzing?"

She paused and listened.

"No."

She dropped the wood onto a pile of other sticks and twigs she had already collected. Sembado stood up gingerly, and walked down the sand to the water's edge. He scared a flock of gulls as he went, and watched them scream down at him as they circled overhead. Foamy white bubbles washed over his feet as the waves crashed and fizzled up the glistening beach. He instinctively looked around before exposing himself, and urinated into the salty shallows; his dehydration was evidenced by his dark and pungent urine.

He returned to find Kaluna had arranged the twigs and sticks into a multi-tiered box. He watched her use the sharp corner of a stone to dig a small indentation in a spare piece of driftwood.

"What are you doing?" he asked with genuine curiosity.

She did not respond, but pursed her lips and continued to concentrate. She set the wood aside and used the rock to carefully whittle a second stick to a relatively sharp point. Sembado stood, befuddled, with his hands on his hips. Kaluna set the driftwood in front of her and positioned herself on her knees beside it. She bowed to it like an altar, the sharpened stick in her hands. Sembado's ignorance began to aggravate him and his confusion grew as Kaluna began to spin the sharpened stick quickly between her hands. She had the pointed end of the stick planted firmly in the divot she had dug in the driftwood. Her hands worked artfully from the top of the stick to the bottom as she twisted it back and forth between her sun-kissed fingers. Sembado slowly sat down as the mysterious demonstration developed. The last few days' malnutrition started to show on Kaluna's sweat-beaded brow. The pain in her cramping forearms spread across her face in the form of a bitter grimace. Sembado was just about to tell her to stop her struggling when an amazing thing started to happen: small wisps of smoke began creeping out from under the end of the stick. The success emboldened

Kaluna, who fought past her discomfort with renewed fury.

"That small, hairy bark," she commanded breathlessly. "When I pick up the stick, put a small amount in the hole."

Sembado obeyed, pulling a large pinch of the woolly material from the assortment Kaluna had collected.

"Okay," she said as she lifted the stick just out of the hole.

Sembado quickly stuffed half the material into the small hole, and pressed it firmly. He pulled his finger away quickly as his brain registered how hot it was. He put his finger in his mouth as Kaluna returned to her task. The material in the divot smoked further.

"A little more," Kaluna demanded.

Sembado deposited the remainder of the furry bark in the hole more carefully than before. Kaluna jammed the stick back in the hole and spun it more furiously than ever. Smoked billowed out from the hole.

"Get ready to add more on top," Kaluna said.

Sembado collected half the remaining bark shreds in his hand, and waited excitedly. Kaluna lowered her mouth to the smoke and blew ever so carefully. Sembado watched her pouting lips as they breathed life into the thick smoke. She continued to work her magic until the stringy material suddenly caught flame. Sembado shouted in excitement before carefully sprinkling more of the bark on the burgeoning fire. Kaluna collected the smaller twigs and leaves and packed them into a loose ball. She held it over the flames until it caught. Sembado then watched in excitement while Kaluna used two longer sticks to pick up the flaming ball of kindling and deposit it into the small boxy structure she had premade. She and Sembado took turns adding small twigs and other bits while the outer structure caught fire.

"Not too much," Kaluna cautioned. "You'll smother it."

Sembado held his handful of scraps back and observed her blow more forcefully on the existing fuel. Kaluna showed him how to lean more sticks against the assembly while maintaining open airflow. Kaluna sat back and let her arms rest while instructing Sembado how to add progressively larger pieces.

"We will need more of the big pieces to keep it going tonight," she said. "Make sure it's the drier stuff."

Sembado sprang up, eager to participate in the maintenance of the fire. He took off down the beach in search of more wood. Within ten minutes, his arms were full and he returned to make his deposit. Kaluna was fiddling with the sharp rock again, but Sembado did not stay. He moved further down the beach where he found a small group of old dead trees. Several of the branches broke under his weight and he happily dragged the larger boughs back to Kaluna. He sat for a break as his mouth-breathing had reached its effective limit.

Kaluna was prying the crab carcasses open and twisting the pale meat around two sticks. She carefully handed the first completed skewer to Sembado.

"Don't let it fall or burn," she said.

Sembado held the flesh over the fire with focused intent. He moved it from side to side as it started to pop and sizzle. Kaluna finished her own skewer, and started to roast it as well.

"Yours should be good," she said.

Sembado carefully handled the hot crab meat off the stick before popping it in his mouth. He breathed out quickly with his mouth open in an attempt to cool the hot flesh.

"Well it's gonna be hot!" Kaluna laughed. "It's fire."

Sembado tried not to choke as he swallowed the first piece. He blew on the remaining skewer before eating the succulent, white meat; the sweetness was surprising. He closed his eyes and savored the tender morsels as he worked through the rest of his humble meal. He set his skewer aside, and when Kaluna was finished with hers, he added some of the larger limbs that he had collected. The sun sat low in the western sky as he left Kaluna to gather more wood. He returned to the dead trees to further his search. The bases of the trees looked particularly compelling. He grabbed the main trunk of one with both hands; his fingers just barely touched. He tried shaking the tree to and fro, but it was rooted firmly in the sand.

He stopped for a moment when the buzzing returned to his ears without notice, but this time it was louder. He wiggled his fingers in his ears and opened and closed his mouth, but the buzzing continued. He tried to see if it was coming from around him, but the dimming light offered little detail of his surroundings. Suddenly, the buzzing stopped.

He looked around one more time before returning to the task at hand. He stepped back and kicked at the tree with his bionic leg. The tree shuddered with a cracking noise. He positioned himself for a more powerful blow, and kicked again. Several loud cracks later and the tree leaned to one side. Sembado used one final kick to break the tree free from its base.

Sembado returned to the camp with two of the small trees in tow. Kaluna shook her head and laughed.

"We'll have to break those up," she said.

"Don't worry," he said, patting his prosthetic. "My leg makes a good wood breaker."

"It's called an axe," she laughed.

"Whatever," he said as he took a seat by her side. "I heard that buzzing again. It was louder."

"Probably an insect of some kind," Kaluna said. "You've probably never heard them before."

"I remember some from your island," Sembado protested. "Maybe you're right. Hey, what are you working on now?"

"I'm trying to recreate something Mahana showed me once," she replied. She had two of the domed crab shells open and was scrubbing out the remaining connective tissue with wet sand. Sembado stoked the fire while she got up and went to the water line. She returned with both shells rinsed out; one was full of water. She had Sembado hold both shells out of the sand while she used a hooked piece of wood to pull part of the fire away from the main blaze. She worked carefully to maintain the embers of the secondary fire. She took the water-filled shell from Sembado and carefully set it over the glowing coals. She stoked the smaller fire carefully, taking care to keep its size manageable. They watched the awe-inspiring sunset while the water heated. Their dancing fire battled with the sky to produce a more captivating appearance, but could not provide the greens and blues and purples that stretched high over their heads. It was nearly nightfall when the water in the shell started to bubble and steam.

"Okay," Kaluna said. "This would be a lot easier with a sheet of plastic or something, but we can only try with what we have."

She had Sembado hold the second shell just outside the fire's reach. When he was in position, she stood up and unfolded the cartoon map. She carefully held it over the simmering shell, careful not to get it too close to the flames. She grasped it delicately by opposite corners with a third corner in her teeth. She allowed the fourth corner to dangle over Sembado's empty shell. He crouched down low to avoid the excess heat that emanated from the fire. From his low vantage, he could see the underside of the map begin to collect beads of water; it almost appeared to be sweating. Kaluna pulled the map a little higher as her fingers became uncomfortably hot. The beads of steamy moisture continued to condense until her movement caused one large drop to break free and slide down the underside of the paper. It collided with smaller droplets as it went, each adding to its size and momentum. The large, collective drop paused momentarily at the hanging corner before falling into Sembado's waiting shell. He looked up at Kaluna with a grin. She was concentrating too much to respond. Several toiling minutes later had produced barely an ounce of distilled water, but Kaluna had to take a break. Her hands and jaw were sore from their awkward and prolonged position.

"I think I sweated out more than we made," she said dejectedly.

"You've had a long day," Sembado said. "Why don't you have the water and get some sleep."

"We'll split it," she replied stoically, and sipped at the crab shell modestly. "But I'd be happy for some sleep. Keep an eye on the fire, would ya?"

Sembado helped her retire to a more comfortable position with the hill to their backs, and the fire between them and the ocean. She nuzzled in next to him. He was careful to keep the firewood within reach of his one arm; he embraced her lightly with the other. He let the fire die down slowly as he rationed what wood they had left.

The stars above shined brilliantly. A happy smile spread reactively across his face as he took in all the twinkling pinpricks. He sat and watched the moon rise and climb high into the night. The nearly full orb moved slowly across the sky as the night became dark and a chilled breeze blew off the water. He slowly dropped his head against Kaluna's. Somewhere in the distance, he was sure he heard the buzzing.

***

Sembado opened his eyes to the sight of Kaluna blowing on the black embers from the night before.

"Oh no," he said. "I'm so sorry! I let it go out!"

"It's okay," she said calmly. "It's a lot easier to restart from the embers. See?"

She gave one more hard breath and a glowing nugget popped to life. She recoiled from the fire, touching her fingers to her temples.

"Ugh, my head," she said quietly. "We really need more water."

"Maybe there's a river or creek nearby," Sembado said.

"I just wish we could be in better shape here before we spread out," Kaluna said. "More food and water, you know?"

"Well we aren't doing too well here," Sembado replied. "Maybe there is more of both nearby. Can we bring the fire with us somehow?"

"I really don't think I'm up to that kind of walk yet," Kaluna said. "And neither are you."

"My nose is feeling a lot better," he added, breathing in deeply through his nostrils.

"We can wrap a stick to make a torch," Kaluna said with her eyes closed. Her headache consumed her. "Maybe with part of your shirt."

"Yea, sure," Sembado said, peeling off his garment immediately. Kaluna opened her eyes just long enough to start laughing, but stopped when it made her head worse.

"What?" Sembado asked.

"Your arms and chest," Kaluna said tenderly.

Sembado looked down to see his red, sunburned arms contrasted against his sallow chest.

"Oh shut up," he laughed. "Not everyone can be beautiful and golden brown like you!"

Kaluna accepted the compliment sheepishly. She helped Sembado tear the tattered shirt Barton's people had given him into strips. They wrapped a few of them around a long smooth branch and reserved the rest for later.

Suddenly, the buzzing returned; it was too close for either of them to ignore.

"See!" Sembado exclaimed. "Do you hear that?"

Kaluna craned her neck all around to search for the source of the noise.

"That's no insect," Sembado added. "Listen, that sounds electronic...or mechanical. There!" Sembado pointed just up the beach. He and Kaluna gawked at a small white object that hovered in place about forty feet above the sand. It had four small arms with tiny little blades that produced the buzzing noise as they spun rapidly. Sembado squinted at the small black fixture on its belly. It seemed to be swiveling and spinning in place.

"Deeks, I think that's a camera." Sembado said quietly as his eyes widened. "I think we need to go...now!" he added emphatically.

Kaluna continued to watch the drone warily as it buzzed loudly from its great height.

"Look!" she exclaimed. "It's leaving."

She and Sembado watched the drone drop three feet vertically before awkwardly disappearing over the hill.

"Yeah!" Sembado said. "Let's not be here when it gets back. Forget the fire. Let's move!"

He pulled Kaluna away from their small camp with one hand, the unlit torch in the other. Her dehydration and fatigue did not allow her to object.

***

Sembado kept up a hurried pace throughout the morning as they tried to put as much distance as possible behind themselves. The beach offered a clean, open path, but they soon met their first obstacle in the form of a rock outcrop that pushed straight out into the waves, cutting off the beach entirely. Sembado's first instinct was to wade out into the water and simply walk around the edge of the point, but the crushing waves and persistent tide kept him from going more than a few feet before he was forced to return to Kaluna. Kaluna insisted they rest in the shade of the rocky overhang.

"I think we'll have to go up and over," Sembado suggested, pointing to the grassy bluff above. "I think there was an old path just back that way."

Kaluna sluggishly followed him back to the dirt path that led up the cliff. The path was worn smooth, but every few steps, there was a wooden plank jutting out of the hillside. Sembado and Kaluna reached the top and took in the spectacular view. The land above the beach was an eerie ruin-scape that had been commandeered by the trees. Hollow shells of ancient homes played host to a random collection of palms, pines, and fruit trees. Kaluna led Sembado to a tree that was covered in juicy, ripe oranges. They each ate three of the succulent spheres before filling their arms and moving on. Their pace increased up where the sand could not impede them, and they quickly traced the top of the beach bluffs in two hours. Sembado watched the high ground fall away one more time before it was truncated by a large, noisy creek.

"Fresh water!" he yelled, grabbing Kaluna's hand and doubling his pace.

They reached the creek and followed it back up the hill until they were safely out of the salt water's reach. Kaluna found a stony spot to sit and drink while Sembado splashed excitedly. They gulped and wallowed and refreshed themselves. Sembado crawled to the side and laid on the cool, pebbled creek bank while Kaluna submerged herself directly in the main flow. They sat quietly while the creek babbled by and met the crashing waves below in noisy spurts.

"I think we should try and set up here like before," Kaluna said. "We've got water and cover this time," she added, indicating the thick canopy of trees that lined their segment of the creek.

"It's certainly less open than the beach," Sembado agreed, eyeing their surroundings. "Do you think you could start another fire?" he asked.

"Maybe we skip that part for now," Kaluna replied. "The smoke could draw unwanted attention. And besides," she added with a sheepish grin, "my arms are tired."

***

Sembado returned from relieving himself the next morning to find Kaluna organizing and stacking small logs.

"I thought you weren't going to make a fire," he said.

"I'm not," she replied. "I'm trying to make us a place to sleep. See the frame? I'm adding these smaller branches to fill in the openings."

Sembado watched Kaluna fill in the large openings in the framed structure before helping her finish the roof and walls with thick, leafy foliage. They completed the shelter in time for lunch, which consisted of more oranges, sun-dried kelp, and water. They sat on their matted, leafy mattress and ate quietly. Sembado listened to the birds sing and flutter overhead while he watched a few defiant rays of sun cut through the cover and dance across Kaluna's face and chest. Bright diamonds and triangles highlighted her golden brown skin with a creamy yellow hue. He leaned his head against hers as he chewed up some more kelp leaves. She reached for his hand and entangled her fingers in his.

"Do you see what the oranges have done to our fingers?" Sembado asked as he turned her hand over in his. Their fingernails were covered in a powdery yellow film.

"It'll wash off," Kaluna said as she pulled his hand close to her chest and pushed up against his arm with her head. They stretched out and rested for the remainder of the afternoon, exchanging intermittent kisses between extended spells of sleep.

Chapter Thirty-Eight
Headed South

Sembado walked down the beach. The sun beat down on his neck; the fluffy, white sand was hot on his feet. Up ahead he saw Kaluna talking with a mysterious figure. Sembado could not see the man's face. He hurried his pace and called out to Kaluna, but his voice was a hoarse whisper. He ran faster, his bionic leg pushing him along through the loose sand. He called out in vain and waved his arms frantically as the man began to lead Kaluna away. The stranger took her by the hand and led her down to the waterline. Sembado hurried faster; his bionic leg shot him forward ten feet at a time. The man had Kaluna wading out to her knees as the crashing waves grew as high as her chest. Sembado reached the water, just yards away from where they were when an overwhelming buzzing noise came from above. An entire fleet of four-bladed drones dropped out of the sky to hover in his path. Dozens and dozens of the little white machines formed a floating net between Sembado and Kaluna; their tiny black cameras swiveled and focused on Sembado's face. He desperately punched and kicked at the flying terrors as the mysterious man led Kaluna deeper into the relentless tide. The

301

buzzing drones moved as one as they closed their gap to Sembado. Their obnoxious whine reached a climax as individual drones started to dart out and attack Sembado. Their blades cut his face and arms as he swatted them away. One drone shot across his face so close that he briefly saw his reflection in the small, black camera lens. Kaluna's dark hair momentarily floated on the water's surface as the stranger finished leading her to her death.

Sembado sat up in fright. His forehead was sticky with sweat. Kaluna lay next to him in their small, leafy shelter. He breathed in deeply as he focused on his true reality. He tried to force the desperate anxiety of his dream away, but the buzzing and humming of the drones persisted. He craned his head around inside their small hut as he realized the buzzing noise of the drone's blades was actually approaching them. Sembado laid back down next to Kaluna and carefully shook her awake. She opened her eyes lazily; the loving smile faded from her face when she recognized the call of the drone. Sembado rolled over on top of Kaluna, and braced himself on his hands and knees.

"I'm going to collapse the shelter," he breathed silently. "It could hide us better."

Kaluna agreed with an inaudible confirmation, and Sembado used his bionic leg to strike the shelter's main support with one, destructive blow. The walls of the small hut fell away as the roof folded in on Sembado's back. The leafy panel struck him in his arched shoulders, but he was able to support it. He lowered his body onto Kaluna's and let the leaves and branches settle around them; the small mound of leaves and branches blended into the surrounding undergrowth as planned. They looked into each other's eyes and breathed quietly as the drone's sound grew louder. A second, quieter buzz indicated that an additional drone had joined the search. Sembado looked into Kaluna's fearful gaze. Their leafy cover bathed their faces in a green tint, but her irises were their usual piercing jade. Her eyes grew wider as the dual tones of the searching machines reached a terrifying and unnatural harmony. Sembado's concern intensified with Kaluna's labored breathing; too much movement would render their camouflage useless. He closed his eyes and took her lips in his own; she returned the embrace, and began matching her breathing to his. They opened their eyes just long enough to search each other's gaze before closing them again and continuing their loving exchange.

The quiet tone of the second drone died away while the closer one moved just above them. Sembado thought that he could feel the leaves on his head and back shutter for a moment, but he continued to concentrate on the warm, tingling sensation that enveloped his body when kissing Kaluna. Their parted lips danced passionately as the sound of the drone moved away, faded to a distant hum, and then died entirely. They reluctantly stopped their encounter so that Sembado could clear the brush from on top of them. He rolled off of Kaluna and laid on his back, breathlessly. They stared up at the early evening sun beams that broke through the canopy above.

"I had a terrible dream," Sembado said, reaching for Kaluna's hand. "That's what woke me up. I could hear the little machine in my dream. There were a hundred of them. They were keeping me from you."

"Well it was just a dream," Kaluna said, squeezing his hand.

"You were being taken away," Sembado continued. "Some strange man was walking you into the ocean by your hand."

"What?" Kaluna asked. "Like trying to drown me?"

"Kind of," Sembado replied. "You weren't struggling. The two of you were just walking straight into the waves until you disappeared. I woke up and the drone was getting closer. How do you think they found us?"

"Well hopefully they didn't," Kaluna responded as she rolled up against his side. "I think we were camouflaged good enough."

"Yeah, but they just happened to be in this area too?" Sembado asked. "We saw the first one miles from here."

"Well I'm pretty sure I heard two this time," Kaluna said. "Maybe that first one on the beach was completely different."

"I think I heard two also," Sembado said nervously. "And if there's more than one then there could be hundreds...or thousands! We don't know who they belong to or what they want. I'm not sure if they're piloted or autonomous. We had independent sub-droids that would regulate traffic and stuff. Maybe those are similar. I'm pretty sure that first one on the beach had a camera though.

That means someone is watching what it's recording. I don't like that. I don't think we should be staying in one place any longer. My nose is better. We've rehydrated. Chances are we will find more streams like this along the way, but I think we should start moving south."

Kaluna rested her head on his chest, but did not respond immediately.

"I can't imagine those things have any trouble seeing at night," Sembado continued. "So I don't expect day or night travel to matter for that reason alone."

"Let's wait until tomorrow," Kaluna said. "I don't want to move at night. We're about to lose the moon and we have enough shade during the day to keep you out of the sun."

"Gee, thanks," Sembado chuckled.

***

The next morning, they drank their fill of water and ate the remaining oranges before moving down to the beach where the mouth of the creek met the salty Pacific. They waited until the morning sun broke above the hills before they waded across the small delta and let the sun's hot rays dry their legs. When they were dry, they moved up under the tree line above the beach where they made faster progress on a hard, dirt path. They passed several tide pools where flocks of gulls were excitedly fighting over the trapped sea life within the rocky crags.

Two hours after leaving the mouth of the creek they reached another rocky outcrop. They crested the hill that overlooked the beach and looked over the south side of the cliff. Below was an ancient and derelict harbor filled with half-sunken and dilapidated yachts. Sembado and Kaluna carefully worked their way down the hill, weary of the crumbling beach town that was well hidden in the jungle that led inland. Ruins of palatial homes were barely visible between the thick network of palms and undergrowth. They made their way past the harbor as a pack of wild dogs crisscrossed the overgrown lane before them. Sembado and Kaluna advanced cautiously as the dogs retreated to the shadows and watched with curiosity. The brindled canines moved around behind Sembado and Kaluna as they passed, and followed them for another mile. Kaluna watched the dogs while Sembado navigated them forward. Up ahead, he saw an old crumbling bridge. As they approached it, he saw that it crossed a wide, fast moving river. He moved forward, leading Kaluna by the hand while she continued to watch the dogs' progress. Sembado stopped where the abutment met the bridge. The crumbling, grassy pavement of the road gave way to equally decrepit concrete on the bridge deck. A loose net of rusted reinforcement showed through in several large, open areas while loose chunks of the gray concrete clung to bended strands in other places.

"Think we could pick up the pace?" Kaluna asked; she had not looked ahead yet. The dogs were circling and pacing. One of them bobbed its head up and down while another cocked its head from side to side at the sound of Kaluna's voice.

"I don't think we want to go much faster," Sembado replied, drawing her attention to the state of the bridge.

"How about those heavy pieces there," Kaluna said, pointing. "Those should hold us."

Sembado inspected the line of stout looking girders that spanned the bridge. He picked a line and started to move across; Kaluna picked a parallel set of supports as she finally turned her back on the pack of dogs. The dogs showed no interest in crossing the bridge, but watched a while longer before breaking off and chasing a rabbit back the way they had come. Sembado and Kaluna shuffled slowly across the bridge, careful not to trip on the tangle of concrete and steel. The open spaces in the bridge exposed the rushing torrent just feet below the bridge deck. It took Sembado a full twenty minutes to waddle across the bridge; his powerful prosthetic was more of a liability than an asset in the delicate situation. Kaluna waited for him at the other end; they held hands while they found a shaded place to sit and rest.

They stayed in place until midday, feasting on a bush of dark berries. They alternated between the beach and the old roads above as they moved their way south. The sounds of another gurgling creek led them to a new river, but it was lined with broken, weathered concrete slabs, and passed its way through a number of old, muddy tunnels before it reached the sea.

"I don't want to drink from that," Kaluna said darkly. "That does not look pure or natural."

They crossed over one of the tunnels without incident and continued forward. The sun started to fall over the ocean as they picked through a tidal pool for small, boneless creatures to eat; Sembado had to fight off a sea gull that became entangled in Kaluna's hair while it vied for the juicy morsels. They plodded along in the hot evening sun as a cool breeze blew off the waves. The late afternoon moonrise brought the high tide with it, and Sembado and Kaluna worked their way up onto the high road as the water on the beach rose. They moved along an old set of rails that lay parallel through the grass and brush. It ran along the hill that topped the beach, and led Sembado and Kaluna to another stream. The rails stopped short where a bridge would have been if it had not been washed away long ago. The stream was fresh, active, and vibrant. It jumped and skipped over a bed of large, round cobbles before colliding with the rising ocean. Kaluna sat at its bank and rubbed her cracked, calloused feet.

"I think we should move up the creek here and take a drink," she said. "We haven't had any water since this morning."

Sembado led her up the riverbank by the hand. They found a lazy, quiet stretch where they could drink, rinse, and rest in the shade.

"I haven't seen or heard one of those flying robots all day," Sembado said. "You still think we should avoid camping overnight?"

"I didn't say we couldn't sleep overnight," Kaluna replied. "I just don't think we should waste our energy on building another shelter. And smoke and fire still seems like a hazard to me."

"Well I don't think we're going to find a much better spot before nightfall," said Sembado.

He allowed Kaluna to rest while he found a small grove of trees. He returned with his arms full of oranges, pears, and olives.

"Not sure if this is all edible, but I figured I'd collect what I could," he said.

Kaluna showed him how to eat the olives while avoiding the pits. He was much happier eating the pears for their lack of peeling. They ate a large fruit course before they walked to the beach where Kaluna taught Sembado how to hunt and catch crabs. They returned to their bed-down area at dusk with two crabs apiece. They killed, cracked, and ate the crustaceans before finding a sandy embankment to curl up against.

***

"Sem, wake up! Wake up! Sembado!"

Sembado opened his eyes to Kaluna shaking him; she was crouched down, her eyes darted around wildly.

"I hear more of the flying drones," Kaluna whispered. "A lot of them."

Sembado sat up; his bionic leg twitched reactively.

"Where?" he asked.

"Just listen," she replied.

As Sembado's ears registered the sounds of the surrounding nightlife, one even tone cut through the rest. The buzzing and whirring seemed to come from every direction; the pitch black night of the new moon offered no visual cues to accompany the approaching noise. Sembado looked down the stream's course to where it emptied into the ocean. The stars' reflections in the sea silhouetted countless drones as they bobbed up and down against the shimmering backdrop. Sembado grabbed Kaluna by the hand and pulled her away from the ocean; he fought to keep their pace manageable for her as they worked their way up the stream bank.

The buzzing of the drones persisted as the small machines pursued Sembado and Kaluna. The noise grew from either side; Sembado could now see shadows moving alongside either bank of the river. A new sound joined the commotion. It was a deep, rhythmic pounding. The sound doubled and tripled in volume as its source seemed to multiply; the drones' whirring accompaniment remained.

Sembado helped Kaluna splash across the stream at a low point before cutting up the side of a sandy ravine and onto flat ground. They raced across the open scrub brush, darting in and out of the clumpy growth. The drones circled overhead; the rhythmic pounding converged behind them. Sembado heard shouting behind him; human voices repeated commands to each other. His bionic leg pushed him faster than Kaluna could manage. He paused for only a brief moment so that she could climb onto his back.

Once she was clinging tightly to his shoulders he unleashed the full potential of his powerful prosthetic. He tried to gallop away from their pursuers, but constantly dodging the bulky foliage impeded his speed. The powerful pounding and shouting grew closer. Anger crept into Sembado's mind as his leg started to overheat and send feedback to his brain. Kaluna's escape became his singular objective, but the sounds of his pursuers grew around him as they passed and encompassed him. He finally slowed to a stop as several people circled him and Kaluna on horseback; their drones hovered above.

Sembado fought to subdue his rage as Kaluna climbed off of his back. He extended his hands to guard her. The riders spoke commands to each other quickly before one of them addressed Sembado directly.

"That's a hell of a leg ya got there," the man said from atop his horse. "Where ya headed with a thing like that?"

Sembado breathed heavily, but neither he nor Kaluna replied.

"You've been in a restricted recovery zone since you were dumped on the beach," the man said as he and his cohorts settled their mounts. "But you don't know what that means, do you? But you allowed those island mongrels to take your submarine?"

Sembado and Kaluna remained silent.

"Look," the man said. "This would be a lot easier for everyone if you just told us where it is you're headed so fast. You've been makin' pretty good progress to the south. You got a destination or are you just wanderin' in from beneath the surface?"

Sembado and Kaluna exchanged a glance. She nodded her approval to the man.

"Yes, we've had a whole mess of you folks floating in lately," the man said. "What happened to your home under the waves? You ruin that one too?"

"We're trying to reach some friends," Sembado said.

"That's what I thought," replied the man. "Can't just be the two of you. Where are they?"

"We are trying to find them," Kaluna said. "They are supposed to be in San Diego."

"Well then," the man replied. "You're quite a ways north aren't you?"

"We got lost," Sembado said earnestly.

"Evidently," said the man. "Well, it'll take ya forever fighting through the wilderness like this. Why don't you come with us? We'll have you in La Jolla in less than a day's ride."